R0201583663

10/2020

These Low Grounds

D0167950

PALM BEACH COUNTY
LIBRARY SYSTEM
3650 Summit Boulevard
West Palm Beach, FL 33406-4198

These Low Grounds

WATERS EDWARD TURPIN

Dover Publications, Inc.
Mineola, New York

Bibliographical Note

This Dover edition, first published in 2020, is an unabridged republication of the work originally published by Harper & Brothers, New York, in 1937.

Library of Congress Cataloging-in-Publication Data

Names: Turpin, Waters E. (Waters Edward), 1910– author.
Title: These low grounds / Waters Edward Turpin.
Description: Dover edition. | Mineola, New York : Dover Publications, Inc., 2020. | This Dover edition, first published in 2020, is an unabridged republication of the work originally printed by McGrath Publishing Company, College Park, Maryland, in 1969. | Summary: "These Low Grounds tells the story of the lives and struggles of four generations of an African American family, beginning with Martha, a freed slave who becomes a housemaid, through her great grandson Jimmy, who is an athlete with dreams of becoming a teacher and returning to his hometown in Maryland to improve the lives of his fellow citizens. Originally published in 1937, These Low Grounds was the forerunner of family history legacies such as Alex Haley's Roots"— Provided by publisher.
Identifiers: LCCN 2019050653 | ISBN 9780486843490 (trade paperback) | ISBN 0486843491 (trade paperback)
Subjects: GSAFD: Epic fiction.
Classification: LCC PS3539.U875 T47 2020 | DDC 813/.52—dc23
LC record available at https://lccn.loc.gov/2019050653

Manufactured in the United States by LSC Communications
84349101
www.doverpublications.com

2 4 6 8 10 9 7 5 3 1

2020

To my mother
Rebecca Henry

Chapter 1

I

Martha unbent from the washtub, roused by a frightened clucking, and made hastily for the front lawn. "Devilish chicken-stealers!" was her first thought.

At the corner of the house the rooster, Toby, scurried past, and at the same moment something thudded into Martha's middle. She sat down, breathless.

Facing her, also on the ground, was a man, a dusky mulatto, who blinked foolishly and gave off a strong odor of liquor.

Martha scowled fiercely. "What you a-doin', a-chasin mah Toby?" she demanded. "Is you one dem fug'tives? Go 'long wid you befo' Ah calls mah missy an' she gits you put in jail!"

The man continued to blink stupidly. But his wits were not too dull. Even through the fog of whisky he could tell that Martha was as good-looking a woman as he had seen in many a day. His connoisseur's eyes took especial note of two provokingly shapely legs revealed to indiscreet advantage.

Martha jumped up hastily, embarrassed by his stare.

"Ah done tolt you to git 'long wid you, ain't Ah?" she said, impatiently.

"Ah warn't trying' to steal yo' chicken," muttered the man. He erected himself in sections without taking his eyes off Martha. "You sho is purty, gal!"

Martha glared at him, but now the glare was a little forced. "Ah ain't axin' you fo' no sweet talk!" she declared. "Git 'long wid you."

The man stood brushing himself, quite at ease. Suddenly he grinned engagingly.

"When you's tired bein' mad," he said, "gimme somep'n to git clean wid. Mah marse'll gimme glory-be efn he catches me like dis."

"Ah ain't gonna git you nuffin'—nuffin'!" answered Martha, struggling to maintain a frown. She'd had time to take in the fellow's good looks. Tall and slim—broad shoulders—slender waist—aquiline features—eyes jet black and yellow flecked. Not many men came cut to that pattern. And his clothes didn't look like any clothes she'd seen on Baltimore Negroes; they reminded her of those worn by Joseph, the butler back home on the plantation.

He was still grinning. "Aw, honey, don't take on so," he said, soothingly. "Ah jes' come to town yestiddy from down Tidewater way, Virginny—"

"You-all from Virginny?" Martha's anger gave way to curiosity. "Dat's where Missy and me's from. Looka yere, man, you ain't tryin' to fool me, is you? What's yo' name?" It had been a time since she'd seen anyone from the Tidewater.

He breathed easier. "Mah name's Joe," he said. "Git me somep'n to brush wid an' Ah'll tell you all 'bout it."

Martha sped indoors and returned with a whisk broom.

"You see," Joe began, "Ah comes from Stanbrough Manor—"

"Den you-all's plantation is right next ours," Martha interrupted.

"You means you's one o' ole man Owens' people? Doggone mah skin! Den you must be Mis' Lucrece's gal dat went away wid 'er when she come north to be a nurse."

"Dat's right."

Joe's excitement mounted. "Look yere—you-all know dat Marse Hugh Allen done come up yere jes' fo' to see Mis' Lucrece?"

"So you's his nigger?"

"Yassah! Ah'm his vallay."

"Why fo' Marse Hugh want to see mah Missy?" Martha wanted to know. "Her don't have nuffin' to do wid de likes o' him. Her's too busy."

Joe looked wise. "He make like he jes' come up on bizness. But Ah knows he ain't fo'got how he use try to be her beau!"

"Huh!" Martha put a world of contempt into the exclamation.

"He 'lows he's a-comin' to see her t'night." Joe handed the brush to Martha and looked at her speculatively. "How'd you like me to come, too? Huh?"

Martha shrugged. "Don't make no diff'ence to me."

Joe moved slowly away, then turned.

"Ah'll be yere—you hear me?"

As he gained the walk, Martha peered around the corner of the house, her teeth a white streak in the brown of her face.

II

It was spring. Joe came that night and other nights in the weeks that followed.

One evening Martha was hooking Lucrece into a new gown. "Missy—," she began.

"Yes, Marty?" And as Martha seemed not to hear, Lucrece repeated: "Yes, Marty?"

"When is Marse Hugh goin' home, Missy?"

"Do you mean when is Hugh going home, or when is *Joe* going home?" parried Lucrece. Her calm gray eyes were bent quizzically on her maid.

Martha looked up shyly at her mistress from beneath lowered brows. A smile played across her mistress' serene countenance.

"Wal, Ah did kindah mean dat, too, Missy."

"They're leaving day after tomorrow," Lucrece informed her, and turned to leave the room.

"Missy!" The cry was almost a scream as Martha dropped to the floor, sobbing.

Lucrece knelt beside her. "What's the matter, child? Is it—" The question was irrelevant—Lucrece knew before Martha shook her head affirmatively. "Why that's nothing, honey," she comforted. "There's only the two of us, and there's plenty of room for a baby."

"But, Missy, dat ain't it. Ah wants mah chile to have a pappy. Ah don't want 'im to be bo'n—'cause de Good Book done say it ain't right."

"Precious much the Good Book has to do with babies! Besides, you can't have Joe, honey. You know that."

Martha was silent for a moment, drying her eyes. When she looked up at last she was calm, and there was no mistaking the resolution in her voice.

"Missy, how long Ah bin wid you?"

Lucrece frowned, trying to recall. "Why, I don't know exactly, Martha. About fourteen years, hasn't it been, since we came to Baltimore? Why?"

Martha ignored the question.

"Has Ah ever done wrong sense Ah bin wid you?" she continued. "Hain't Ah always looked atter you? Is Ah ever axed you fo' nuffin'?"

"You've been wonderful, Martha. And I appreciate everything."

They arose and faced each other, two mature women who had been together since the plantation days of their childhood and youth.

"What is it, honey?" asked Lucrece, gently.

Martha replied quietly, in an even voice: "Ah wants Joe, Missy. Ah wants to git married. Efn you'll buy Joe—"

"Hugh wouldn't sell him, Marty. Besides, what do you want with him? He's no good. I can see that plainly."

"Ah wants him, Missy!" Martha was stubborn.

Lucrece's expression of amused impatience changed to one of resignation.

"All right. If you can make Joe stay, I'll make Hugh sell him."

III

So Lucrece bought Joe, and Martha got what she wanted. The birth of her child, Carrie, was almost simultaneous with the outbreak of the war. Her work called Lucrece to the battlefields. Then shortly afterward Joe left home blithely with a band of colored volunteers made up of Freedmen, and Martha was in tears.

Chapter 2

I

Lucrece came home—a Lucrece whose hair was iron gray and whose high, thoughtful brow was faintly lined. She had known Shiloh and the Wilderness.

Sherman had marched to the sea in spite of stubborn, gallant resistance. Grant had haunted Richmond until harassed Lee could no longer bear the misery-ridden faces of his soldiers. Western Maryland rested easily, at last, from the hoofbeats of "Beauty" Stewart's phantom cavalry. There had been Appomattox, and now there was peace.

The little house in Baltimore, where Martha and Carrie lived with Lucrece, returned to a semblance of order. Martha went out to work by the day for wages—this was Lucrece's idea; Martha saw little reason in it—and during Martha's absence Lucrece looked after Carrie. She could not stand the routine of nursing now—could not bear the faces of the sick. She preferred to spend her time teaching Martha's golden sprite of a daughter her letters.

Joe had not returned. He had not been heard from during several years. At first Martha had grieved. But she couldn't do that for long. She had Carrie to think of, and the future. The future involved a plan—a way to spend her glittering savings. She was going to buy a house. Then she and Carrie would have a piece of property like every provident Negro who looked ahead. It was a burning ambition.

Martha realized her ambition before she hoped. For when Carrie was eight years old Lucrece died. And her will provided that the proceeds from the sale of her own house should go toward a last payment on Martha's. So Martha and Carrie moved into the eastern section of Old Baltimore where Freedmen Negroes—those who had earned or been granted their freedom before the war—lived beside newly emancipated Negroes in a curiously mixed settlement.

II

Carrie's teacher had died—a gentle young Negro whose pioneer zeal had demanded more than his weakling body could perform—and Carrie and Martha were returning from the funeral. As the hired carriage drew up to her house Martha saw a man and woman standing on the porch. She stared aghast, then ran forward with a glad cry and threw her arms about the man.

"Joe!—Joe!—Is it you, honey?"

Joe grinned complacently—the same Joe, a little more dissipated, not so elegantly dressed.

"Sho, honey. Didn't you-all know Ah'd be a-comin' home some day?"

"Lawsy! Ah done said all 'long you done bin kilt in de war!" Martha hugged him closer.

"Dey couldn't kill dis yere chile—nossuh!" Indicating the woman, he said, "Dis yere's mah sister Sue."

Carrie stood watching, bewildered. She had never known her father.

"Looka yere, honey—dat ain't our baby, is it?" Joe pointed to the child.

Martha assured him it was.

"She sho is purty! Come yere to yo' pappy, honey." Joe stretched out his arms invitingly.

Carrie hesitated. She was not sure that she liked this man. However, she sidled up to him and allowed him to kiss her cheek. He smelled just like a man she had come upon one Sunday morning in the gutter.

"You-all come on inside," invited Martha. "Dis yere's mah house," she added, proudly.

"Yeah?" exclaimed Joe, interestedly. He threw the woman Sue a sharp glance which was answered by a casual raising of the eyebrows.

"Yassuh!" assured Martha. "You-all jes' make you'self to home, an' me'n' Carrie'll fix up somep'n fo' you." She passed into the kitchen, and soon the scent of frying fish spread through the house.

Joe settled himself beside Sue on the sofa.

"Look yere," he said, "don't you let on to her you ain't mah sister, see? Dis yere's a place fo' us to live, and efn you don't let on, it'll be all right, see?"

Sue looked at him evilly, but did not answer. Joe was not satisfied.

"Lissen yere! Ah gits run outn Richmond on 'count o' you messin' wid white men. Didn't Ah have a good barber shop an' was makin' good money? Ah always kept you in classy style. So now you gots to help me! You hear?" He paused to see what effect this had.

Sue gave an impatient sniff.

"Now what we does is dis: Ah gwine start a barber shop yere. Efn you is mah sister, Marty ain't gone mind you stayin', an' you kin git some work to do, see? She don't have to know de diff'rence."

Sue heard him through absently, her gray-green eyes fixed on a corner of the room, as if the plan of immediate action lay there.

"Whyn't you tell me you was married?" she demanded, her voice husky with anger.

"How come you gits yo'self messed up in Richmond, huh?" Joe countered.

Sue stared again into the corner, and came to a decision.

"Lissen. Ah gwine stay yere"—she paused as Joe brightened—"but ain't gwine be nuffin' 'twixt us! Ah gwine git a job—efn Ah kin. An' efn Ah cain't—wal, Ah cain't." She shrugged indifferently.

Martha's cheery voice broke into the conversation at this point, calling them to the kitchen. At the table, each one ate in the company of his own thoughts. Carrie was shyly attentive, Sue sullen, Joe speculative as he balanced the charms of one woman against the qualifications of the other. Martha was frankly curious. As Carrie cleared the table her questions tumbled forth: Where had Joe been? Was he wounded in the war? Why had he never tried to communicate with her?

Joe delayed his answers to ask whether Martha had any liquor in the house.

Martha's brows drew together uneasily. "You still drinks heavy, don't you, Joe?" she questioned.

Joe feigned a cough, and the effort brought on a genuine paroxysm which caused a shadow of anxiety to flit across Martha's face.

"Ah only takes a li'l' attah meals, honey," he explained. "It keeps mah ches' mis'ry down." He shot an appealing glance at Sue as that outraged woman gave a contemptuous snort.

Martha was too concerned to notice. "Oh, honey, you ain't bin sick, is you?"

"Wal—no—jes' a li'l' mis'ry in mah ches', dat's all," said Joe.

"Missy give me her likker when she died, an' Ah ain't teched none of it yit. Ah'll git you some." Martha hurried upstairs and returned with a small jug and two glasses which she placed on the table. Sue eyed the second glass appreciatively while Joe poured himself a generous portion.

"Go on, honey, help yo'self," offered Martha, shoving the glass toward Sue. The woman hesitated primly for additional assurance, which Martha gave, then tilted the jug expertly over her arm.

Another drink and Joe had the necessary courage to begin his odyssey:

"Honey, you knows Ah always was sorry fo' leavin' you, but you see Ah warn't mahself. When Ah goes to git dem vittals dat day, Ah stopped past de back do' o' de tavern. Dem waiters dere was all up in de air 'bout 'listin'—said dey wants to fight fo' freedom. Dey was a-drinkin', an' Ah jines in wid 'em. De next mo'nin' Ah wakes up an' Ah's got on a unifo'm an' we's somewhar outside Wash'ton."

One battle had cured Joe of a taste for war and sent him to hospital with a chest wound. When he had been there about a month he left. The Stanbrough plantation was near by, so he went there and found Hugh dying. Joe stayed through the war, until Hugh's sister came to take charge. Then he and Sue drifted on to Richmond.

"Ah didn't know efn you was married ag'in a-no—" Martha interrupted with earnest assurance of her fidelity.

Joe saw that he had hit upon the right track. "So Ah thought Ah'd jes' stay whar Ah was. But de Klu-Kluxahs done got so bad Ah picks up wid Sue an' left. So yere Ah is, honey!" As a concluding gesture he emptied his glass.

This was not the trim and jaunty young rascal she had known. Years of dissipation had left their mark on Joe; his clothes were untidy. He was obviously evading the question of his belated return. But Martha still felt tenderness toward her first and only lover. She went to him now and hugged him hungrily.

"Dat's all right, honey. We's gwine start whar we left off, ain't we?"

Joe cast a glance over her shoulder at Sue, but she had left the table with a roll of her eyes and was sauntering into the parlor, her hips switching in studied nonchalance. Joe read "finis" in the movement and resignedly enveloped Martha in his arms. After all, he decided, he might have done worse.

III

Joe wanted to start his barber shop. It wasn't ambition that urged him to work, nor was it a desire to help Martha in meeting living expenses. He missed the gossip and the back-room gambling and the chance a barber-shop window afforded to review the passing feminine show.

But Joe had no money. So he went first to Sue.

It was two weeks after their coming to Baltimore, and in this time Sue had bestirred herself—not too violently. But so perverse is fortune, her half-hearted quest had rewarded her with an easy job in a small, prosperous family. For two days, like the proverbial new broom that sweeps so clean, she did admirably. (She was a good cook, if a bit sloppy.) But on the evening of the second day, a big black sailor, in port for the first time in months, accosted her while she was on her way home from work. She glanced over his huge well-knit frame. A whiff of the liquor tingled into her nostrils. His toothsome grin enticed her. . . . The next morning she awoke alone in a dive on the docks. Languidly, more out of curiosity than desire to do the right thing, she dressed and approached her place of work, to have the kitchen door opened by an angular Swedish woman.

"Oh! Guess Ah'm in de wrong place," Sue giggled tipsily.

"You ban right!" asserted her successor with an energetic slam of the door.

Thus Sue was relieved of the burden of toil. But because she suspected rightly that Martha would not understand, she left the house each morning as if she were going to work. There was a "blind pig" some blocks away where she could spend the day idling with the proprietor's wife and drinking what she could get gratis. Then, night coming on, she would ply her ancient trade. She did well.

Now, listening to Joe's request for money, she oscillated her gray eyes violently. Joe's hopes oozed.

"Lissen, man," she told him, "Ah'm doin' enough keepin' mah mouth shet, ain't Ah? What's de mattah wid yo' woman?" With that she flounced off.

Lacking other alternatives, Joe went to Martha. She was dubious and said so. But she couldn't resist Joe. She loved him. She went, therefore, to Max Abrams, an immigrant Jew, who lived at his place of business in the heart of the Negro section.

Max was something of a phenomenon in the neighborhood. He was a short, slightly built man, with definitely Semitic features and eyes that took shrewd account of everything they saw. An accident had left him partially crippled in both legs, but had done nothing to daunt his intrepid spirit. Among the Negroes he was liked and admired. He was the only white man they knew who permitted them the use of his first name—and this in itself was a cause of wonderment.

"Vell, Marda, *wie geht's*?" he greeted from the back of his store as he caught sight of Martha and Carrie making their way through open barrels of flour and sugar. He liked Martha. She wasn't lazy and she always paid her bills promptly. "*Ach! Und* how *ist das schöne Mädchen* tonight, *hein?*" he beamed upon Carrie, tendering her a piece of licorice twist.

Martha nervously scanned the rolls of cloth against the fly-specked walls. Now that she was here, she didn't like the idea of the loan at all. Maybe Max wouldn't let her have it. This thought, which should have comforted her, agitated her. Joe needed the money. Joe must have that shop! Joe would make good. Joe— Joe. . . .

She wasn't versed in the arts of business, so she came right out with her request. Max listened intently, considered this woman, her husband, whom he had estimated fairly at first sight.

"But, Marda," he cautioned, "*wenn* your husband—he don't make *der gut*—" His expressive hands completed the warning.

Martha's head came up and her gaze did not flinch. At that moment she was like a carven figure in heroic proportions. She said what women in similar situations have said through countless ages:

"Mah man'll do all right!"

Max smiled and nodded ruefully. "*Lieb ist über alles.*" His voice was resigned. He became all business. Terms were agreed upon (more lenient terms than Max's better sense dictated), the mortgage was drawn up, and the money was handed over to Martha. Then Max leaned upon his scarred counter, his shoulders drawn up to their highest, and with a hint of pity watched Martha and Carrie depart.

IV

In justice to Joe, when he stood for the first time in his starched white coat and freshly creased trousers, he had every intention of making good. And for a while there was substantial promise of success. Customers poured in, the best people of the settlement—butlers, hostlers, coachmen, and other domestics. Even Max Abrams came to get his hair-cut and shave and add prestige to the establishment; also the Reverend E. J. Jones, shepherd of Shiloh Baptist Church. Soon all the Negroes of any means had their private shaving-mugs deposited on the shelves of Joe's shop. Martha glowed proudly, while the children of the neighbors were glad to be associated with Carrie.

By the end of the first year half of the debt to Max was paid, including the small interest rate required. Max was surprised, but made no comment. Maybe he had been wrong.

V

Joe was industriously applying an after-shave lotion to the fat, shiny-black face of the Jamesons' well-fed butler when a surprised voice twanged from the door:

"Looka yere! Efn it ain't ole Joe!"

Joe glanced up quickly. Exclaiming his delight, he abandoned the fat man's chin and leaped to meet the newcomer.

"Jake Tillery! You yaller son of a—" Joe disregarded the No Profanity sign on the wall, which had been placed there at the request of the Reverend E. J. Jones.

The man facing Joe was of Joe's height, slim, and of that mulatto coloring which is described by Negroes as "dirty yaller." His eyes were light hazel, his head small and egg-shaped. Adorning it was a mat of sandy kinked hair through which ran a razor-made part—a single canal in an arid waste. The shop loafers, commenting on the elegance and extreme cut of his clothes, opined that he was "dressed out de barrel." Although the man was ugly, it was not this that made him repugnant. There was something else—some indefinable quality of evil that lurked in his slinking movements and emphasized an unwholesome look of dissipation.

He and Joe entered into an animated conversation that ignored the Jameson butler until that worthy, growing disgruntled, wrenched himself out of the chair like a sulky bear, finished wiping his jowls, replaced his stiff collar and black tie, and stalked out.

"So you gots a wife, eh?" Jake was saying. "Looks like you done struck it rich, man!"

"Ah'm a-doin' fair-to-middlin'," Joe admitted, complacently. Just then a cough caught him. He went to a little cabinet and poured two glasses of liquor. "Yere, take one wid me."

"Luck to you," toasted Jake, briefly.

"Hopes you lives fo'ever, an' hopes Ah never dies!" responded Joe.

As they drained their glasses, a tall, thin-faced, dark-brown man came in, dressed in the sober garments of the divine calling. He eyed Jake suspiciously and glared reprovingly at Joe.

"Brethren," his high-pitched voice intoned, "'wine is a mocker, an' strong drink is raging'! Brother Owens, whyn't you walk in de path more'n you does? Hain't Ah done tolt you . . ." The Reverend E. J. Jones was just warming to his temperance talk as he divested his frock coat and standing collar.

A true child of Satan, and not relishing this baptism of verbal holy water, Jake signaled to Joe that he would return later, and sauntered out. He wasn't interested in morals or souls.

Not far from the shop he encountered something more to his taste. It was Sue. She cruised up the dimly lighted street just as Jake turned the corner. He looked likely. She assumed her most enticing manner. Needless to say, Jake was open to any promising suggestions. He returned her scrutiny. Then he looked again. There was something familiar. Where had he seen those weaving movements before?

Sue's simpering, wide-eyed look changed to one of astonishment.

"Fo' de Lawd's sake! Jake!"

"Yeah," said Jake, laconically.

"Look yere, honey, what you a'doin' yere?" Sue's eyes sparkled as she pressed a hand caressingly against his chest.

"Klu-Kluxers," answered Jake, shortly. He was thinking. Sue must be doing well, if her clothes were an indication. Better sound her first, though. . . .

"What you doin'? Workin'?" he asked.

Sue grinned. "Nope. Seem like Ah jes' cain't git no job." She winked knowingly. "But Ah'm doin' purty good."

"Look yere, baby, Ah jes' got in town an' Ah'm broke. Ah had to use all mah money gittin' 'way from Richmond." His voice became syrupy as he drew the unresisting Sue to him.

"Whar was you goin', honey?" His eyes were half-closed, like a cat's when it has scented a mouse.

Sue's hands played over his back and arms. She laughed invitingly.

"Ah reckon Ah was a-waitin' to go wid you, honey," she cooed.

"But Ah ain't got no money—"

Sue interrupted him to pull up her dress and point significantly to a bulge under her stocking.

"Keep yo' money, big boy. Ah knows you gots some efn dey's any in de world. Ah don't want yo' money. . . ."

Jake grinned as they swung up the street.

VI

It didn't require much effort on Jake's part to persuade Joe to open a gambling-den in the back room of the shop. He would have opened one long ago had it not been for Martha.

Jake put it this way: Business was good and Joe needed a helper on Saturdays. He, Jake, had some money with him (chiefly his share of Sue's earnings from clients he sent to her), and would buy another barber chair. In return he would receive a percentage of the increased custom.

Martha listened to the plan with misgivings. She didn't like Jake, and she didn't like the way he eyed Carrie whenever he came to the house. Moreover, Joe, since Jake's coming, had taken to drinking more heavily. Still, Joe vowed that Jake was a good barber and his best friend, and he was out of work. Finally Martha was prevailed upon. And Jake set about putting his ideas into practice.

He installed the second barber chair. Then he turned his attention to the back room, adding to its furnishings a long oblong table covered with green felt, a pair of smaller tables with chairs, and two powerful nickel lamps. To insure privacy—more to be desired than fresh air—he sealed the two windows, but left the door available as a means of hasty exit.

The first Saturday night passed smoothly. Jake whispered invitations to a picked group, counseling quiet, and deserted his duties in the front of the shop to act as game-keeper, or cut man, and maintain orderly play. At one o'clock everyone left quietly by the back door.

When they had gone the partners entered into financial calculations. Within a few hours they had made more money at the game than they had made all day in the shop.

"Man-dee!" exclaimed the elated Joe.

Jake, hardened gambler that he was, remained calm. "You ain't seed nuffin' yit," he prophesied. "Wait'll you start makin' *real* money, man. Dis yere's chicken feed."

Even Martha was pleased when she was informed next morning of the brisk upturn business had taken. But though she greeted Jake more amiably, she still held him at a distance.

VII

Business continued good—so good that there was a tendency to forget the caution to quiet. Strange conversations drifted from the back room to the customers out front.

One Saturday the Reverend E. J. Jones came in for his pre-pulpit shave and hair-cut, his Bible under one arm, somber preoccupation veneering his thin, ascetic face. He sat down in the chair next to Joe's and relaxed with hands clasped across his narrow chest—a prophet in repose.

"Whar's yo' pardner?" he inquired.

Joe wavered nervously from one foot to the other as he clipped his customer's hair. He couldn't afford to let the Elder know of the gambling, and he couldn't keep him waiting—equally hot fires burned, as it were, at his front and rear. Finally he went to the door leading into the den and opened it a crack.

There was a low hum of voices mingled with the faint click of dice. Then: "Come, li'l' bitches, come! Hah—you sev'!"

Sometime in his vanished youth the Elder must have watched the dice, for his relaxed frame galvanized immediately into action. He leaped from his chair with astonishing swiftness and pointed a long, bony finger at the discomfited Joe.

"You gots gamblin' back dar!" he declared in a piercing voice. "Why fo' you gots it, Brothah Joe?" And he went on to deliver his best tirade, ending with bristling promises of hell fire and brimstone. Then he stalked out of the shop.

Joe rushed into the back room and drew Jake aside.

"We gots to stop dis game fo' tonight!" he panted. "De Eldah done found out 'bout it."

Jake shook his head. "Efn Ah stops dat Big Sam when he got his luck on he sho start somep'n."

Joe argued feebly, but Jake was firm. He saw money for himself in sight and he was against pampering the pastor in his aversion to gambling.

"Wal, fo' de Lawd's sake, keep 'em quiet!" Joe gave way. "Efn Marty find out 'bout dis, she'll jes' nacherly raise hell, sho!"

VIII

Martha was finding out at that very minute, for the Reverend Jones had not felt his duty ended with the impromptu sermon to Joe. He came upon Martha over the washtubs and delivered himself promptly in as scathing terms as he could command.

When he paused for breath Martha was wiping her arms on her apron.

"You come wid me!" she said, and there was a menace in her voice.

But the Reverend E. J. Jones was not made of the same metal as Isaiah, the dauntless prophet. He visioned the treatment he might receive at the hands of the angered gamblers, and that particular brand of martyrdom held no charm for him.

"No, Sistah Martha, Ah ain't gwine wid you. Ah'll preach me a sermon dat'll break dat thing up!"

So Martha was alone when she appeared at the shop door a few minutes later.

"Hullo, honey," Joe greeted her uneasily. "You ought'n' to come out wid no coat on—you'll git yo' death o' cold."

The solicitude was lost on Martha. "Whar's dat gamblin' a-goin' on yere?" she demanded, abruptly.

She took her stand in the center of the shop, feet braced widely apart, hands gripping her broad hips. This was a Martha Joe had never seen. He was frightened.

"Whar is it, Ah says?" Martha's deep voice was dangerous.

Joe did not have to answer. A voice from the back room boomed, "Walk, you bitches, walk!"

Sweat broke out on Joe, and it was not caused by heat from the pot-bellied stove. He tried to intercept Martha's lunge for the door, but with one sweep of her hand she sent him sprawling. A violent twist and jerk of the knob flung the door open, and Martha stood poised on the threshold, like an angry brown goddess about to scatter destruction on her sinful subjects. The effect was instantaneous.

Hand raised high over his battered, dirty hat, Big Sam stared at this apparition which had appeared so suddenly. His big eyes popped to their uttermost, and his thick-lipped, open mouth froze on an unspoken command to the dice. The cane with which Jake shuffled the cubes broke its hopping, anticipatory antics, and lay like a miraculously petrified snake on the green cloth. Men forgot their haggling over side bets. The drunken, slobbery-mouthed youth with the consumptive face and hang-dog expression stopped annoying Jake for a free turn at the dice at the expense of the game-keeper. More than a score of eyes, displaying various degrees of consternation, peered through the smoke haze at Martha in a stagnant silence.

"Git!"

Like a clap of thunder the word leapt at them. With one instinct the men turned like automatons toward the door at the back of the room. Jake attempted to stop the exodus.

"Hold on, men! You don't have to go. Ah owns part o' dis place! An' dis yere woman ain't got no rights to order you out!"

He turned on Martha, his hazel eyes ugly, his brows drawn upward in a way that boded no good. "You git to hell—" and that was as far as he got.

Two swift strides brought Martha in front of him, her face an agony of wrath. She seized him by the throat. She shook him until his yellow skin paled to green. Then she flung him against the table. The men who had paused in their flight now scrambled for the exit.

"Git what belongs to you an' don't lemme ketch you 'round yere no mo'! An efn you comes near mah house, niggah, Ah'll kill you!" With that Martha stormed through the door into the front room and swept out to the street. In passing, she favored Joe with a withering roll of her eyes.

Jake was busily recovering the scattered money when his partner joined him.

"Reckon dat 'bout breaks up de whole shootin'-match, Yaller," ventured Joe, easing timidly into a chair.

"Yeah," agreed the kneeling Jake without looking up.

"Reckon we bettah count up an' split de kitty, den," suggested Joe. He coughed nervously.

Jake arose slowly. He arranged the gathered coins into small neat stacks on one of the card-tables along with the square box containing the "cuts." His eyes fondled them. He passed a caressing hand over them, much in the manner of a father patting the heads of his children. Then he squinted at Joe and asked in low, cold tones:

"What kitty you talkin' 'bout?"

Joe licked his dry lips. He had a foreboding that all was not well. Words would not come.

"You see dat?" Jake pointed to the wrecked table. "Wal, dat's yo' kitty! Yo' woman done bust it an' you gots to pay fo' it! See?"

"But dat ain't cost much as dat money, Jake!" protested Joe.

"Go haid 'n' take yo's, den," Jake invited, grimly sarcastic. His eyes held the same hateful gleam that had burned at Martha. His right hand, like a hydra-headed serpent, glided stealthily toward his hip pocket.

Joe shivered. He had witnessed that glinting, upward flash of steel once before at Richmond, and remembered the bloody aftermath. In his haste to be gone he stumbled over the door sill.

Jake shrugged contemptuously, swept the stacks of money into the box, and departed.

IX

True to his word, the Reverend E. J. Jones preached a sermon exposing Joe's moral failings, and his obedient flock cried their "amens" in vigorous approval. When he was finished Joe had lost a great portion of his clientele. And as the days passed other customers—those upon whom Martha's fury had descended—drifted over to the barber who was Joe's only competitor. Martha had not foreseen this effect of her action.

Idleness settled upon Joe and he turned more frequently to his bottle. He hadn't even Martha's sympathy for comfort; contempt was at last eating away her blind love for this weakling. She refused to sleep with him—his slobbering embraces revolted her.

One cold night he fell into a drunken stupor and lay in a gutter until Martha found him and carried him home. Already honeycombed with tuberculosis, he lingered two feverish weeks, then a hemorrhage spurted out his life.

Chapter 3

I

Martha spoke to Carrie across the dinner table. It was the Sunday following Joe's burial.

"You cain't git off to school dis year, chile," she said.

Carrie's bright eyes dulled. She had set her heart upon going to the Institute.

Martha went on: "We's got to pay our debt. Efn we works hard dis year, next year you kin go. Warn't fo' dat good-fo'-nuffin' Joe you could a-gwine dis year! Missy told me dat man warn't no good!" She took Carrie's chin in her roughened hand and lifted it gently. "Lissen, chile," she said, bitterly, "don't nevah let no no-'count man make no fool outn you! Ain't no man no-'count! Y'ear me?"

II

They made an heroic effort, but after a year bent over their tubs the mortgage was still unpaid. And Carrie's hope of attending the Institute was little nearer realization. The ceaseless drubbing toil was hardest on Carrie, and for hours and days at a stretch the girl would be plunged into the black moods that are the affliction of adolescence. Was all her life to be cut to this dreary pattern? Was she to go on forever rubbing, rinsing, bluing, ironing, delivering clothes? She saw no other fate in store. And it wasn't fair! It wasn't fair! Lucrece had put the thought of schooling into her mind and the young Negro teacher had fostered it. She was a good student—bright and quick. She was wasting herself over endless batches of clothes.

So she fretted. Spring gave way to summer, summer to autumn, autumn to winter. And each day was hopelessly like the one just past.

Then one morning, before the Christmas season, she was in the back yard hanging out a basket of clothes when she heard a cry.

"Carrie! Carrie!"

In the kitchen she found Martha collapsed beside the ironing-board, on which a sheet was smoking.

"Mah—arm—honey," Martha panted. "It—ain't—"

Carrie took one look at her mother's twisted lips and sped toward the front of the house, where footsteps sounded. Fright leaped in her heart.

In the dining-room she collided with Sue.

"Lawdy!" Sue exclaimed when she saw Martha's drawn face. "It acts like mah uncle Mark's when he was strick.

Help me git 'er to de couch," she directed Carrie, "an' den you run git de doctah."

III

Sue was in deep conversation with Jake in a basement room not far from Martha's house. It was Jake's new place of business.

"Look yere," he was saying, "didn't you tell me dat Joe tolt Martha you was his sistah?"

"Yeah, but—"

"Nev' mind de *but*—you jes' stay his sistah! See?"

"Yeah—but don't dat make me have to take care dat gal, Carrie, efn Martha dies? Ah ain't used to—"

"Nev' mind what you's used to! Don't you see, you fool?—efn de gal comes to you, so's de house!" Jake paused to see what effect this would have.

Sue slapped her fleshy thigh. "Dog-gone! Dat's right, ain't it?" She thought a minute. "Look yere, Martha mo'gaged dat house to set Joe up in dat shop. S'posin' dey ain't paid it off?"

"Wal, Ah was figgerin' dat you an' me could kindah hang together," Jake confessed. "Ah gots a li'l' pile what Ah done made yere—an' dey's mo' comin'. What say, hon'?"

Smiling her agreement, Sue snuggled against him and explored his lean body with plump fingers. Jake responded abstractedly but with expertness. Then with a kiss, and a pat on a rounded buttock he sent Sue on her way and turned to the task of tidying the den. In one corner he spied a slimy pool where some one had unloaded an excess of liquor.

"Damn pigs!" he exclaimed, disgustedly, as he reached for a pail of sawdust.

IV

Martha's death profoundly affected a number of people. It left Carrie to the questionable protection of Sue, with no one to turn to for love and understanding. It gave Sue and Jake a home to which their wits did not entitle them. Incidentally, it afforded the Reverend E. J. Jones with a theme for one of his most eloquent sermons. Martha had not attended church after the night of the gambling-den episode, and this digression from the Path of Light—according to the Reverend Jones's interpretation—in all probability contributed directly to her demise.

Martha was buried beside Joe. The Sisters of the Shining Star in the West Lodge stood about the fresh mound and chanted "Till We Meet." Then all took their ways home, to be submerged again in the affairs of their separate lives. It mattered to no one that Martha symbolized a link between their present freedom and their past condition of slavery;

or that Martha and her valiant kind are rare personalities in any age.

That night Sue moved her belongings from a room over the blind pig to the neat house for which Martha had broken herself. The mongrel had usurped the kennel of the thoroughbred.

Chapter 4

On a certain morning during the rainy season between winter and spring—when the fog banks steal up the Chesapeake and fall over Baltimore with a clinging, dripping embrace—Jake awoke out of alcoholic slumber and growled disagreeably. He looked at the clock. Seven. Hell! He'd slept only five hours! He was about to settle back into his pillow when his attention was caught and held by Sue's face, and he bent upon her the gaze a man directs toward a woman of whom he has had too much; an unfavoring, searching scrutiny. What he saw did not tempt him.

Whisky had swollen the pale-yellow countenance. Sleep had flung wide her loose-lipped mouth, displaying stained teeth that had never known a brush. Her hair was a sodden mass. With a jerk of the covers Jake revealed her body, but the sight of that ungainly mound of flesh only increased his distaste. His lips curled. He lay back and stared at the ceiling.

In two years Jake had prospered. His gambling-den had more than made its way—it had cleared the mortgage on Martha's house. The house itself, straying from its original purpose, had proved a lucrative asset, for single rooms were let regularly for the use of transient bawds.

Jake was pleased with his achievement. But lying in bed this morning he reflected that success entitled him to a woman more pleasing than the one beside him. One thought led to another until in a moment of decision he stepped cautiously out of bed and made his way to the door.

Down the damp, smelly hall he stole, past the corner bedroom where Big Lil lay with her consort of the night, past another room whose door was open, revealing a state of towering disorder—Callie had sneaked out early without paying his percentage of her fee. At a third door he stopped and listened, then exerted a steady pressure.

Carrie wakened to see Jake's evil yellow face so close that twin streams of heat from his distended nostrils pounded against her neck. She did not scream, but her black eyes clouded with hate. Jake misinterpreted her calm.

"Honey," he whispered.

Grasping her shoulders, he attempted to kiss her. Immediately ten fingernails raked his face, leaving livid streaks in their wake, while strong flashing teeth clamped the point of his chin in a painful vise. With one spring a slender brown fury leaped from the bed,

"Ef you don't git out o' here, Ah'll call A'nt Sue!" she warned.

Jake was disconcerted but not convinced; he moved toward the girl, then stood swaying on the balls of his feet while reason battled with liquor and passion. Finally his long training over the gaming-table decided in favor of reason. He did not relish facing an aroused Sue, and he knew that Sue countenanced no liberties with Carrie— some obscure motive prompted her to take the rôle of protector very seriously.

Jake backed quietly to the door and left.

Carrie sat on the bed and drew the quilt about her shoulders. She knew what Jake had wanted. The women and men who came to the house had been a liberal education, and Sue on one occasion had informed her bluntly on the functions of sex, concluding with: "So you keep clear o' dese menfolks—dey don't mean you no good." The advice had been unnecessary. Carrie was not attracted to the men she saw about her. It was easy, with Sue's cooperation, to meet their suggestive smirks with indifference. For Carrie was as Martha had been. A tidal wave might some day engulf her, but there would be no promiscuous giving.

But the moment had come to take stock of her situation. She wanted to get out of all this—the filth, the smell of whisky . . . everything. She had not forgotten her first bright hopes of school. She wanted to know things— things Lucrece and the young teacher had known. She wanted to do things—not just cook and keep this hateful house in a semblance of order.

The mirror reflected a pleasing young person of sixteen, slender but not angular, light brown in color. If she gathered her hair into a discreet bun and wore a dress that would conceal the absence of curves, perhaps she would look older. She would try. For Carrie had made up her mind.

"You goin' to git yo'self a job!" she told her reflection. "Efn you wants to go to school, you gots to git out of here and git some money!"

The kitchen clock on the shelf said a quarter to eight as she stepped into her slippers and eased noiselessly out of the door. From the alley she turned up the rain-slicked pavement at a rapid pace, unmindful of the puddles beneath her feet. Somewhere ahead was a job.

II

Mrs. Josiah Hobarth was having a most disagreeable morning. The fog would have been enough—it always depressed her and brought on an attack of asthma. But in addition to the fog there was Gretna. Gretna, her hired girl, had calmly left the evening before, after informing her: "Ole und me, ve ist married to be diese nacht."

Mrs. Hobarth had pleaded for a few days of grace until she could get some one else, but the girl had been firm.

"Nein, mum, Ole, he ist no vant for me to hire out now. Ole, he say dat for him I vork now."

And that had ended the matter. Ole, the hack-driver, arrived for Gretna's belongings and they departed. And because of them Mrs. Hobarth was in the kitchen this morning, cranking viciously at the clinker-clogged grate of the stove. It gave at last, but when she attempted to start a fire the damp wood did nothing but smoke. She was dirty and perspiring from her exertions. Upstairs, Mr. Hobarth wanted to know where she had put this shirt and that tie.

The good woman could have screamed.

It did not appease her to hear a timid knock at the door, accompanied by an equally timid brown face at the window pane.

Rising impatiently, Mrs. Hobarth swung the door back so violently that the knob slipped from her hand and dislodged a piece of plaster from the wall. This damage to her newly painted kitchen was the crowning exasperation of the morning.

"What do you want?" she almost yelled at the girl on the doorstep.

Carrie shrank within her cloak and forgot her curtsy. She had had no idea it would be as hard as this! "Do you need a girl?" she blurted, in desperation, wide-eyed.

A sigh escaped Mrs. Hobarth. A smile ironed out the wrinkles which irritation had caused. She stepped aside and motioned Carrie into the kitchen.

"Can you cook?" she asked.

"Yes'm," answered Carrie.

Her sharp eyes caught the smoke wreathing from between the lids of the stove. She stepped over to it, turned the damper straight with the chimney, and opened the bottom door. Ashes seeped from the pile beneath the grate. She shoveled the pile into a pail, then swept up the floor.

When she turned back to Mrs. Hobarth approval was written in every line of that lady's plump florid face. A little smudge on the tip of her nose looked like an isolated polka dot in a pinkish dress. Carrie tried to suppress a smile, but failed.

"What are you laughing at?" the woman asked, good-humoredly.

Carrie decided to tell the truth.

"Yo' nose is black, ma'am," she answered, as soberly as she could.

Mrs. Hobarth bustled hastily to the mirror, and after one look at herself burst into laughter that shook her like so much gelatin. The laughter cleared the air of the last vestige of gloom.

"I'm Mrs. Hobarth. I don't know what sent you—but the Lord knows I'm glad you're here! Now, if you'll cook breakfast for Mr. Hobarth and me, we'll have a talk later about you. You'll find things in the cupboard and the pantry. Just eggs. And Mr. Hobarth likes biscuits. Can you make them?"

"Yes'm!" grinned Carrie, happily, darting for the pantry.

III

That night between sips of whisky Sue listened to Carrie tell of her job.

"Huh!" Sue grunted. "Seems like you'd a stayed yere. You didn't have nuffin' to do but pass a li'l' likker 'round. 'Co'se, you suit yo'self. Ah promised yo' mammy Ah'd look to you. Ah done de bes' Ah could. Efn you gits tired, you come on home. See?"

"You bin real nice, A'nt Sue—but Ah wants to make enough money to go to school."

Sue made a face. "What you want go to school fo'? Ain't nuffin' but a waste o' time."

"Ah'm goin' to school!" Carrie replied, doggedly.

"All right—all right! Go 'haid!" said Sue, placatingly. She dashed off the last few drops of her liquor. "We gwine move from yere," she went on. "Jake says dat meddly Mandy Dobson talk too much. We gwine down by de docks— Jake says bizness bettah. So efn you gwine stay whar you works, you better take yo' clothes wid you tonight."

Cheerfully Carrie packed her few belongings and went back to the Hobarth home. She thought the tie broken that bound her to Jake and Sue.

Chapter 5

I

Spring brought light breezes up the bay and fresh foliage and new grass to tempt the robins to the Hobarths' small lawn. It brought Keith Hobarth home from the New England college where he had completed his freshman year.

Keith had neither the stolid, methodical quality of his father, who had made a small fortune in the meat trade, nor the social ambitions of his mother. He was a quiet, rather aloof young man—attractive in appearance and with a poise beyond his years.

He noticed Carrie the first night at dinner. And in the days that followed he found innumerable threadbare excuses to visit the kitchen. He wanted a snack to eat; he wanted to lend her some of his school books since she liked to read. . . .

Carrie, seeing through his pretenses, was worried. She had a good job that would bring her within the reach of school. And she wanted to keep it. School was much more important than any man she had ever seen. Besides, there had been instilled in her the consciousness of racial difference, and this was not easily shaken.

The crisis came one Sunday morning, a fortnight after Keith's return. He had begged off church, saying he wanted to walk over to the Falls. In a short while he stepped through the door of the kitchen.

"Busy?" he inquired, blithely.

Carrie looked up, startled, from the potatoes she was peeling. Dismay followed swiftly on surprise. She started to rise, then remembered the pan in her lap and sat down again.

"Ah thought you'd gone to church, Mr. Keith."

"You know why I didn't go?" he asked, leaning against the table. A furnace raged inside him.

"P-please don't stay, Mr. Keith!" Carrie's eyes lifted pleadingly to his.

The soft beauty of the up-tilted brown face stripped the boy of all his youthful restraints. With a single swift movement of his hand he swept the pan from her lap and jerked Carrie to her feet into his arms. He was bending his head to her lips when—

"Keith!"

It was like the cracking of an oaken beam. The voice, reverberating across the room, put to flight Keith's passion and left him cold and limp. Carrie sank weakly into a chair.

"Go into the parlor, Keith!" Mr. Hobarth's large, fleshy face was aflame. He turned to Carrie. "I don't know whose fault it is," he said. "I don't care. I thought from the first you were too good-looking. I figured my son was attracted by you." The man's anger took possession of him and he stormed on: "I went over the colored neighborhood yesterday. Why did you tell my wife that you were from Virginia?"

Carrie did not answer. What was the use?

"Well, I know now where you came from, and you can go back! Your kind is dangerous to have around—even if it ain't your fault. Such as you are a result of that damn slavery."

He paused for breath.

"I'll pay you for a month. Now get your things and get out of here!"

Carrie dragged herself to her room that had been her very own for so short a time: a sanctuary securing her from the noise of harlots and their drunken companions. With deadening fingers she bundled her effects, adding at the last moment one book, a volume of Home Science. Then she hastened down the stairs and out of the house.

Josiah Hobarth watched her go, an annoying sense of injustice pricking at his conscience. But with a gesture he rid himself of the thought and turned toward the front of the house where his son waited.

II

On the sun-lit yet gloomy journey to the harbor front, two forces in Carrie's nature battled for supremacy. A sea of pessimism engulfed her. Self-pity stifled the spirit of Martha and left her a prey to all the weak elements that were her heritage from Joe. The flame of her ambition, that had struggled so desperately to maintain itself, made one last effort, then died.

In such a mood Carrie turned into a smelly alley-street that paralleled the waterfront. It was lined on either side by warehouses and stables that frowned down upon the few squalid dwellings, much as children scowl at their enfeebled elders who have lingered too long. From the first of these decrepit houses came the sound of a wheezy reed organ, a guitar and a whisky-cracked soprano—all blended in a doleful tune. The voice was unmistakably Sue's.

Carrie knocked at the weather-washed door, from which the paint was peeling. Instantly the discord within stopped. But no one answered the knock. Carrie called:

"Open up, A'nt Sue!"

There was a pause. The door slid open a trifle, and Sue peered out cautiously. Through the haze of her liquor she recognized Carrie. She swung the door wide, grinning her welcome. In her own way, she had learned to love this child of Martha's.

"Come on in, honey!" she cried. "What you doin' yere? Got de day off?"

"Gimme a drink," said Carrie, shortly, dropping her bundle.

"Drink? Sho. Water in de back room, honey."

"Ah wants likker! Likker!"

Sue blinked her amazement. Carrie had never touched whisky, even though it had always been accessible to her.

"What's de mattah—" Carrie's scowl halted Sue's query.

"All right, honey . . . all right. . . ," she soothed, and staggered through dirty drapes to the back room.

Carrie deposited her bundle on a chair, sat down and looked about her.

The room was about ten by eight feet. The floor was bare, except for two spotty, ragged mats which sprawled like grimy poodles asleep in the sun. The walls, in the more seemly days of their past, had been papered, but now were shedding in patches. As if to offset this evidence of deterioration, flies had obligingly dotted the surface with an effect that suggested a pattern. Several people, in varying degrees of intoxication, lounged in the chairs along the walls, regarding Carrie curiously.

A pock-marked, scrawny yellow woman sat in the corner, with one arm flung about the bullish neck of her companion. At the organ was a light-skinned youth, lean and fidgety, with a brown-paper cigarette swinging limply from his mouth. Four women, unpaired, after one look at the newcomer, went back to their lusty snoring. They were resting for the evening, when men would be coming from the harbored boats in search of diversion.

Sue brought in a small demijohn of rum and set it on a side-table along with some glasses.

"Help yo'self, honey—but you bettah go slow, seein's it's yo' first."

Carrie ignored this counsel, poured a brimming glassful and drained it at a gulp; poured another and drank that. Sue's eyes rounded in astonishment.

"Lawsy, chile! You gwine to git drunk sho's you bo'n!" she warned. "It makes me drunk to watch you!"

"Ah don't care!" Carrie avowed, tempestuously. She approached the organist.

"Play that song ag'in," she ordered.

The youth turned readily to the organ and struck from it a few groaning, preliminary chords, then swung into the tune Carrie had heard from the street. The bull-necked black man disengaged himself from the skinny arms of the yellow woman and strummed an accompaniment.

"Sing it, A'nt Sue!" laughed Carrie, crazily.

Sue caught up the refrain, which told of a certain brown-skin "papa," for whom a dolorous brown-skin gal was longing. The verses were mere jumbles, liberally supplied with obscenity. But the whole wove a rhythmical pattern which beat into Carrie's liquored brain until she began to hum along with Sue. As she caught the words she sang louder in a deep contralto, and as she sang she swayed her trim hips in time to the music. The guitarist's eyes were dark slits. His yellow companion sulked angrily.

Heavy boots fell upon the steps outside, the door was jerked open, and Jake waved four men into the room. He evinced no surprise at Carrie's presence.

"Mistah Hen'y Taylor"—he introduced the first man, a black giant with huge, square jaws and incredibly thin lips. The awakened women eyed him appreciatively.

"Mistah Zack Wheelah." That stubby one hunched his shoulders a trifle and grinned.

"Mistah Hank Tate an' Mistah Slim Hackins." Tate and Hackins were too drunk to display any interest and remained placidly blank.

Jake finished the introductions by turning to the women:

"An' dis is Jinny." Jinny was chocolate-colored and robust.

"An' dis is Kate—" A midgety, faded-yellow jade smiled invitingly; she wasn't choicy.

"Dis yere's Josie." Cynical lips twisted across a colorless face, like a streak of blood on a piece of bleached putty, and hard eyes fixed themselves on the weak-faced Hackins. He involuntarily staggered over to her.

"An' Cassie," Jake ended. That squat, black one grinned the width of her broad face. Hank scampered to her, like a mouse to a piece of cheese.

"Who dat?" asked the big man, indicating Carrie. Before Jake could answer, Sue confronted the fellow.

"Dat's mah niece—why?" Her tone challenged. The huge man looked at her and looked away.

"Nuffin," he said, and strode over to the robust Jinny. Wheeler, of necessity, took his place with the uncoupled Kate.

"Go on an' sing, Carrie," bade Sue.

III

There were times, during the days that followed, when the old urge for an education would revive in Carrie; but never to remain for long. Too much of her father's spinelessness had been engendered by her first failure. The injustice of the Hobarth incident so shadowed her thinking that it served as an immediate check whenever she considered getting another job. She fondled the notion that all the world conspired against her. The notion became an idea and in time a fixed state of mind.

A contempt for everything and everybody fastened upon her and soured her. She despised Sue for her slovenliness. To Carrie the woman was filth personified. She loathed the seafaring men, their leering faces and lust-flamed eyes. They made her feel naked. Some of them would come alone and insist that she sit at their table. Sue assured her that she didn't have to if she didn't want to. But Carrie derived malicious pleasure from watching them try to make her drunk. She devised a scheme by which she increased Sue's liquor profits and at the same time rid herself of annoyers. Next to the wall under each table she placed a wide-mouthed crock. The first two or three drinks she drank outright—she developed a surprising ability to control her liquor— then when the man became too stupefied to notice, she deposited drink after drink secretly into the crock. The ruse delighted Sue.

But though she loathed these others, it was Jake for whom she had a consuming hatred. She hated the cold precision with which he robbed his less brainy opponents over the crap-table. She hated the swift snakiness of his lean fingers as they curved about the dice. She hated the way he cut quarters, instead of nickels, from the winnings of a half-drunk illiterate. And, above all, she hated and shrank from the assuredness of his stare, which seemed to prophesy that some day she would be his in spite of her antipathy. She answered that stare, however, with a defiant scorn which was heartened by the knowledge that Sue's protecting bulk stood between them.

Thus Carrie kept her physical chastity, like a luster-less gem in a setting of corroded metal. She attached no value to it. She simply didn't choose to part with it.

Then, in about a year and a half, out of the lowlands of Maryland's Eastern Shore came Jim Prince.

Chapter 6

I

Summer had carried over greedily into September; time of hot, sultry days and nights cooled by breezes off the Bay; time when farmers from the harvested fields of Virginia and Maryland come to Baltimore town seeking buyers.

As soon as you saw him, you knew that Jim Prince was not of an urban breed. His spanking-new clothes, the extreme cut of them, their flashy pattern, the self-conscious manner in which he wore them—all attested his bucolic origin. Further evidence was the exaggerated swagger of his narrow yet powerful shoulders, which sloped as if they were eternally lifting a heavy load. His young copper-brown face bore the imprint of toil, and the face harmonized with veined, hard hands that were obviously unaccustomed to handling dice. The very curve of the knotty fingers suggested rather a plowshare or hoe. And despite thorough scrubbing, despite the odor of cheap tonic on his freshly cut hair, he smelled of earth—clean plowed earth.

After a short time spent in Jake's gaming-room, Jim Prince left. Clearly, it was no place for one who appreciated a dollar, and Prince did. He drifted into the front room.

Two women looked up hopefully as he entered, but he dismissed them with a glance and strode over to Carrie, who was absently fingering chords at the organ. She looked at him without interest and returned to her aimless music. Nothing daunted, Prince leaned against the organ and let his eyes rove leisurely over her head and shoulders. She frowned.

"Well?" she demanded, peevishly.

He grinned, and his grin had an infectious quality.

"Mah name's Prince—Jim Prince," he informed her in a twangy, lilting drawl. "Everybody titles me Prince, though. Ah'm from de Sho'—East'n Sho', Maryland, down to Shrewsbury and Deerfield way." He paused, waiting for Carrie to exhibit some interest, but the organ wheezed on in unconcern.

"Mah ole man he sent me to Balt'more, 'cause he's poorly, to look attah de wheat- an' corn-sellin'. Ah'm jes' 'bout finish now an' thought Ah'd have me some spreadin' joy. But dat cat-eyed hound in dar, he done tried to take me fo' a good thing. So Ah thought Ah'd git out 'fo' Ah lose mah haid." He bent confidentially over Carrie. "Now cain't 'mongst-you help a fellah out what wants a good time?"

Carrie smiled crookedly as she gave him a hard-eyed stare.

"You better go on home, big boy, whilst you still can. These buzzards'll pick you just clean's a bone efn you hang 'round!" Why she advised him so, she didn't know. Perhaps it was because of his youth; perhaps because of his clean virility—two qualities which the other men lacked.

He began to protest: "Oh, you don't have to worry 'bout me, honey! Ah kin take care mahself, all right. All Ah wants is—is—"

"All you wants," Carrie finished for him, with cool bitterness, "is what all the rest of the men wants what comes here! You wants a woman—to drink wid an' to sleep wid."

Prince was seized with embarrassment.

"Ah'll drink wid you. But"—Carrie looked him straight in the eye—"that's all."

She left the room and returned with a bottle, beckoning him to a near-by table. Prince took the drink she offered, but sputtered and choked trying to down it.

"You ever drink likker befo'?" asked Carrie.

"No—only Thanksgivin' an' Christmas an' New Year's," he confessed.

"Huh!" grunted Carrie. "What Ah ought to do is make you drunk an' take all yo' money from you! But Ah reckon Ah'm jes' too chicken-hearted. . . . You git outn here 'fo' some wench takes all you gots!"

"You reckon so?" queried Prince, already dizzy from his single drink.

"Yeah, Ah reckon so!" declared Carrie, emphatically. "One mo' drink an' you ain't able to stand on yo' feet! Come on!"

"But Ah'm all right!"

"You better git on a boat an' leave fo' the Sho' efn one's goin' tonight!" With that she shoved him out into the alley.

II

He came again the next day. Sue was taking her daily nap, and Jake was out. It was too early for the other women.

"Thought you was on yo' way back to the farm?" Carrie looked up from the dress she sewed. She was neither glad nor annoyed at seeing him. "Rest yo' burden, since you's here," she invited. She motioned him to a chair.

Prince sat down and stretched his long legs. He grinned his slow, boyish grin, but said nothing.

"What's the matter?" asked Carrie. "Boats stop runnin'?"

"Nope, dey still runnin'," Prince assured her. He cut a piece from a plug of tobacco, and thrust it into his mouth, careless of the sharp edge of the knife. "Jes' didn't feel like leavin' today," he concluded.

"Oh, you wants to git robbed anyways!"

"Ain't nobody gwine rob me," vouchsafed Prince, searching for some place to deposit a mouthful of juice.

Gingerly, with a foot, Carrie shoved a filthy cuspidor from beneath a table.

"What you come here fo', then?" she asked.

"'Cause Ah wanted to see 'mongst-you ag'in," was his blunt answer.

"Lissen, big boy, didn't Ah tell you nothin' doin', last night? The rest o' these women do *that*—not me! Ah ain't no piece o' meat to buy!"

"Is Ah said anything 'bout *dat*?" he countered, unruffled. "An' who says Ah buys?"

"Huh! That's what they all come here fo'."

"What you stay yere fo' efn you don't like it?" retorted Prince.

"Where Ah goin' to go?" demanded Carrie. She put the dress aside and took up the conversation in earnest. "Lissen, big boy, Ah reckons this place is the only one fo' me. Ah was bo'n fo' bad luck, that's all!"

"Luck's in de Lawd, an' de devil's in de people," drawled Prince, and he spat squarely into the cuspidor.

"Huh! That's what you think, but Ah knows better! Lissen." And Carrie sketched the details of her life: her mother's death, its consequences, her failure to keep a job, her longing for an education. Prince listened sympathetically.

"Ah ain't got no eddication," he said, "'cept'n a year or so. Ah kin read an' write an' count. An' mah ole man, he ain't got no l'arnin' a-tall. But he sho is smart. He warn't freed by no white mens a-fightin' fo' him. Nossuh!" Prince went on to tell how his father had worked seven years for his freedom and five more for that of his wife; how his father had struggled to make his small plot of ground yield, adding more and more land, until now he owned "a purty tol'able farm."

"But de ole man's failin' fast," Jim concluded. "Co'se, he allows he kin still keep up—but 'tain't so. He home now 'thout nobody to look attah him. Ain't bin no woman in de house since Ma died."

Despite herself, Carrie had become absorbed in the narrative. It lifted Jim Prince out of the category of all the men she knew and made an individual of him—some one clean and wholesome. She felt belittled beside him.

"It must be nice down there," she ventured, wistfully, and for the first time she smiled whole-heartedly at him.

"'Mongst-you would like it!" he exclaimed, eagerly. "Some o' dese days," he prophesied, "Ah'm gwine have one o' de best farms on de Sho.'" And Carrie could not help but feel that his was no idle boast.

"Looka yere—uh—," he stammered. "Looka yere, how'd you like to be down dat way? 'Mongst-you don't b'long in no place like dis." Prince indicated the dingy room which even Carrie's industry could not much remedy.

"Do you reckon Ah wants to stay here?" came the disconsolate reply. "But where am Ah goin'? Ah cain't git no job after what happened at the Hobarths.'"

"Ah don't mean fo' you to stay in Balt'more," interposed Jim. "Ah means fo' you to go home wid me. We needs a woman 'round de house—me an' Pa—"

"You means you would—marry me?" Carrie cried.

"Co'se Ah means dat!" answered Jim, firmly. He leaned forward eagerly.

Away from the filth and the smell of raw liquor and stale smoke. Away from the debauched men and crawling women. Away from Jake's hateful face and hot eyes, from Sue's sloppiness. Away—to where she could see clear skies and clean earth, instead of drab gray walls of warehouses and crumbling bricks. . . . The picture caught and held her for a moment. Then her habitual pessimism blotted it out rudely.

"No. . . . No. . . . It wouldn't work. It mought fo' a while . . . but wouldn't last long. Ain't nothin' never goin' to last wid me! Guess Ah b'longs here."

Prince pleaded. He coaxed and argued. But Carrie remained listlessly determined. Finally he arose.

"Guess Ah'll leave tonight on de twelve-'clock boat. Good-by."

Carrie made no answer.

III

The weather had changed overnight. A blustery northeast wind rushed from the Bay, sweeping debris before it. It was not a cold wind, but it bore a chill which made the alley-dwellers close their doors. The ragged urchins who usually played about the doorsteps had carried their activities inside.

Sue was enjoying one of her alcoholic naps. Jake puttered about the gaming-table, making minute repairs. Carrie was at the organ. As she played she hummed softly, thinking of many things—of Jim Prince and his farm and her own dreary lot.

Suddenly Jake's voice purred above her and his fingers caressed her shoulders.

"You sho sings purty, gal."

Carrie's fingers died on the keys.

"Take yo' dirty hands offn me!" she commanded, her voice metallic.

Jake said nothing, but pressed himself against her back and gripped her firmly.

"You hear me?" Her voice rose to a higher pitch. "Ah'll call A'nt Sue!"

"Go 'haid," snickered Jake. He held her more tightly.

"A'nt Sue! A'nt Sue!" called Carrie.

There was no answer. Jake laughed.

"Go 'haid! Holler!" he mocked.

Carrie struggled to gain her feet and Jake shifted his hold to her wrists, twisting them violently. The girl kicked and tried to bite, but without success. She felt herself weakening.

"Let me go!" she cried.

As if that were a signal, a long form hurtled through the door and leapt on Jake, while sinewy fingers, like cables, wrapped themselves about the gambler's freckled neck. Like a bag from which the contents are pouring, Jake sank to his knees, his pale eyes bulging.

From across the room, where she had been flung by the impact of the men's bodies, Carrie recognized the distorted face of her rescuer, who at the moment seemed intent on killing Jake.

"Jim! Jim Prince!" she screamed.

The great fingers loosened slowly, and Jake dropped to the floor.

Prince picked up the limp form. "Show me whar he sleeps—an' git me some likker," he ordered Carrie.

Carrie led the way upstairs. When he had dumped his burden on the bed, Prince took the bottle and poured some of its raw contents into Jake's gaping mouth. Jake gurgled and spat feebly.

"Git yo' clothes together," Jim told Carrie.

"Mah clothes?"

"Git yo' clothes!" His voice snapped. "Whar's yo' A'nt?"

Carrie jerked a thumb at the other bedroom. "She's in there—drunk."

"Kin she read?"

"A li'l."

"Wal, you jes' make a note sayin' you's gone," commanded Prince. "Hurry up!" he added, before she could begin to quibble; "it's 'most time fo' de boat!"

Chapter 7

It is a low, flat land, the Eastern Shore of Maryland. It crouches there between the Chesapeake on the west and the state of Delaware on the east. Toward the south the green waters of the Atlantic wash lazily—lazily, that is, until one of those northeastern gales frightens the ocean out of its calm. At such times, gigantic billows blast the frail man-made bulwarks and wipe away, as by the sweep of an angry god's broom, those little clusters of frame houses and hotels which are the sea-shore resorts. And the tidal waters of the Choptank, the Miles, the Shannon, the Tred-Avon, and others of the rivers, flood the inland towns, driving the population into the upper rooms of their dwellings. Then the refuse from the outhouses floats in the streets until the waters subside. And the crops of the farmers are ruined, and their live-stock lost.

It crouches there, the Shore, like a sulking, neglected child, with its scattered hamlets, towns, and villages.

Some of them have caught the modern spirit; others lie in dull contentment with their lot beneath whatever kind of sky the fates provide. The farmers plow, plant, and reap. The river men snatch their produce from the streams. The canners pack their tomatoes and peas. And natives of all persuasions are born, live, propagate, decline, and are buried beneath the low, flat land, in order that their children may take up the thread of life.

Carrie loved these autumnal lowlands to which Prince had brought her. She loved the steady sameness of their flowing fields fringed by pine woods. Somehow the monotony of the landscape reassured her—gave her a feeling of security.

She liked, too, the way the sun regulated her life. She arose at dawn, there were so many things to do. There was the fire to be made; breakfast to be cooked; the chickens to be unroosted; the cows to be milked with Jim's coaching. At noon, Jim and his father would come in from the field, preceded by their eager mules, smelling of the manure they had been spreading. And it was a treat to watch them gobble up the meal she had prepared. After dinner the two men sat on the back porch and chewed their quids— the old man whittling aimlessly, Jim scanning his land in contemplation—while Carrie washed the dishes and went about her housework. Then back to the fields they would go, to return with the sunset and the chickens and the leisurely plodding cattle.

When supper was finished the three of them gathered about the big kitchen stove which roared with pine logs. Carrie might read aloud from old newspapers, the Bible, or from the one book she had brought with her. Jim rarely said much, but schemed silently. The old man was different. He could be lured easily into conversation, for he loved to talk of the past: scenes and events on the plantation. Weddings, christenings, fugitive slaves, floggings, deaths—he recalled them all as if they had been catalogued within his mind. Carrie never tired of listening to him. And she understood why Prince was so proud of him. He had known toil. He had faced years of grinding disappointment. He had met life bravely, with a purpose in mind, and he had won his reward.

Later, when deep night settled, Prince would help his father to bed. Then after locking the doors and banking the fire, Prince and Carrie would follow. And in bed, with the feel of Prince's arms about her, Carrie found contentment.

But Sunday was red-letter day, when, after morning prayers and a simple breakfast of warmed-up food—the elder Prince would allow no cooking on the Sabbath—they would attend church. The journey was made in a fringe-topped carriage, in a silence that was rarely broken, for Sunday was the day of meditation. Carrie, in her best dress of sober gray, sat beside her husband, in store-bought clothes and celluloid collar. The back seat was given entirely to Father Prince, who always wore the swallow-tail coat that denoted his deaconship.

Yes, Sunday was red-letter day because the church, which nestled on the western extremity of Shrewsbury, focused all the social life of the little community. One was made or broken by his standing with other church members, and by the number of church activities in which he engaged.

Carrie warmed immediately to the kindly welcome that met her from all sides on her first Sunday. Another week and she had joined the choir. Then the minister, discovering that she was a capable reader, appointed her church clerk. A class was given her in the Sunday school, and she assisted the organist. As a final crowning recognition, the Reverend Holland's wife saw to it that she entered the charmed circle of the Ladies' Aid. This last marked a seven-league stride along the social pathway. If some of the sisters begrudged a newcomer such signal favor, Carrie was too happy to notice.

II

Within the first year of Carrie's marriage, old man Prince left them to join his wife, and for a time there was a great void in the small family. Then young Jim came to make welcome and exacting demands on his mother's time. Because of the child Carrie lost her old haunting fear that her happiness could not endure. And more and more she became a part of Prince's life. His ways were her ways; his mode of thought and ambitions hers.

Chapter 8

I

It was near the time of Carrie's second child, one evening at the close of the reaping season, when there came a terrific pounding at the door.

"Mistah Jim! Mistah Jim!"

Jim hurriedly opened the door to admit a frenzied woman.

"Please, Mistah Jim, save 'im—save mah boy! He's all Ah gots!" She careened crazily about the room, whimpering so that little Jim crept frightened to his mother's side.

"Wait!" Prince gripped the woman by the shoulders. "Now—tell me what's de matter, A'nt Hester!"

"Dey's attah him—Ben!"

"Who's attah him?" Prince demanded.

"De white mens! He an' Mistah Will Redden had a fuss an' Ben struck 'im on de haid wid a wheel-spoke attah Mistah Will shot 'im in de chest! Ah gots all de do's an' windows lock in our house whar Ben is. Oh, Mistah Jim—Ah b'lieves he dyin'!"

Prince turned abruptly to the back stairs, and in a minute returned with an old flintlock rifle. There was a look in his eyes that Carrie remembered having seen once before—the day he was bent on choking the life from Jake.

She flung herself upon him. "Jim!" But he shook her off and was gone. Shortly there was heard the sound of swift hoofbeats. Then silence.

The old men of Shrewsbury will still tell you how Jim Prince reined his lathered mare to a stop in front of the pool-room that night and rushed into the place like a raging boar; how he mounted the single table at a leap to harangue and plead and storm at the men who stood with up-turned faces—faces that were every shade from deepest black to near-white. Some of the men were angry, some sullen, some indifferent—all were frightened. None showed the least disposition to act for two centuries of the lash had taken their toll of manhood.

"Don't 'mongst-you see dat efn we lets 'em lynch Ben, dey'll do de same to any of us?" Prince shouted at the height of his impassioned speech.

He waited for an answer, but none came. Only fright took possession of all the faces now. Even Big George, a known fighter, at whose side the endangered man had worked, said nothing.

Then Jim Prince cursed them, with the frenzy of a despairing man. The veins in his face and neck filled, and down his cheeks ran angry tears.

"Ah'll go by mahself!" he finished, leaping from the table.

They acted then. They closed about him and a crashing blow felled him into blackness.

On the porch of the Prince homestead, A'nt Hester and Carrie turned haggard faces toward the finger of flame which had suddenly leapt into the sky. From the same direction there came faintly on the wind sharp cries of a human being in agony. The cries were mingled with a babble of hysterical shouting.

"Dey got 'im! Dey got 'im!" The words were torn from A'nt Hester as she dropped, mercifully unconscious, to the floor.

Had they got Jim also? Carrie lifted tortured eyes to the sky and prayed while pains of premature labor gripped her. From the lane came slow hoofbeats. And the flame slid downward, losing itself in the jagged top of the pine wood.

II

That grim night in late October changed Prince's outlook on life.

How he managed to get Carrie and her child—born two months before its time—upstairs, he never knew. Nor how he revived A'nt Hester to a condition of usefulness and rode for the doctor. But when he had done what had to be done he sank into a fever, to emerge three days later an older, harder man. A path of white directly through the center of his crinkly hair bore witness to the horror which had impressed itself upon his spirit.

"How's Carrie?" he demanded, and before Dr. Stevens had a chance to answer: "Ah gots to git outn yere—gots to git dat fodder in 'fo' it rain."

"Now, now, Jim," answered the doctor, quietly. "Carrie and the new little lady are coming 'round all right now. And you don't have to worry about the work, either. Big George is taking care of that."

"Big George!" snarled Prince, remembering.

"I know—I know," nodded the doctor. "All a damn shame! Damn shame!"

"Dey wouldn't *none* of 'em help me stop it!"

"I know—I know," the older man repeated. Then: "Listen, Prince, it won't do any good for you to get yourself all stirred up again. Those men you tried to move the other night they don't speak your language. They're just like the common run of humans—fear is their strongest feeling. You might as well know now, Prince, that there is one law your people must learn the meaning of—the law that says that only the strong shall live!" The man of science looked squarely at the man of the soil. "Don't mistake me, Prince. I don't mean that every man should get himself a club or a gun and go around doing away with whoever he thinks

to be his enemy. No, not that. But you've got a farm here—
one of the best in the county. That's your strength, Prince,
if you have the gumption it make it so. Understand? . . .
Now you stay in this bed until I tell you to get up!"

His words fastened in Prince's mind, in a soil already
prepared for them, and took root and grew. Obsessed
by a single idea, the man's character changed. He grew
inhuman, suspicious, and nothing could distract him from
ceaseless work. There was something almost symbolic in
his passion to show his independence and self-sufficiency.

Chapter 9

I

When Prince had been married fourteen years his material assets might have been listed as follows, in the order of their importance to him:

One large well-stocked and producing farm, an accumulation of the land of farmers less astute than himself.

Farm hands who were so in his debt that payment of their wages was optional.

One general merchandise store to which nearly all of the colored population of the town was in debt.

One livery stable, patronized by both colored people and whites.

One son, who would soon take his apprenticeship on the farm.

One wife, who did most of the laundry for the well-to-do white people of the town; she was also midwife, dressmaker, and social leader.

The best-looking house in the section to which the Negroes had moved from the outskirts of Shrewsbury.

Two daughters who would soon be able to work out as hired girls.

This last item was not just to Prince's liking. He had never quite forgiven Carrie for bringing these female children into the world. He had wanted boys to share the burden of managing the Prince estates. Furthermore, Prince had always suspected that Evenezer's last minister had had something to do with the fact that little Martha bore no resemblance to either Blanche or young Jim. She was too yellow and she was too frisky. And her hair was straight and luxuriant—the young minister's hair had been of just that quality. About that time, too, Carrie had practiced a lot on the church organ. . . . So Jim Prince put two and two together and arrived at an ugly four.

Now Blanche and Jim were different. Blanche was serious and steady, and in time would make an excellent domestic servant. As for young Jim, people were prone to say that his father had "spit 'im out." He looked like his father. He talked like his father. He even walked like his father, and was as shrewd and smart. If Prince loved anyone, he loved this son of his.

The boy stood before Prince in the store one afternoon—slim, nut-brown, with small bright eyes and sharp features.

"Pa, I'm going to finish school here in the spring. . . ." He paused, not knowing how to put it. "I been thinkin'—I mean—I'd like to go to the Institute next fall."

Prince knew where that idea had come from. There had been a brilliant young teacher in town from the Institute with a quartet of male singers, and during the week that he held meetings at Ebenezer Church he had fired the community with his talk of vocational education. But Prince had other plans for young Jim, who would soon be fifteen and old enough for farm work.

Seeing that his father was about to speak in disagreement, young Jim hurried his slow speech. His eyes were shining. "After that I could help you here with the business an' the farm. I'd study hard an' learn everything."

Big Jim pointed beyond the window to the turned-up earth. "You see dere?" he questioned. "Wal, you gots to dig down in dat 'fo' you kin l'arn 'bout it. Ain't no books gonna l'arn you." Then he waved his arm to take in the store and a desk which was a miracle of neatness. "Ah didn't l'arn from no books how to do dat, nuthah. You cain't l'arn right from books. Dey's all right, mebbe, but efn you wants to l'arn somep'n you gots to do it—an' keep on a-doin' it!"

"But, Pa, the man said that's what they do at the Institute," countered Jim. The light in his eyes was fading.

"Ah heard 'im speak. But Ah don't see no use o' wastin' fo' years down dere, when you kin l'arn right here. 'Sides, look at de money it cost."

"But, Pa, you can afford it."

"How you know what Ah kin affo'd?" demanded Prince, testily. "Don't you be gittin' uppish jes' 'cause you ain't starvin'. An' don't you lissen to dese no-'count niggahs what figgers Ah got heaps. Ah says you ain't goin'! Ah knows what's best fo' you. . . . An' you better start checkin' dem 'counts."

Young Jim went to his mother to enlist her aid. But Carrie, who would gladly have had her own dream realized through her son, could not move Prince. His word was law and there was no repeal. It had been many years since he had admitted Carrie to equal partnership in his life. Yet she continued to worship him, remembering her deliverance from Sue and Jake.

So when the spring plowing began the boy went under the tutelage of Big George, who could turn the deepest and straightest furrow in that section. Plowshares were toothpicks in his giant hands. Day after day Jim kept pace doggedly, until his muscles hardened. But he grew thinner, and through the long summer months of planting and cultivating he had no appetite. Dr. Stevens, happening by, counseled a change of climate, but Prince wouldn't hear of it. The boy was brooding because he couldn't have what he wanted, that was all. Work would cure any silly fancy in time. And the father, warped by the passion of a single idea, honestly believed what he said.

When the harvest season came young Jim was working in a field beside the main turnpike, and for a week he waved good-bys to his classmates who were departing for the Institute. He did not complain. For when the spirit is dead, disappointments do not hurt so much.

II

Jim Prince had not reckoned all the possibilities of his money-making program. He had not known that galloping consumption has a fertile field in adolescence. Now he sat, still and tortured, watching young Jim's life go out, and there was nothing he could do about it, though he was the richest colored man in town.

Old Dr. Stevens pulled the cover over the disease-ravaged young face.

"If you'd taken my advice about sending him away, Prince, we might have saved him." He tried to make his voice matter-of-fact. If he could only teach these colored people to work on an illness in time!

Ike Johnson returned from his second year at the Institute to read the resolutions. "In the spring of life, he left us at springtime," he ended. Then they buried young Jim between his grandparents.

Chapter 10

I

Jim prince was hard before. Now, after young Jim's death, he became mean. Those who had been jealous of his prosperity grew to hate him. They hated him for his pretense of superiority. They hated him for the way he drove his womenfolk to work for him. They hated him for his grudging aid during the hard times of an economic depression. In truth, it was only his formidable array of power that saved him from violence at the hands of his neighbors.

It was hard times which gave Prince an unaccustomed leisure, and the leisure induced his thoughts to wander, with the result that he took a mistress. As far as Carrie was concerned he had no excuse, for Carrie was as comely as when he first saw her. Perhaps it was simply the next inevitable step in an aggressive career. Work, marriage, success, leisure—then a mistress. Many a man might confess to the same sequence of events.

His choice was the young Widow Jones, also a member of the choir, who had been much in Prince's debt since the death of her husband. In the beginning she had employed her wiles—a fetching smile, an inviting roll of her dark eyes, and a coo—to solicit leniency when money payments were due. These overtures from a woman not his wife were too much for Prince's male vanity. One thing led to another.

Then the gossips got busy—across the back fences, in the barber shop, in the pool-room, in the very church pews: "Did you hear . . ." "Ah heard . . ." "Dey tells me . . ." "Everybody knows. . . ." For months it went on, and as is usual, Carrie had no inkling of it. She was too busy. Then like an explosion knowledge of the situation crashed into her consciousness.

The Ladies' Aid Society was meeting at the parsonage to see what could be done about that bane of church finances, "current expenses." Carrie came late, and pausing on the porch for breath—it was mid-July—heard her name, then a gust of laughter. The next words rooted her to the porch floor.

"Everybody knows 'bout it 'cep'n' Sis' Carrie. An' Prince, he a deacon, too—an' her a-singin' in de choir right wid de man's wife! Lawsy!" This was Sister Jenkins, who knew everything as soon as it happened, or was miserable.

Rachel King spoke up, a mouselike woman whose liaisons even Carrie knew about: "Did 'mongst-you see dat dress she had on last Sunday? Dey ain't givin' dem 'way like dat wid times like dey is—nossuh! An' po' Sis' Carrie she ain't had nuffin' new fo' years!"

"Dat man o' hern sho keep her nose to de grindstone," said Sister Jenkins.

"Yass," agreed Rachel, "he jes' tryin' to see how much money he kin get. Stingiest man in town! Worked dat boy o' hisn to death, an' tryin' to do de same to his wife. 'Spect he gwine put dat biggest gal to work soon's she gits through wid school. He's a mean man!"

Carrie was stunned. As they went further into the details of Prince's shortcomings, she backed slowly from the door and down the steps. It was a dark night, lighted only by stars. She walked, with no sense of the direction, guided only by the white picket fences which, alternating with honeysuckle-covered wire, bounded the front yards. The honeysuckle gave off its delicate lovely scent but Carrie did not notice. One fact throbbed in her brain: Jim, her husband, was "runnin'" with a woman. All else they had said counted for nothing. Only Prince's unfaithfulness held any significance.

Suddenly the light from the store gleamed into the hot gloom of the night. Automatically Carrie turned in through the door. The few loafers, leaning against the posts of the entrance, winked meaningfully at each other.

"Where's Mistah Jim?" asked Carrie of the sober-faced youth behind the counter. At her voice, his sleepy eyes widened, searching her face.

"Is you got a cold, Mis' Carrie?" he inquired.

"Where's mah husband?" repeated Carrie, impatiently. The clerk started back, stammering: "'Dee-deed—Ah—Ah don't know, Mis' Carrie!"

Carrie glared at him a moment. Then her shoulders slumped and she turned away. Out in the night again she took up her aimless walk. It led her home.

Standing before the white, green-shuttered house, she heard a party of straw-riders go singing by. Their gay young voices mocked her. That first summer, she remembered, she had had her only straw-ride. They had been young then, she and Prince. Young? Why, she was young now—only thirty-four.

But your husband's with another woman, came the answering thought, like a persistent imp.

She fought it off. Maybe they were just talking, back there in the parsonage. Of course they were just talking! Didn't they gab like that about everybody? They were jealous, that's what it was. They were jealous because she had gotten the man that nearly all of them had set their caps for!

But you haven't got him, reminded the imp.

I have!—I have!

In her bedroom Carrie undressed slowly before the mirror, and as she did so she surveyed herself critically, as she had done that morning when she went in search of a job in Baltimore. There was the same golden-brown skin. Although she was a little stouter, that only lent more pleasing curves to her figure. Her hair, loosened from its knot, fell in a rich shawl about her shoulders. There was nothing to be ashamed of, she decided.

A confident smile was on her face as she dimmed the light and lay on the bed, partially covered by the thin sheet. She waited. The reedy calls of crickets darted through the open window. Recurrent waves of sweetness ascended from the honeysuckle vines. The hours tolled. Finally sleep conquered her.

Once she awoke, conscious of the heat from Prince's body. She turned, but his back was to her, and he snored.

Another woman—got your man! Another woman—got your man! Another woman—got your man! The hateful refrain thudded through her brain and fell upon her pride with bruising force, second after second, hour after hour.

II

Prince had immediate evidence of Carrie's knowledge of his indiscretion. First, when he awoke next morning—it was the Sabbath—he thought it strange to find rumpled sheets but no Carrie. Then the aroma of baking rolls came from below. That explained it. Instead of biscuits, they were having fresh rolls this morning, and Carrie had risen early to prepare them.

"Sho gots de best wife dis side de Chesapeake," flashed across his mind, for Prince was partial to freshly baked rolls. But with the thought his conscience was unpleasantly stirred. He recalled what the walls of the Widow Jones' house had seen as recently as last night. Then he dismissed all consideration of the matter to turn over for another nap.

He awoke a second time to find Blanche insistently shaking him by the shoulder.

"Mamma says breakfast is ready," she informed him. "Here's yo' hot water fo' yo' shave," and she placed the pitcher on the washstand. Prince's elder daughter never addressed him as "papa" when she could avoid it.

Downstairs, Carrie and the girls waited for him to lead the family prayers—a regular Sunday-morning custom. Carrie did not pray after him this morning, and he sent a surprised glance at her, for always before this she had followed his supplication with one of her own. The girls gave their short, incoherent utterances, after which Prince led the Lord's Prayer. Again Carrie was silent.

At the table she ate little, but watched Prince's every movement with a brooding attention. Her black eyes, at intervals, concentrated squarely on his face. He felt them bore into him when he bent down to his food. When Blanche went upstairs with Martha to dress for church, instead of getting immediately into his deacon's garments, Prince delayed in the kitchen.

"What's de matter, honey?" he inquired. "Ain't you feelin' good?"

Carrie stared at him until his eyes dropped, then turned to the task of clearing the table. She had not uttered a sound. He squinted back at her for an angry moment, and in a flash the realization came that she knew. He made as if to approach her, but, reconsidering, hastened to his room. As he dressed himself absently, he pondered the turn affairs had taken.

"Some hussy's done found out 'bout me an' Amy," he decided. A second suspicion tramped the heels of the first. "Reckon dat woman's done said somep'n to Carrie, herself? Dirty strumpit! She better not!" Just the same, he'd be wise to speak to Amy after church. He wondered who else knew. Hell! if one knew, they all knew! "Triflin' hounds! All dey gots to do is set 'round an' meddle in somebody else's business! Jealous! Every damn one of 'em."

His accusation at the moment carried conviction, for the mirror gave him back a handsome figure—slim, incased in the black swallow-tailed suit that was the emblem of his churchly rank. Deacon James Prince, Shrewsbury's leading colored citizen, looked the part.

Meanwhile, Carrie, putting on her grey muslin dress and outmoded straw hat, had reached a conclusion of her own. She resolved to speak to the Reverend Johnson at the close of the morning services. Perhaps he could persuade Prince to give up the widow. This hope, rising out of despair, drove some of the gloom from her face, and by the time they had walked to church she was able to summon a front with which to march up the aisle to her place in the choir.

They were a little tardy, as became the most distinguished family of the congregation, and their entrance created a flattering stir. The two girls came first, primly schooled, their stiffly starched frocks of pink and white standing out over their pantaloons like umbrellas. When they were deposited in the pew, Prince took his place at the right of the pastor on the rostrum and perfunctorily bowed his head in prayer. The unctuous smile of the Reverend Johnson greeted him with a special benignity, for was not Prince the only wholly solvent member of his flock?

It happened this morning that the pastor took his text from the incident of the Nazarene's writing in the sand. The distressing state of national, international, and local affairs the Reverend Johnson attributed to the loose and lascivious living of mortals. He listed the vices. Then he crowned his message with the thought that current hard times were but writings in the sands by which the Almighty let each one know that He was not to be deceived by an outward show of good works.

Try as he might, Prince could not but imagine that all eyes were fastened upon him while the pastor was denouncing the sin of adultery. His reason cast the idea aside. Why, he was the only paying member in the church! Wasn't he deacon? The minister couldn't be talking about him. Nevertheless, immediately after the service Prince hurried in search of Amy. He had to stop this talk.

Carrie, on the other hand, had been cheered by the sermon. It bolstered her hope that the minister would throw his moral support toward the solution of her own domestic difficulty. She stopped him as he left the pulpit and told her story, haltingly, head averted.

"Please, Elder," she ended, "cain't you do somep'n 'bout it?"

The Elder stroked his chin meditatively. Had he known his sermon would precipitate such a situation as this, it never would have been preached. He wasn't a timid man in the pursuit of his divine mission. And he was, essentially, a good man. But for all his consecration to his calling, the Elder was cautious. He knew of the financial support given the church by Prince. It would be unwise to incur the man's enmity, especially in times like these. It would be equally indiscreet to ignore Carrie, who was a choir member, a substitute organist, and a powerful financial agent in the Ladies' Aid. The good cleric was, indeed, in a dilemma.

"It's a ticklish situation, Sister Carrie." His ministerial voice matched his troubled moon-like face. "But for your sake I'll speak with Brother Prince. Maybe it's all just a lot of gossip."

III

The Reverend Johnson was never quite able to pray away the effects of that brief consultation he had with Jim Prince the next afternoon. It always brought the jingle of thirty pieces of silver echoing down nearly two thousand years of church history.

"Brother Prince," he began, after first clearing his throat ceremoniously.

Prince looked up from his desk where he was making entries in a large, blue-backed ledger. The sum of the money owed him had aroused him to an ugly frame of mind. He was clearly annoyed by this visitor.

"Wal?" he demanded.

The Elder fingered his tie uneasily. This was going to be trying! He coughed again.

"Wal!" Prince repeated, and this time he squinted squarely into the cleric's face.

The exclamation acted as a vocal stimulus and the pastor blurted his mission:

"Er—uh—Sister Carrie's been telling me you ain't been walking as straight in the path as you used to—"

Prince leaned back in his chair, listening to the coaxing, pleading tones of righteousness. As he did so, he thumbed the leaves of the ledger until he came to the J's.

"Brother Johnson," he interrupted. Shifting the blue book around so that the Elder could see it plainly, he pointed to the total entered under the caption,

Reverend I. Johnson

It amounted to fifteen dollars and seventy-five cents. The visitor opened his mouth, shut it again, and gulped.

"My son—he's at the Institute—and these are hard times, Brother Prince," he offered lamely.

"When's de interest due on de church mortgage, Rev'end?" asked Prince, shutting the ledger. Again the Elder gulped.

"Well, to tell the truth, Brother Prince, it's due next week," he admitted. He mopped his face with a large white handkerchief.

"Don't worry, Rev'end, Ah'll take care o' dat," assured Prince. "Now—what was you a-sayin' when you come in, Rev'end?"

"Why—why—nothing, nothing, Brother Prince." The words were spoken over the shoulder of the swiftly retreating cleric.

Chapter 11

I

July blistered into white-hot August. A drought—scourge of farmers—was on. Wheat drooped away into tinder. Corn-stalks crackled in the dry breezes. And little green tomatoes dried up until you could hear their seeds rattle, while panting cattle lowed beseechingly. Nature, in this hard, uncompromising mood, decided to relieve little Annie Burns a month early of the child she carried, and old Dr. Stevens stopped by for Carrie, as was his habit when there was a childbirth in the colored section.

"Damn shame to bring babies into the world, hard as times are," he commented as he whipped his horse to a gallop.

"Yes," agreed Carrie, "'specially when there ain't no pappy."

"How'd she get in trouble?"

"She was workin' out on Miles' farm—hired gal. Them dev'lish men out there'll ruin any gal!"

The shack where they stopped was a drab unpainted affair with rags stuffed here and there at broken windows. Inside was dirt and confusion.

Guided by a whimpering noise, Carrie and the doctor went into a farther room where a mulatto girl lay groaning on a soiled, rumpled bed. Beside her sat an old hag-like woman, the mother. It was she who was whimpering.

"Get her out of here, Carrie," ordered the doctor.

The woman, protesting, accompanied Carrie to the kitchen, and while Carrie washed kettles and pans and swatted at flies, heaped torrents of abuse on her daughter's betrayer. Carrie only half listened. She was thinking of her own life with Prince, and of what her mother Martha had said about men, "Dey ain't none of 'em worth it." How many women had to learn that for themselves! And now that she had learned, how long could she stand it? How long? . . .

A little later Dr. Stevens was washing his hands after a battle that had ended in defeat.

"First two we ever lost, Carrie," he said, remorsefully. "Guess I'm getting too old."

"'Tain't yo' fault, Doc' Stevens," comforted Carrie. "They jes' didn't have the right kind o' vittals befo' the chile come."

Carrie did her best to restore order to the house—no mean task. Then on her way home she stopped by at the parsonage to inform the Reverend Johnson that his services were needed. She did not linger over her message, for recent events had shaken her faith in the brotherhood of Christians, and Ebenezer Church would do without her in the future.

II

Jim Prince wiped his mouth and pushed himself back from the table.

"Kin Blanche cook tol'able fair?"

"Why?" countered Carrie suspiciously. She'd seen one of the Miles' farm-hands come out of the store on her way home from the parsonage the afternoon before.

"Wal, Ah gots a job fo' her, efn she kin cook purty fair."

"Where's the job?" Carrie's eyes narrowed.

"Out on Miles' farm. Two dollars a week ain't bad fo' times like dey is—"

"She ain't goin'!" Carrie's tone was final. She pushed her plate away and resolutely faced her husband across the table.

The two girls, on either side of their parents, cringed before the rising storm. They knew what to expect when the big anger vein snaked up the center of Prince's forehead, as it did now.

"Why?" he thundered, half-crouching in his chair. His fingers bit like claws into the table cloth.

"She ain't a-goin'!" repeated Carrie. Her eyes, dead black dots, seemed to recede into the brown mask of her face. "You know why Annie Burns is dead. Them dev'lish men out on Miles' would do the same to Blanche. You knows it. But she ain't a-goin'—you hear me? She ain't a-goin'!"

"Huh! Jes' 'cause dat gal was frisky wid de mens ain't no reason why Blanche got to be," answered Prince. "'Sides, Ah'm losin' money every day 'count o' de drought. Ain't no—"

"That's it! That's it! You wants to work her to death like you did Jim! But you ain't a-goin' to do it! You hear me, Jim Prince? *You ain't a-goin' to do it!*" Carrie's voice rose to an hysterical scream.

Then Jim Prince made the big mistake of his life.

"You dirty bitch!" He sprang to his feet, and sent his chair crashing against the wall. "Ah brung you down yere from dat whorehouse an' made you what you is—a 'spectable woman! An' now you tryin' to tell me how to run mah 'fairs! Mind you' own damn business! Dat's what you do!"

Carrie flinched as if from a sudden blow. All the tenderness, all the gratitude she'd had for this man, withered like grass under a scorching sun. Words droned from her, like the wintry winds that moan over the lowlands.

"Ah don't owe you nothin'—nothin', Jim Prince! Ah worked fo' you, didn't Ah? Ah didn't complain 'cause

Ah didn't have no clothes like the rest o' the women. An' Ah ain't complained when you bin runnin' 'round wid another woman, have Ah?" She broke off, sobbing, and sank into her chair. "Ah knowed it wouldn't last! Ah told you so when you first asked me to come home wid you."

Prince was not to be moved by his wife's tears, but her reference to the Widow Jones infuriated him. He made a second mistake.

"You gots a nerve!" he snarled. "Efn Ah is runnin' wid a woman, Ah ain't got no bastards by her. An' dat's mo'n you can say. Jes' 'cause Ah ain't never said nuffin' 'bout it, you thinks Ah don't know. But Ah knows you got dat Martha by dat Rev'end Thomas. You dirty—" He stopped short and involuntarily stepped back.

A swift change had come over Carrie. Her head had shot erect. Veins stood out on her face like agonized serpents, while little gibbering sounds issued from her twisted lips. She bent forward in her chair, crouched, then advanced slowly upon Prince. Her whole body was shaking and hot tears streamed down her cheeks.

Then Jim Prince made his final mistake. He had never laid an angry hand on Carrie, but now he stepped forward and gave her a resounding slap. When he tried to grasp her arms, Carrie with a wild scream launched her body headlong into him. The impact caught Prince squarely and knocked him breathless. He fell backward with a groan, and Carrie followed up her advantage by slashing her finger nails across his face. Her strong teeth imbedded themselves in his throat; her fists rained blows upon his head.

When she felt Prince grow limp under her, Carrie rolled over on her side. As her anger ebbed, fear gripped her. She looked at the still form of her husband. She felt frantically for his heartbeat. Nothing! Panic-stricken, she leapt to her feet and spun in a circle. Her eyes lighted on the girls, who still crouched in their corner.

"Git mah clothes an' you-all's together, quick!" she gasped.

Blanche stared at her father but made no move to obey.

"Git the clothes, Ah say!" screamed Carrie.

Blanche made for the doorway leading to the stairs, with the small Martha in her wake. Carrie rushed out of the house and down the street to the Prince livery stable.

Jim-Ed James was cleaning manure from the eight stalls and gossiping with Charlie when he sighted Carrie dashing through the wide door. In his astonishment at her disheveled appearance his chew dropped from his mouth and he sidled cautiously out of her path.

"Hitch me two hosses to that carriage!" she commanded. "Hurry!" For the bewildered black hostler only stood there popping his round eyes stupidly.

"Wh-what's de matter, Mis' Carrie?" he questioned.

"Gimme them hosses an' that carriage, Ah tell you! Them two." She pointed out a fine pair of blacks, trim, sleek animals, the pride of Prince's stable.

"Mistah Jim he don't—," began Jim-Ed.

"Efn you wants to keep yo' job, you better do as Ah says!" Carrie silenced him.

He hunched his shoulders resignedly and soon had the carriage and horses ready.

"Wimmin sho is quare crittahs!" he commented as Carrie and the blacks disappeared through the stable door. "Ain't never seed her act like dat befo'!"

"Huh! What you care?" rejoined his companion, "She ain't yo's, is she?"

III

Prince came to shortly after Carrie left him. His anger had flown and knowledge of his foolishness weighed upon him.

"Carrie!" he called.

Hearing movements in the room above, he stumbled into the hall. Blanche and Martha were coming downstairs. At sight of her father, Blanche dropped a large bundle she carried and it rolled to Prince's feet, scattering dresses, shoes, and other apparel.

"What you doin'?" demanded Prince.

"Mamma told me to get all our clothes together," answered the girl timidly.

"What fo'? Where's yo' mamma?"

"I don't know."

Galloping hoofbeats drew Prince's attention to the street. He saw Carrie get out of the buggy and tie the blacks to the horse-head hitching-post. Then she rushed into the house, almost colliding with Prince.

"What you fixin' to do wid dat team?" he greeted her.

Carrie breathed her relief at seeing him alive but her face hardened.

"Ah'm goin' away—that's what Ah'm fixin' to do!"

"You ain't no sich-a-lie! You's mah wife an' Ah ain't gwine let you!"

"Ah ain't askin' you to let me. Ah ain't askin' fo' nothin' no mo' from you!"

"You cain't take dem hosses!" cried Prince. "Ah'll have de sheriff attah you!"

"Ah'm yo' wife, ain't Ah? What's yo's is mine! Git them clothes, Blanche!"

Prince changed his tactics.

"You cain't go an' leave me like dis, honey! You knows Ah loves you."

"Don't you talk to me 'bout love, man!" Carrie burst out. "Ah'm leavin'! An' them hosses an' that carriage Ah counts as pay fo' eighteen years' hard work—an' fo' you not ownin' yo' own chile—an' fo' you a-comin' home from another woman! Ah'm leavin', an' efn you tries to stop me Ah'll kill you! You hear me? Ah'll kill you!"

With the bundle in one arm and little Martha under the other, Carrie stormed out of the door and down to the carriage. Blanche followed.

Attracted by the shouting, a knot of curious neighbors had collected, most of them women. Carrie turned on them with a laugh.

"There he is!" she cried, pointing to Prince, who leaned weakly on the porch railing. "There he is. You kin all have 'im now—the biggest man in town!" She cracked the whip and the carriage lurched down the street in a spreading sheet of dust. And the laugh hung insanely on the hot air.

Chapter 12

I

It was the same Jake Tillery, except that on this warm Sunday afternoon in August he was a very frightened man. The beads of perspiration on his forehead were not alone the product of muscular exertion. If the truth were told, this nattily dressed, middle-aged man—who looked younger— was trying to put as much distance as was possible between himself and something. That was why, every so often, he snatched a look over his left shoulder in the direction of the clump of woods bordering the white shell road that led southward from the thriving town of Eastland. After he had rounded a bend about two hundred yards from the woods, and there was no sign of pursuit, he collapsed in the meager shade of a scrubby little mulberry tree.

While he wiped his face and nursed bruised lips which seemed recently to have come in violent contact with some hard object, he hurled invectives at unnamed individuals. Then, having relieved himself to his satisfaction on that score, he turned the stream of vituperation upon himself. He was a thus-and-so and a thus-and-so forever.

"You must is gittin' ole an' clumsy," he muttered, "lettin' a country buck ketch you wid three dices! Keep on— you gwine have to work yet!" He emphasized the "work" with abhorrence, and at the same time surveyed his well-kept hands, the palms of which were smooth and tender. "Reckon you better gone to Her'ford an' ketch dat boat to Balt'more—guess de coppers done fo'got you now. Wish somebody'd come 'long wid a buggy so's Ah kin git past dat meetin'-ground. Dat man sho want to cut me bad!"

He could not have done better had he rubbed Aladdin's lamp, for in answer to his wish, a cloud of dust swirled around the next bend in the road, headed in the direction from which he had just come. Soon, two dust-laden, black horses, drawing a carriage, trotted up to where he stood waving his arms.

"Lady, kin you-all give me a lift to town?" he inquired, politely, of the road-weary Carrie. She looked at him distrustfully, then bade him get in. As he clambered up beside her, each recognized the other.

"Jake!" exclaimed Carrie, recoiling instinctively.

Jake stared open-mouthed.

"Fo' de Lawd's sake, Carrie! Whar you bin all dese years?"

Her first notion had been to drive him away. But surprisingly enough, Carrie felt no fear of this man now. So she started the horses on their way.

"Ah bin livin' down to Shrewsbury way wid mah husband an' family. How's A'nt Sue?"

Jake coughed slightly before answering. "Oh, she's all right—Ah guess."

"Where is she?"

"She's in Jessup's cut." Jake stated this much in the manner that he would state a wager in a crap game.

"Jessup's cut . . . ?" puzzled Carrie.

"Yeah—you know—de penitentiary. De coppers is gittin' meddly on 'count o' de new commissioner o' police. He done started to clean up things. So when dey comes to close our house, Ah skipped. But dey caught Sue."

They were passing the woods now and could see the gathering of horse-drawn vehicles on the edge of the clearing. The sound of fervid singing reached them.

"Camp-meetin'?" inquired Carrie. Jake nodded affirmatively and breathed easier as they passed the scene of his late misfortune.

"Whar you gwine? Visitin'?" he asked Carrie.

She shook her head.

"You says you comes from Shrewsbury? An' yo' husband ain't wid you? How come?"

"Ah ain't got no husband," stated Carrie, unemotionally.

"Ain't got . . . What's de matter wid 'im? Dead?"

"Ah left 'im," said Carrie.

"You left . . . Oh . . ." A craftiness spread over his yellow, speckled features. He struck out carefully to offer consolation. It worked. For four days Carrie had been meandering blindly about three counties, headed in a northwesterly direction, and she had wanted someone to whom she could talk about her troubles. She had found neither the courage nor the inclination for more than casual conversation with the hospitable tenant-farmers who had given shelter to her and the two girls. Now she poured out the whole story to Jake.

Jake listened, interspersing sympathetic remarks, while his agile mind worked swiftly in an entirely different direction.

"But whar is you goin'?" he questioned, pointedly.

"Ah don't know," she answered. She looked back at the two girls. Martha was asleep in Blanche's arms, worn out from the inaction of a journey which had had in the beginning every appearance of an outing. The child was constantly fretful now, except when she was asleep, and Carrie worried, knowing she was not well. She had to find a place to pass the night.

"Look yere," offered Jake, as the idea he had been pondering took form. "Whyn't you come to Her'ford wid me? Dey say dat's a town what has good pickin's. You an' me kin go there an' git set fo' de winter. Dat's when de oyster-shuckers comes to town. Dey bin tellin' me dem mens spends dey money like water when de season's busy. We kin start a boardin'-house an' make money hand over fist!" His hazel eyes glowed at the scheme. "Ah gots some money, an' you kin sell yo' hosses an' carriage. We kin start on dat. Huh?"

Carrie's brows knitted in suspicious doubt. She hadn't forgotten the Jake she had known.

Jake, divining her meaning, added, quickly: "You don't have to worry 'bout me—we'll jes' be partners."

"Ah ain't worried 'bout you," she informed him, a hard quality in her voice. "Ah jes' want you to know that you ain't dealin' wid no fool! Ah done had one man to take 'vantage o' me, but ain't no mo' goin' to! See? Ah'll go in wid you—be yo' partner—until you starts gittin' wrong! An' when you does, we quits! See? Now, where's this town?"

"Turn left in de next road an' keep goin.'"

Jake grinned. "She ain't young no mo,'" he told himself, "but she sho gots her good looks yit."

II

Herdford, at present, drowses through the years with a medieval air of disdain for civic progress. But this little water-locked hamlet was not always so. If you stop along its one paved street—Front Street, the natives call it— and inquire of any old inhabitant, he will tell you of days when the diminutive Eastern Sho' town was the seat of the county; how it used to be a center of the oyster-packing industry before Milestown, over on the Miles River, and Deerfield and Kent Island usurped the honors. He may also point out, with sorrowful pride, the site of the old military academy, now burned down, opposite Sam Newton's general store. The Public Lot, they call it—a grove of maple, hemlock, and walnut trees overlooking the placid ripples of the Avondale River. Dusty chronicles record that once, in Colonial days, Herdford was considered a possible site for the city of Baltimore. Possibly because of disappointment that they were passed by, the lowlands remain rustic, except for the enterprising towns of Eastland, Shrewsbury, and Bainbridge.

Even today Herdford seems to resent that early intervention of Providence which stole from it the right to be the queen city of Old Maryland. Like a jilted and faded old lady with her hope-chest, it sits there between its two rivers, the Avondale and Town Creek, on a peninsula shaped like a boomerang, dreaming, perhaps, of the glory that might have been its own; spurning the industrial opportunities offered it by capitalists who realize the commercial value of its location. "Nope!" says thin-lipped, grizzled Kirkland, from the porch of his green-shuttered, Colonial cottage facing the Methodist church. "No-siree!" drawls Hallock, and his age-molted eyebrows will meet over the shrewd gray eyes of his highland ancestors, and he'll probably mount his ancient bicycle and pedal down to the town pier to see if his crab-steaming box is full. Ole Lady Nanny Crichard will respond in like manner, and others of the landed aristocracy who trace their lineage back to those sturdy Scotch-Irish and English emigrants that first forded Town Creek and settled on this curving spot of land.

These settlers were a conservative and complacent lot. Along Back Street, that rutted dirt and shell road that faces Town Creek and parallels Front Street (the present avenue of the aristocracy) they built their homes after the style of those they had left on the western shore of the Chesapeake: two-story houses, some flat-roofed, others with roofs severely triangular. Time and the elements have necessitated repairs, but on the whole these buildings remain as they have always been, representing the original architecture of the town. And it is here that the hardy crabbers and oysterers live.

Some of the emigrants were farmers and created during the slave era the fertile fields one sees on either side of the ten-mile pike bending westward from Eastland to Herdford. But it was the combined oyster- and crab-packing industry which ultimately pumped the life's blood through the town's lazy veins. For the products of the rivers offer an all-year occupation.

On the whole, though, Herdford is a sleepy town—quaint, lazy, smugly self-satisfied; scoffing at the forward strides of its neighbors in order to distract attention from its own dullard ways.

III

"Here she is," said Jake.

He pointed over the field at his right toward a winding river on whose shores could be seen the tops of houses partly hidden by trees. The girls looked curiously in the direction of their new home, but Carrie was busy at the moment whipping the horses past a stretch of pine woods. The fragrance of the pine eluded her; she noticed only the forest gloom and a ceaseless whispering that struck unpleasantly on her ears. "Go back!" the woods seemed to say. "Go back!" She experienced a sense of relief when the woods gave way to a field of green sow beans. Yet the whisper lingered in her ears.

"Look out!" Jake's voice rasped in her ears. She reined the horses to an abrupt stop.

"Look at dat." He pointed to an object in the road, a giant cat crouched on its haunches like an image carved in ebony. Cold emerald eyes blinked in regal disdain at the skittish horses. To Carrie, with the sinister command of the woods still echoing, the animal was a thing of menace.

Jake snapped the spell by clambering down and flicking the whip threateningly. The cat arched its back and spat before it relinquished the road. But even when they had driven on its icy eyes followed them forbiddingly. Carrie, looking back, shuddered in sharp fear.

"You ain't sup'stishous, is you?" bantered Jake. But his tone was false.

They had come to the little neck of land which forms a natural bridge of oyster shells between the termination of Town Creek and a soggy marsh. Sailboats snuggled on the curving shore. A musty odor emanated from the swampy waste. At this point the town abruptly began.

"Yere comes some colored folks," said Jake. "Ah'll ask dem whar we kin git a place to sleep fo' de night."

An old couple approached dressed in their Sunday best. The man reminded Carrie of Father Prince. His white beard fringed a kindly weather-beaten face from which his eyes peeped brightly out, like shiny brown marbles—age had not found him easy to destroy. He leaned heavily on a gnarled stick.

"Good attahnoon to you." He lifted an ancient black felt hat from a shiny pate in courtly deference to Carrie, and nodded cordially to Jake. The woman smiled and bobbed her knee in a rheumatic curtsy.

"Speak a leetle loudah," the old man piped in answer to Jake's query. "Ah'm a leetle deef—bin so fo' goin' on nigh to fo'teen years. An' she"—nodding toward his wife—"cain't hear none a-tall."

Finally Jake made him understand.

"Oh—'mongst-you wants lodgin'!" he exclaimed. "Ah reckons you kin git it down to Tilton Street. 'Mongst-you keeps right down dis yere street 'twell you comes to Gus Hagen's corner sto'—but you don't turn dar! You keeps on 'twell you comes to de bank an' de colored church an' den you sees de Public Lot right in front o' Sam Newton's corner sto'. An' you keeps right on past de white chillun's schoolhouse 'twell you gits to a li'l' teeny street—but don't turn dar nuthah, 'cause dat'll take you smack into Back Alley. So 'mongst-you keep right on 'twell you pass Jim Pratt's big white house an' right past de post-office—de next street to yo' right is Tilton Street!"

Carrie thanked him for his explicit directions and started the horses.

Tilton Street sloped gently downhill. For the most part it was unshaded—worm-eaten tree stumps testified that the inhabitants had more use for fuel than for beauty, but now and then trees in a front yard marked a family not so pinched by the hard times. The first three houses had some of the airs and graces of those along the main street. They seemed to be striving to hold aloof from the dwellings just below them, which had frankly abandoned all pretence of refinement.

Carrie brought the dusty blacks to a stop in front of the most superior house on the street—a white-and-green cottage that was like a resplendently attired gentleman in a crowd of tramps. There was a demeanor about it at once haughty, condescending, and apologetic. Two neatly dressed children, a boy and girl of Martha's age, stopped their play to stare at the callers. A man, who had a certain cocksureness about him that reminded Carrie irritatingly of Prince, left the porch and approached the carriage.

"'Mongst-you be strangers in town?" he ventured as an opening. When he was assured that they were, he introduced himself. "Mah name's Tom Winters—Cap'n Tom, they calls me. Is there somep'n Ah kin do fo' you?"

Jake stated their need.

"Well, Ah tell you," Winters said, after judicious stroking of his sideburns, "you kin put up fo' the night down to foot o' the street wid Mis' Gussie. That's the only person what takes lodgers this time o' year. You see that big field yonder to that big red house? Wal, Gussie she live right cross from there. . . . 'Mongst-you say you from down to Shrewsbury way? Ah used to run a barber shop down to Deerfield befo' the smallpox broke out there. To be sho, now! An' all mah folks come from down to Upper Hill. . . ."

But Jake had slyly jerked the reins and the tired horses pulled away before Winters could go more deeply into his personal history.

IV

Gussie sat in a creaking chair propped against her disreputable shack—a living replica of a Mongolian belly-god. To Carrie, she looked a little like one of Prince's brood sows. She sat there, with a litter of cats and scratching chickens about her, swinging a fan and cursing the flies which swarmed about, attracted by the odor which her great fat body gave off.

"Dam' crabs!" she swore. "Makes dese flies light on you same as bees on honey!" She appraised Jake with a sweeping scrutiny. Carrie she eyed with hostility.

"Is you Mis' Gussie?" Carrie stepped back a pace to get out of range of the unpleasant odor. The fat woman noticed the movement.

"Efn you plans to stay in dis town," she said, "you mought's well l'arn to git used to dis yere crab stink, 'cause ain't nuffin' you kin do to git it offn you once you works in 'em." Then she attended to Carrie's question: "Yass, Ah'm Mis' Gussie—an' you kin leave off de Mis'. What do 'mongst-you want?"

Carrie told her. "Wal," she wheezed, "Ah kin put you up fo' de night, but Ah ain't sayin' as how it'll be so comf'table. Ah warn't 'spectin' nobody befo' oyster season on 'count o' de drought done stopped de cannin'-house from openin' up. You kin stay efn you like. . . . You plannin' on shuckin'?" She looked dubiously at Jake's smooth, slender hands.

"We was thinkin' 'bout openin' up a boardin'-house, efn de season's good," answered Jake.

Gussie turned a shrewd eye on Carrie's good looks. "H'm—'mongst-you man an' wife?" she asked.

"No!" replied Carrie, emphatically.

"Oh. . . ." The fat one's tone was a little more cordial. "What kind o' a boardin'-house you gwine have?" and she raised a significant eyebrow.

"A boardin'-house!" snapped Carrie.

"All right—all right. . . ."

With a heave Gussie struggled to her feet. At the small doorway of the house she took a sidewise stand, then with the skill of long practice eased herself through.

The interior was what one would have expected from a view of the yard. The room they entered was stuffy and low-ceilinged, so small that it seemed some part of Gussie must protrude at any moment. The walls had once been whitewashed, but now the surface hung in loose brown patches which occasionally became detached and fell to the floor. A multitude of flies buzzed about the remnants of a meal which lay on a dingy table. Against one wall was a greasy couch holding the inert form of an under-sized man. Gussie delivered a blistering epithet in his direction as she waddled past in search of a bottle and glasses.

"Drink up, folks," she invited. "Ah'm goin' up to git you-all's rooms ready." With that she unlatched the door to the flight of narrow stairs and began her laborious way upward, attended by a cloud of flies.

"Come on an' drink," said Jake, already on his second glass. His spirits were nothing dashed by the squalor of the surroundings. This was what he had known with Sue.

Carrie started to refuse, but hesitated. She hadn't had a drink since she left Baltimore—nothing stronger than the sweet wine Prince kept in the house for festive occasions. Why should she refuse now? The old life with Prince was gone. She was starting all over again . . . to be her own boss . . . to do just as she pleased.

She went to the table and poured a stiff drink. Then another.

"Mamma, can we have some, too?" piped Martha.

Carrie lowered her glass for a moment, but thought: "Oh, hell! Ah'll do what Ah wants! An' efn Ah ketch 'em drinkin' Ah'll hide 'em good-fashion!"

Blanche watched her mother in amazement.

Jake, his eyes ablaze, poured Carrie a third drink but did not offer it to her. *He was smart.*

"Time you gals was in bed," Carrie said, recalling her maternal duties. "Do you hear me?" The whisky was rapidly taking possession of her and making her temper short.

"Yes'm!" Blanche pulled Martha to the stairs.

Now Carrie began to drink in earnest, in short, quick swallows.

"Jes' like old times," Jake ventured, lighting the stub of a cigar.

"Yass," agreed Carrie, absently. She smiled.

"Never reckoned Ah'd see you ag'in, sartin."

"Nope—reckon so. . . . You still gamblin', eh?"

"A li'l'," Jake admitted. "Ah calc'lates to make somep'n in dis yere town." A thought struck him. "Look yere! Ah ain't seed no signs o' a saloon when we was a-comin' down de street. Reckon we could sell likker in de house when we git started? Ah could go to Balt'more an' git some good stuff. Den we could cut it."

Carrie nodded drunkenly. "'Course—'course," she assented.

Gussie came grunting down the stairs. "Yo' rooms is ready," she panted. She gulped a drink, then offered the bottle to Carrie. "To ease dat hiccup, honey," she explained.

Carrie acted on the suggestion. Suddenly the room began to perform crazy antics. Now it rocked like the boat had done that night on her way from Baltimore with

Prince. Now it whirled like the big ferris wheel at the carnival to which Jim had taken her that first summer. Finally she sagged forward on the smelly table. From afar off she heard Jake tell Gussie that he'd take care of her. After that she knew no more.

Blanche awoke just before dawn to the humming accompaniment of mosquitoes and the fretful activities of bedbugs. Sitting up, she peered through the darkness for her mother. But the space she had purposely left on the far side of the bed was vacant.

Chapter 13

I

Carrie lost no time in disposing of the horses and carriage, and with the proceeds she bought a house. This was the way it happened:

Sid Hooper, proprietor of the livery stable on Front Street, saw the blacks and marked the excellent condition of the carriage. The sight aroused covetous desire. But Carrie had not listened in vain to Prince's bartering in horseflesh. She drove a hard bargain. At first the white man feigned indifference. He said "naw-sirree," and hemmed and hawed. But Carrie found his Achilles' heel when she threatened to drive to Eastland for the sale.

"Wal," he finally conceded, "I'll give ye two hundred an' fifty dollars an' not a dern cent more!"

"Mister," Carrie answered, "you don't want them horses an' that buggy—that's sartin! Ah knows Ah kin git three hundred easy. So Ah reckons Ah'll go on over to Eastland." She turned away.

"Hold on yere—hold on!" exclaimed Hooper. He raked his chin with a nervous hand and drowned a cluster of stable flies beneath a squirt of tobacco juice. "Take three hundred—an' I'm a dern ole fool!"

Carrie paused as if reflecting. She was really delighted. "All right—let's git the papers ready," she said with elaborate reluctance.

Sid Hooper eyed this soft-spoken woman probingly. What the devil did she know about a bill o' sale?

"Looka yere—ye be a stranger in town, ain't ye?" he asked.

Carrie nodded.

"Ye goin' to work in oysters?"

"Ah was reckonin' on runnin' a boardin'-house."

"Oh . . . I see. . . ." Sid eyed her appraisingly, taking in all her points of beauty. There was not a great deal exposed in those days of ground-sweeping dresses, but even then the practiced eye could discern much. "Ye got a house?"

"No. Ah jes' got in town yestiddy."

Hooper's face lighted. "Yestiddy? H'm. . . . Looka yere, I got a house—a brick house—down thar jes' offn Tilton Street. I'll sell it to ye cheap. Ye kin have it fo' two hundred an' fifty dollars an' a lease on them grounds for as long's ye like. That'll give ye fifty dollars left outn the whole bargain—an' ye cain't do better'n that ef ye go in all the nine counties! What ye say?"

Carrie looked her incredulity. She had seen the house that morning. It seemed in good condition except for broken windowpanes. And for two hundred and fifty. . . . But her appreciation of a good bargain was strong.

"Ah'll give you two hundred," she stated, calmly.

"What!" Hooper sprang from his desk. "Ye mean to stand thar an' offer me two hundred dollars—for a *brick* house?"

"Never mind," answered Carrie, coolly and with a shrug, "jes gimme the money. There's other shacks. . . ."

Hooper wilted. She was too much for him. And, for reasons known throughout the town, he wanted to be rid of that house. If he allowed her to talk to any one . . .

"All right—all right," he said, and the bargain was closed.

So Carrie came into possession of the Red Brick House. But the bargain, that appeared so desirable at first glance, was not altogether satisfactory. Big Gussie made clear the weakness of the deal.

"Lawsy, honey!" she exclaimed, when she heard Carrie's news. " 'mongst-you ain't gwine live in *dat* house?"

"How come Ah ain't?" Carrie wanted to know. "Ah bought it!"

"Lawsy, chile! Dat house is ha'nted!"

"Ha'nted!" Jake and Carrie exclaimed in one breath.

"Sho! Law-aw-dee! Lissen yere. . . ." Gussie went into a long story, the gist of which was as follows:

The Old Brick House had been built by a tonger (one who gathers oysters by means of long-handled rakes, or tongs) ten years or more ago. He and his wife lived happily there for nearly half a year. Then, after two days' search, fellow tongers found the man's bloated, blue-faced body on the far side of the Avondale. His widow remained in the house for a week following the accident then she suddenly sold it to Sid Hooper and left town.

The house stayed vacant for perhaps six years before Lottie Turner rented it in a fit of defiance to escape her mother's counseling tongue. Some three months later, on a gusty March day, two truant schoolboys spied a bobbing, hairy object under Gallion's wharf. It was Lottie's water-grayed body.

No one dared to occupy the Old Brick House after that incident. But there was another happening to augment the eerie legend. One dark night Tilton Street had been startled from its peaceful slumbers by piteous cries of "Murder! Murder!" In the morning the fainthearted residents investigated the Old Brick House, from which the cries had come, and verified their expectations. A tramp lay dead on the porch with blue marks of fingers on his swollen neck. In the pockets of his ragged trousers were found seven pairs of dice; when thrown, all of them turned up "seven" or "eleven."

So for the past three years the Old Brick House had stood deserted. Boys had used its windows for target practice until they yawned like the dark mouths of caves. The natives hurried past it after dark, whistling vociferously. In the early hours before dawn, crabbers and tongers, if possible, traveled another route to their boats lying at the wharves on Town Creek. The Old Brick House was a pariah.

"Ah'm tellin' you," Gussie concluded her sanguinary history, "it's dead bad luck! Efn 'mongst-you wants to keep outn trouble, you better not live in dat place!"

Carrie and Jake were visibly shaken. But Carrie thought of the money she had spent. Two hundred dollars was too large a sum to be sacrificed.

"Damn de ha'nts!" she exclaimed.

II

A month later, one warm afternoon in September, Jake sat on the porch. He was more than satisfied with his lot. He was inclined to be complacent.

Under Carrie's capable hands the house had undergone a transformation. It was no longer vacant-eyed. The windowpanes had been replaced and now showed bright new curtains. Every room had been calcimined and the floors had been scoured until they looked like bread-boards. Some second-hand furniture completed the change. From all appearances, the Old Red Brick House was no longer the meeting-place for troubled spirits.

But more pleasing to Jake than the house was his conquest of Carrie. Her mature charms were vastly more alluring than her youthful charms had been, and Jake fancied himself as the Great Lover. He did not take into account Prince's long neglect. He did not know that to

Carrie he was but as sweetened hot water when no tea is available.

Carrie came to the door, a dust-cap protecting her hair, and stood there a moment, surveying him in silence. A small pucker gathered at the bridge of her nose. She spoke softly—too softly:

"Ah needs some mo' wood, Jake."

Jake started at the sound of her voice, then eased back into his chair.

"All right, honey," he said, but there was no honey in his voice. "Ah'll cut a li'l' attah while. . . ." He settled more comfortably on the end of his spine.

"Ah needs it now," said Carrie, still softly. But the pucker deepened.

"Oh, cain't Blanche chop some?" offered Jake, plaintively. He didn't move.

This was the proverbial last straw. For the past four weeks she had put up with his sloth. Now her leashed feelings broke loose.

"Lissen yere, man!" she grated through clenched teeth. "Efn you thinks you gwine squat 'round this house a-doin' nothin' all the time, you gots another think comin'! This is *mah* house! You ain't put a red cent in it! Now befo' you sleeps in *mah* house another night, you's gwine to give me some o' that money you said you had when Ah picked you up! An' efn you cain't cut a li'l' wood now an' then, you kin git the hell out! An' stay out!" With that, Carrie slammed her way back to her work.

Jake was shocked; so much so that he arose like one who suddenly realizes that the object he sits upon is an intensely hot stove. The ultimatum echoing in his ears, he made a direct line to the back yard and, in the same breath, industriously engaged the wood-pile. The chips flew. But soon his fine flare of energy died and his hazel eyes narrowed rebelliously. His masculine vanity had been bruised.

That night after the girls had gone to bed, Carrie soothed his injured pride by wiles she had never before exercised. She did it as an experiment. She held no tenderness for Jake, but she went through the process of cuddling and caressing as a scientist tests a theory. It sufficed, for Jake, completely deceived, handed over nearly all his money into her keeping.

Carrie was progressing rapidly in ways that would have surprised members of the Ebenezer Ladies' Aid. The obedient wife of Jim Prince, so soft-spoken and retiring, who had walked so decorously in the conventional paths, was disappearing as if by magic. And in her place there was emerging the Carrie Prince who is still a subject for discussion among the older gossips of Herdford.

As a property-owner she had credit at all the stores. So she bought silks and calicos from which she created dresses that aroused waves of jealousy among the feminine population. Puffed sleeves exaggerated her magnificently wide shoulders and emphasized in contrast her slender waistline which sloped into shapely hips; while tight bodies revealed to perfection the mature beauty of her bust. Carrie was aware of her good looks and she made the most of them. As she emerged from the sarcophagus of unbecoming garments, her whole demeanor changed. She studied her carriage, until her walk became a movement in voluptuous rhythm. There was no obvious switching of the hips, but through suggestion Carrie achieved a most telling effect, and her passage down the street was a signal for the turning of heads. One man, in a poetic mood, said she was like "a willow tree when de wind hits it." The women were less kind. "Look at the hussy strut!" they grumbled among themselves. But Carrie, holding her head high in the pride of her newly found power, went her oblivious way.

III

It required only one visit to Gallion's crab-house to decide Carrie against picking crabs, and anyone who has done this work will not readily condemn her. It is an odious labor.

The crab-house sat on that point of land known as The Island, at the juncture of the Avondale and Town Creek. Originally a swampy waste caused by the tidal flow, it had been built up to usefulness by an accumulation of oyster shells. A neck of soggy land isolated it effectively from the town of Herdford proper.

Gussie went along with Carrie in the capacity of guide, and enjoyed her rôle to the full. She was hugely amused when at the door of the crab-house she saw Carrie's nose go up in delicate disdain at the overwhelming stench which greeted them. It was no wonder. There is nothing more revolting than the smell of steamed crabs, and the day was hot.

"Dat stink'll stay right yere twell dey starts to shuckin' oysters," Gussie said, cheerfully. "An' Ah don't know what's de worst—crabs or oysters."

They continued to the wharf, where a large oblong wooden box swung on iron rods and gave off jets of vapor from under a stained sailcloth cover. This was where the crabs were steamed, Gussie explained. The steam was supplied from a boiler near by.

Two boats bobbed just below the wharf's edge, their masts wrapped in their sails and reclining along the gunwales. A red-headed white man and a Negro talked and joked as they worked.

Carrie moved toward the Negro to see better what he was doing. As she approached he removed his hat.

"Ah'm baitin' mah line fo' tomorrow," he answered her query. Then he went on with his task.

Carrie's first impression was that this was the blackest and the biggest man she had even seen; his teeth the whitest and his eyes the strangest green-gray. Moreover, he was the only man in Herdford who had looked at her without ogling her. She wanted to know more about him.

"What do you use for bait?" she asked, to be saying something.

"Tripe," he answered, without looking up. It could have been a rebuff.

"Why do you throw 'way them pieces?" She pointed to some floating scraps of whitish meat which were being attacked by a cluster of minnows.

The suspicion of a smile flickered across his face.

"Some o' dese crabs," he explained, "dey's like some folks—kindah partic'lar 'bout who dey eats attah. So Ah changes de bait to please dey appetites." The smile flashed out frankly for a second and then was smothered.

"Oh, you's jes' jokin' me!" answered Carrie, also smiling.

The man looked up long enough to sweep his eyes methodically over her figure and take in the full extent of her beauty. This time his smile flashed approval.

"Who is you, lady? Stranger in town, ain't you?"

"Mah name's Carrie Prince. Ah bin yere goin' on a month now."

"Oh—so *you's* Carrie Prince!" He resumed his work with a finality that checked the rejoinder Carrie was about to make.

A boat drifted in with more crabs and the black man shoved away from the wharf to make room for the new arrival. Carrie turned to Gussie.

"Who's that man, Gussie?" Carrie nodded to the drifting boat with its solitary occupant.

"Lew Grundy?" asked Gussie. "Why, he's de head deacon over to Winters' Meth'dist church. An' he ain't no hypocrite. He don't chew or smoke or drink or mess wid women—leastways Ah ain't never seed 'im foolin' 'round. An' you ought hear dat man sing an' pray!"

"Huh! So he's a deacon?" Carrie sneered.

A wizened little man named Tommy Dyke—Carrie recognized him as the drunk she had seen on Gussie's sofa—was busily shoveling the steamed crabs from the box into baskets and rusty boilers which stood about. As if in answer to a signal, more than a score of women and children swarmed out onto the wharf, cursing and jostling each other in their haste to retrieve their receptacles. One old woman was almost pushed into the water.

"Don't you dast tech dat boiler!" an ancient hag screamed. "Dat's mah red string on it an' you knows it! You li'l' hussy!"

A mulatto with Titian hair took a belligerent stand with hands on hips. "Huh! You's so old you cain't even tell yo' own things! Try to tech it!" she dared.

"You young snipper-snaps ain't got no 'spect fo' yo' elders, dat's what!" the old woman complained, sniffling.

"'Spect!" And with that the mulatto snatched up the boiler and disappeared into the crab-house.

Tommy Dyke stood there unmoved by all the clamor. Now and then he paused indifferently to mop his bald knob of a head with a filthy bandanna. When he had finished distributing the crabs he righted the steam box and swung a fresh barrel of live crabs into it.

Carrie peered over the top of the box at the crawling, clawing creatures awaiting a vaporous death. They were making valiant but unsuccessful efforts to climb the smooth sides of the boiler. Every time one would secure a precarious foothold a struggling neighbor would pull it back.

"Dey's jes' like folks," said a deep voice at Carrie's side. "Efn one cain't git out, he ain't gwine let another git out."

She turned to face Lew Grundy. Again she thought she had never seen a man so big, and was disturbed.

"Ain't seed you at church," he observed.

The sense of disturbing enchantment which the man's size evoked was shattered now.

"Ah don't go to church," said Carrie, frigidly, and swayed into the crab-house, exhibiting her newly found grace of deportment.

The incessant murmur of voices interspersed by the cracking of knives upon some brittly substance met Carrie at the door. She saw Gussie's broad, yellow face topping a pile of crabs on one of the center tables. As she stood at Gussie's elbow, watching the picking process, many sidelong glances were cast in her direction.

At first the swiftly moving hands of the four women at the table were to Carrie a jumbled series of quick stabs and slices. For her benefit, Gussie picked one more slowly. She first tore off the obular, pointed back, then picked the meat from its sections. The largest particles she deposited in a separate pan.

"Dat's de lump meat," she explained. "Taste it."

Carrie, selecting an extra large one, found it so delicious that she rapidly followed it with others.

"Help yo'self," bade Gussie. "You'll git sick of 'em efn you stay yere long enough." Taking a big claw, she continued: "Yere's how you git de meat outn dis." She brought her knife down with splintering precision. The shell dropped off and disclosed the yellowish-brown muscle.

"Ain't you scared o' cuttin' yo' hands?" asked Carrie.

"Huh! When you does dis season in an' season out, you don't know what cuttin' yo' hand is."

A high soprano began to hum a dragging tune. Other voices came to its assistance.

> "Dere is rest fo' de weary—
> Dere is rest fo' de weary—
> Oh, dere's rest fo' de weary—
> Dere is rest fo' me!
>
> "On de other side o' Jordan—
> In de green fields o' Eden—
> Where de tree o' life is a-bloomin'—
> Dere is rest fo' me!"

Innumerable verses, improvised by the pickers at different tables, carried the lyric on and on until it wavered and died. Over in a corner, a ray of sunlight fought its way through a splotched window and lighted the reposed faces of two infants. Unmindful of flies and the heat simmering through the tin roof, they slumbered, lulled by the mournful strain.

Chapter 14

Summer broke abruptly about a week after Carrie's explosion to Jake. The sun tried to hold its own, but there was clear evidence that fall was no longer to be denied. Dropping leaves reddened and yellowed the Public Lot and littered the bricks under the arch of maples down Front Street. Wild geese streamed southward over the Avondale. One by one the crabbers laid aside their lines and took their tong shafts and rusty rakes to young Tom Ridgely, the blacksmith, for repairs. Fewer and fewer crabs came into the wharves until, on the last day of September, the rival houses on the Island and on Town Pier sent no blasts shrieking to the skies. The crabs would have peace until the following summer.

With the crabbing season ended, the oyster season was on, and now the town awoke to full life. For two weeks boats, trains, wagons, and all manner of horse-drawn conveyances brought men and women—sometimes whole families—to swell the colored population. Most of the incoming oyster-shuckers were men. They came from Virginia and points as far south as North Carolina. And the majority came by way of Baltimore on the steamers *Avalon* and *Talbot*.

One of these boats touched Herdford every night on its way to Eastland Point, which was the last stop on its route. From Monday to Friday the vessel slunk into Town Wharf at about midnight; then, its obligations discharged, departed with expeditious haste. But Saturday night was different. Saturday night was Jug Night.

No matter what the weather, when the first blast of the steamer was heard, nearly all the men of the town who had reached their majority would take themselves hurriedly to the wharf. Here, in the dim light of the kerosene lamps which perched on the walls of the freight-house, they would wait eagerly for the boat to dock with a great splashing of her side wheels.

Their patience was rewarded when, after passengers and merchandise had been transferred, the stevedores would march single file down the gangplank, each swinging a jug in either hand. The jugs were deposited in the freight-house. Then there was a grand rush as the waiting men bore down upon the freight agent, who shouted out the names which tagged the necks of the containers. Every man eventually was awarded a jug. The greedier ones opened theirs on the spot, slung them over the crooks of their arms and gurgled happily—and as they gurgled the trials of the week washed away.

Sunday night also was a gala night at the wharf, for after a day of rest the residents of the sleepy village were prime for any diversion that chance or circumstance offered. A queen and her imperial train could not have received more homage than the side-wheeler from Baltimore as she swung around Tom's Point into the Avondale from Choptank River. Idlers from Front and Tilton streets dashed headlong to the waterfront. Children raced to see who could get to the wharf first. Their elders, out for a walk, accelerated their pace. And as the boat came splashing to rest, with a final shrill blast of her whistle, horses reared and pitched, and the more timid watchers clutched at each other in giggling fright.

Jim Tutley, the shipping agent, his magnificently curled mustachios erect, was a paragon of authoritative pride on such occasions.

"Haul away!" he would bawl after he had slipped the wide nooses of the lead line over stout pilings at each wharf corner.

From that moment until the boat's departure, the proceedings took on a certain ritualistic cast. The roustabouts rushed here and there, clearing a space, removing a bar—every movement an incident in a prearranged plan. Then the gangplank was shot over the boat's side, a waist-high railing was attached, and a resplendent personage in blue uniform advanced to snarl:

"All off 'at's goin' off!"

First the white passengers disembarked, the women throwing timid glances at the water yawning darkly below. After them came the Negro passengers, the oyster-shuckers—swaggering, teeth flashing. Freight was unloaded, outgoing freight was hauled aboard. New passengers arrived. The gangplank was withdrawn. A shrill whistle. The waters churned. And in a minute more the steamer had rounded the bend toward Eastland Point.

Jim Tutley extinguished the lamps and locked the great sliding doors, and once more the wharf was a patch of darkness against the gently swelling river.

Chapter 15

I

By the middle of October Carrie had all of her rooms rented. She would accept only male lodgers, for the women who drifted into Herdford after the oyster season was in full swing brought memories of A'nt Sue's bawd-house. They swaggered into Carrie's kitchen in their cheap, flashy clothes, and when Carrie refused them quarters they switched out saucily and over to Gussie's, where there were no restrictions. That fat one had an eye for business. How twelve women could live in her squalid five-room shack was a mystery. But they did, and they brought their landlady handsome remuneration.

At Thanksgiving time Gussie bloomed in new finery, and took occasion to twit Carrie for her prudery.

"Ah don't care," Carrie answered bluntly. "Ah ain't goin' to have mah gals a-larning dirt from them hussies. 'Sides, Ah makes enough from mah likker an' rooms an' board."

Jake also protested, only to discover that he had made the wrong move. His stock had never been very high with Carrie. She had refused to permit gambling in the house. Now she had the opportunity she wanted to tell him what she thought of his carrying-on with a strumpet across the way. She did so in no uncertain terms, and when she had finished Jake knew that his brief reign was over.

"You thinks Ah'm goin' to let you run with that Nellie gal over to Gussie's and then bring yo'self to me? Huh! You's jes' as wrong as you kin be. You turns mah stomach, anyways!" She grimaced. "You kin stay yere—but that's all!"

Jake growled evilly, but said nothing.

Though Carrie's life from this point was irreproachable, Herdford saw what it saw and drew its own conclusions. It saw men staggering from the Red Brick House at all hours of the day and night. It saw that Carrie was a friend of Mis' Gussie, a known bawd. It was said that she drank and smoked. It was rumored that by her own admission she was not married to the gambler Jake. Finally, her good looks and her arrogant walk was proof positive that she was not what she should be.

The girls complained that no one would play with them at recess, or sit next to them at Sunday school.

"Never mind," Carrie soothed. "You-all ain't gwine have to stay yere all the time. Blanche, you is goin' to the Institute next year. An' soon's Martha's old enough she's goin' too. Don't you mind."

But they did mind.

II

About this time little Martha became something of a sensation.

The women from Baltimore had brought a new dance to town—the cakewalk—and nothing would do but Carrie and Gussie must learn it. A slender girl with short hair, moody black eyes, a reedy soprano, and a gift with the guitar provided music. When she had had three or four drinks Gussie's poor shack rang to the sound of a lively tune and strutting feet. Gussie's two hundred pounds were a serious liability when the dance called for perilous balancing with knee raised and back parallel with the floor, but Carrie mastered the dance's intricacies with a natural grace.

One Saturday morning as Carrie was scrubbing the kitchen floor she missed Martha's chatter in the back yard where she had been holding conversation with a stray kitten. She called to Blanche, who was upstairs, tidying the lodgers' rooms.

"I don't know where she is, Mamma," Blanche answered, "unless she's over to Mis' Gussie's."

Carrie hurried across the crusted road, to be met with a burst of laughter and the strumming of a guitar.

"G'on, gal!" she heard as she neared the door.

"Lookit dat li'l' un go!"

"Walk dat cake, honey! Bless yo' heart!"

"Her kin whip her mammy, sho's yo' bo'n!"

There in the center of the room, surrounded by an enthralled audience of men and women, was Martha, her braids tossing, her slight body swaying to the rhythms of the cakewalk. Every so often little squeals escaped her. Carrie had her mouth all fixed to scold the child when, with a final turn around the circle, she bent her pliant back parallel to the floor and strutted right into her mother's skirts.

The chastening words died on Carrie's lips at the impish gesture. And Martha's career as an entertainer began. After this, when Gussie had company, the evening wasn't complete until Martha had danced at least one cakewalk.

III

"Larnin' dat chile to dance!" said Laura Titman to Etta Curley. "She ought be 'shame' herself!"

Laura was the portly woman who sold pastries and home-made ice-cream savoring strongly of cornstarch. Etta was a slattern, her good looks destroyed by child-bearing and years of drudging over laundry tubs. Between them they set the pace for Herdford gossip. And they were so generous with their store of information that their opinions were very apt to be shared soon by all their neighbors.

Chapter 16

The Good Brothers' Hall—a magnificent structure of red tin—had had a thorough scouring by the Brothers' wives. Bunting in many colors draped the ceiling and walls of the assembly-room. The platform was gay with paper streamers in honor of the Bainbridge band. Long tables of smooth planks mounted on saw-horses and spread with new oilcloth bordered three walls. An inviting smell of fried oysters pervaded the place. It was December, and the annual oyster supper and dance was in full swing.

On this occasion the colored people of Herdford were the guests of the rival barons of the oyster industry, Kirkland and Gallion. These gentlemen sat now directly in the center of the table at the end of the room, trying for the moment to cloak their differences in a semblance of good-will. To their right was the Reverend Raymond, shepherd of the colored flock. And flanking these dignitaries were the foremen and the tongers of the rival houses. Those of lesser station sat at the side tables, while some of the younger generation, who were of no station at all, lounged in chairs by the door, impatiently waiting their turn at table.

The usual speeches were delivered—polite and labored speeches by the two hosts which combined cajolery with flattery, a long-winded speech by Gallion's foreman, Bud Saunders. Then Kirkland and Gallion slipped thankfully out of the side door and the company, just as thankfully, relaxed for the good time which was the real business of the evening. Conversation got louder. Laughter rang truer. Drink flowed more freely.

Carrie, who had been persuaded to come by Tom Bentley, was thoroughly enjoying herself in a new blue velvet gown of her own making. It didn't matter that little groups of buzzing women indicated her with sly nods and a turning up of the nose. The men more than made up for any neglect by their spontaneous attentions. For them, gossip simply enhanced her charms. They hung on every word she uttered. They leaped to fill her glass with beer from the barrel at the corner of the stage. They swarmed for dances.

There was only one man who had nothing to say to her. That was Deacon Grundy, who sat at the table opposite her and fastened her relentlessly with his gray-green cats' eyes until she felt them sinking into her flesh. She threw up her chin defiantly, angry that he could put her out of ease, and met his look straight. The suspicion of a smile crossed his dark face, and against her will she smiled in return.

Just then a shout rang out.

"Look out! Tom Bentley's gonna shoot!"

The screams of frightened women split the air and there was a mad scramble for doors and windows. Some of the company disappeared beneath tables. Carrie, pinioned between table and wall, looked wildly around for a place to hide, then relaxed in relief. It was a false alarm.

Tom Bentley had a reputation for using his forty-five-caliber pistol on the slightest provocation, so when he rose above Bud Saunders with his arm upraised, a glinting knife in his great fist, onlookers naturally expected action. But there was no anger on his blunt square-featured face.

"Ah tells you, Bud," he was roaring, "dem Broad Creek oysters ain't wort' de trouble it takes to git 'em!" And he brought his huge hand down on the table with a splintering crash. Then he flopped into his seat beside Bud and they continued their spluttering but amiable argument. Both were too lager-logged to realize the disturbance they had caused.

Grinning sheepishly, the guests emerged from hiding and drifted back to their places. And now the Bainbridge band, famed in several counties, struck up in earnest. Soon the floor was crowded with whirling, laughing couples. There were some, however—staunch church members like Cap'n Tom Winters, Etta Curley, and Laura Titman—

who regarded dancing in the light of unholy revelry and took their pious ways home.

Later in the evening Carrie had just finished a solo cakewalk when another incident shattered the peaceful gayety of the occasion. Daisy had stood all she could of Ike's attentions to one of Gussie's women. She had put up with the taunts of her friends long enough, and the time had come to exact her dues. Swaggering out of the corner where she had been contemplating her desertion, she caught her lover by the shoulder and wrenched him from his dancing partner. In a second the three were the center of a crowd.

"Ike Brown, Ah'd like to speak wid you!" Standing there, hands on her twitching hips, Daisy was a menacing figure.

"Sho, honey," grinned Ike, "go right ahead." A quantity of beer had put him in a happy frame of mind. And besides, he enjoyed evidence that his gal was jealous.

"What you means by flirtin' wid dis hussy?"

"Who you callin' a hussy?" demanded Callie, and there was that in her manner which welcomed a fight.

"Look yere, Daisy," began Ike, placatingly, "'tain't no harm fo' me to dance wid Callie—"

"Don't you try to soft-talk me, Ike Brown!" interrupted Daisy. She snatched her arm from his grasp and turned again to Callie. "Yass, you's a hussy! An' Ah ain't scared to tell you so, too!"

Suddenly, from somewhere on her person, Daisy flashed an open razor, and with a quick movement spun away from hands reached out to restrain her. Her face contorted by a snarl that revealed ugly purple gums, she advanced slowly on the trembling Callie.

"Don't let her cut me!" Callie's distended eyes searched wildly for some means of escape.

Then Tom Bentley's bellow broke into the hubbub.

"Drop dat razor or Ah'll shoot sho'n hell!"

There was no question in anyone's mind but that he would do as he said. Daisy dropped the razor, all her bellicosity fled, and turned to the paralyzed ring of spectators.

Bentley pocketed his gun, then the razor. "Take dat gal on home," he instructed Ike.

As the two departed meekly arm in arm, Bentley offered himself as Callie's partner and was accepted.

"Strike up a tune, Jim-Ed!"

And the dancers once more swung onto the floor, the recent incident wiped from their minds. For something of the like happened at every dance.

Chapter 17

I

Carrie listened in ominous silence to the story of her elder daughter.

"What did you say to her?" she interrupted. But Blanche was so choked by sobs that she couldn't answer.

"Oh, stop that cryin'!" Carrie commanded, sharply. "You's too soft—that's what you is!"

"I told Mis' Laura I didn't care!" piped Martha. Nothing seemed to blight Martha's spirit. She was made of sterner stuff than her sister.

"Git me mah coat," Carrie ordered Blanche.

Fifteen minutes later the Reverend Raymond was interrupted in his Sabbath meditations by a knock at the door. He stifled his surprise at the sight of Carrie, who was the last person he would have expected to call. He had heard much of this woman—a Magdalene, if reports were true.

"Come right in, Sister Prince!" His invitation was kindly, for kindliness was his fundamental trait. This was a man whom none of the bitternesses of life could make bitter. His starved ascetic face emanated a quiet enduring strength.

"Don't you 'sister' me!" retorted Carrie disagreeably. She brushed past him and took her position by the squat coal-stove.

"Are we not all sisters and brothers down here in these low grounds of sorrow?" returned the pastor, evenly. "Won't you sit down?"

"How come you let that *Sister* Curley and that *Sister* Titman keep mah gals outn parts on the Christmas program?" demanded Carrie, accenting her words viciously.

"Why," the Reverend Raymond remonstrated in surprise, "haven't they parts? The whole Sunday school is Supposed to take part."

"You knows they ain't got no parts! You knows it!"

"Please, Sister Prince! Won't you sit down and tell me all about it?"

Carrie eyed him sullenly for a moment, trying to decide whether or not his surprise was genuine. Finally she sat on the edge of a chair and slowly relaxed as her host continued to smile ever so faintly.

"Now—," he prompted. He stretched his long legs at ease and waited.

Her heat rising again, Carrie told how Laura Titman, head of the primary department, and Etta Curley, Blanche's intermediate teacher, had neglected to give the girls pieces to recite.

"Ah knows Ah don't go to church. Ah ain't pretendin' to be no saint nuthah. But mah gals got jes' much right to be on that program as anybody else's! Ah gives 'em pennies to put in collection jes' same's the rest!"

The pastor stroked his side-burns thoughtfully during Carrie's angry recital. When she was finally lost for words and simply sat there glowering at him, he began to talk in an even, soothing voice.

"I'm glad you came to me with this matter, Sister Prince. I didn't know a thing about it. But you can be sure that the girls will have parts. The superintendent, Brother Winters, has often spoken of the aptness of your daughters, and I'm quite sure this unpleasant thing was no fault of his. I shall speak to Sisters Titman and Curley at once. Your two girls shall have their pieces tomorrow. Just tell them to stop past here on their way from school, will you?" He paused. "And, by the way, Sister Prince, could I extend to you an invitation to come and worship with us some—"

"Ah don't go to no church!" scowled Carrie.

"Oh . . . I see," still quietly. "But surely you will come to hear your girls, won't you?" He fixed his calm eyes on her until she lowered her own.

"Ah don't 'tend no church," she reiterated, like a sulky child.

When she was gone, the Reverend Raymond stood at the door in puzzled thought, unmindful of the cold. Had he seen tears in her eyes . . . ?

Her head held defiantly high, Carrie strode into the little church that Sunday night before Christmas and took a seat in the middle section of pews directly in front of the rostrum.

This was an outrageous thing to have happen, as was evidenced by the expressions of frozen disapproval on the faces of the congregation. For it was a tradition of long standing in Winters M. E. Church that sinners—and was not Carrie Prince a sinner?—occupied the alcove to the right of the entrance. Two occasions only justified their trespassing in the main auditorium: when they took an offering to the collection table, and when they were moved to seek the mourners' bench. Carrie had neither of these excuses, yet she sat there in sanctified territory as if she belonged, her regal air of obliviousness foiling the sharp, angry glances that were darted her way.

The Winters family—in the pew next to the one Carrie had defiled—were represented on the program by little Reba and young Tom, who declaimed their lines with the sing-song glibness expected of them. Cap'n Tom, who appeared to have been poured into his three-buttoned sack suit of slate gray, and Julie Winters, elegant in matronly black, smiled in complacent pride. Then it was the turn of the young Grimms and Wigginses and Horns to perform, and the pride that had sat upon the Winters' faces visited in succession each pair of parents.

Carrie's Martha had twelve lines which she recited with characteristic sprightliness. But Blanche was the unquestioned celebrity of the evening when her clear young contralto rang out in a solo that was the final number on the program.

"Amen! Amen!" could be heard emphatically from all quarters of the church as the girl took her seat.

This was all that Carrie wanted. It was all she had come for. She looked triumphantly at Etta Curley and Laura Titman as they walked stiffly past, then she gathered her daughters and went home.

This was the only time that Carrie Prince attended the church at Herdford.

Chapter 18

I

A false spring settled over the lowlands after the holidays. Ice that had glazed the surfaces of the Avondale and Town Creek, broke and floated out toward the Choptank. The bare three inches of Yuletide snow thawed into a mixture of shell-and-dirt mud that made the roads wellnigh impassable. It clung to the felt-topped boots of the shuckers as they plowed to and from the rival oyster-houses under the mild mid-afternoon sun.

"Hey, Carrie!" Big Gussie stood in the road, balancing a quart jar precariously in her hand. Carrie poked her head out of her kitchen window. "C'mon an' git some free oysters down to de house. Ah jes' seed Oleman Gallion a-goin' up de street."

Carrie joined her presently with her own jar.

Gussie was full as a tick with gossip, and as they walked along she ladled it out. Carrie listened but said nothing.

"What's you gonna do attah de shuckin' season's over?" asked Gussie when she had drained herself dry of other matters. "Season's over in April."

Carrie thought a minute. "Ah don't know. One thing certain. Ah ain't gonna pick no crabs. Guess Ah'll jes' work 'long easy 'twell Ah gits mah house like Ah wants it. You can't keep nothin' right wid a lot o' men around!"

"Ain't it de truth!" agreed Gussie, and the conviction in her voice would have done credit to an immaculate housewife. Then she launched abruptly into a subject to which she had clearly given considerable thought. "'Course, 'tain't no 'fair o' mine, but why you let dat Nellie gal take yo' man?"

Carrie stopped in surprise. "What man?"

"Why, Jake. Ain't he yo' man?"

Carrie laughed scornfully. "Huh! He ain't no man o' mine! Ah wouldn't have 'im. But Ah knows one thing— efn he don't bring mo' money in fo' his board an' keep, he ain't gonna stay in no house o' mine!"

"Wal, how-dee!" ejaculated Gussie between gasps, for the mud was tiring her. "Honey, you sho gots dis town fooled!" In a minute when her breath was coming more easily she added: "Dey says he was purty good wid de cards an' dice 'twell dey cotched him cheatin' out to Tom Bentley's last month. Nellie says he ain't won none since. Guess he's scared, 'cause Tom told him he'd blow his head off efn dey cotched 'im ag'in—an' Tom'll do dat, too! Dat black man sho don't fool wid you none!"

"Somebody ought to blow his head off!" muttered Carrie. "He ain't no good, he ain't! Nellie want 'im, she sho kin have 'im, 'cause Ah don't!"

II

The low-raftered oyster-house was a smelly, sloppy place that would have turned the stomach of the smart people who relished Herdford oysters in the metropolitan restaurants that were their final destination. Four shelf-like, wooden structures, waist-high, ran the length of the room—one on each side, two facing each other down the center. Upon them were distributed heaps of muddy oysters. The shuckers (there were women as well as men) stood in narrow, body-width stalls that reached to the top of the shelves.

A powerful fellow weaved continually up and down the two aisles with a flat-bottomed barrow—bringing fresh supplies of oysters for the shuckers, carrying off shells that the shuckers had cast aside. The shuckers were skilled laborers but this carrier, by comparison, was a menial of the most inferior order. What he had was strength for a strenuous job.

By the dim light struggling through muddy windows Carrie made out the tall form of Grundy leaning industriously over his shucking-board. At the moment he was competing with his neighbor, a wiry little man with the high cheek bones and swarthy coloring that indicated a fusion of Indian and Negro blood. Carrie left Gussie to talk with Bud Saunders and eased over to Grundy's side.

Grundy and the little man were evenly matched but their methods of shucking differed. Grundy used the orthodox oyster-knife, a slender, thin steel blade, about the length and a quarter of the index finger, which he gripped in his right hand. His gloved left hand held the oyster on the board. First he would insert the knife, guiding it with a muslin-stalled forefinger. Then after a preliminary boring effected with his pliant right wrist there would follow a coordinated twisting of oyster and knife—and a juicy grey oyster lay unshelled, to be flipped into one of two pails at the side of the pile. The actual time of this operation was hardly more than five seconds.

His neighbor's methods required more archaic implements—a small hammer and a long-handled knife (originally belonging to a table set) which had been filed down until it resembled a hiltless stiletto. With the hammer the little man broke the mouth of the oyster's shell, temporarily jarring open the two halves. Then he released the hammer with lightning rapidity, the knife fairly leapt into his hand, and the blade darted like the tongue of an aroused serpent between the two shells. With the same twisting motion Grundy practiced he exposed the oyster, and with the same flip he deposited it in its pail.

The movements of the two men were flowing rather than jerky—a symphony in muscular coordination—

and Carrie looked on fascinated. The men were not unconscious of their audience.

Finally Grundy jabbed his quivering blade into the soggy board at the base of his oyster pile and turned to his opponent with a broad grin.

"Ah beat you dat time, Sam," he rumbled, good-naturedly.

Sam shrugged his shoulders and spat a stream of tobacco juice onto the discarded shells at the side of his stall, while he continued to ply his knife and hammer.

Grundy swung his two pails down from the shelf, disappeared into the packing-room, and returned. Carrie was still there.

"You sho kin open dem oysters," she smiled.

His gray eyes might have seen her for the first time, but he flashed the whiteness of his teeth.

"Ain't you never seed no fast shuckin' befo'?" he inquired.

"Ah ain't never seed no kind o' shuckin'," answered Carrie.

"Whar you bin at?"

"Ah ain't lived near no water since Ah was a li'l' gal," she explained.

"You watch me an Ah'll show you how it's done," he promised. He took an oyster leisurely. "You see, oysters ain't like humans—dey don't like to open dey mouths 'less'n dey jes' has to. Dat's why dey squeaks an' spits when you sticks 'em wid yo' knife. You gots to twist yo' knife like dis so's to make his jaws tired. See? Den you cuts de muscle off'n de bottom shell easy-like so's you don't mess up his guts. See? Dar he is—a big 'un. Want 'im?"

Carrie took it gingerly, but in a minute her expression of distaste disappeared and her face broke into its most alluring smile.

"Will you shuck me this jar full fo' mah supper, Mr. Grundy?" she asked.

"Sho! How'd you know mah name?"

"Oh, Ah larned that when Ah first come to town. Don't you 'member out on the wharf, yonder, an' at the oyster supper?"

Gray eyes met black eyes, smiled, and looked casually away.

The cry of a baby wailed above the buzzing voices and crackling shells. From the side of her husband, felt-booted and mud daubed as was he, a stalwart woman strode to a wooden box by the stove. Catching the kicking infant to her breast, she sat down, crooning softly. But the child's cries shrilled higher and higher.

"Hey thar, Lew Grundy!" called the woman. "Sing dat 'Go Down Moses' fo' dis chile; he's a man-chile efn dey ever was one! He don't like no baby song!"

Coaxing cries came from all quarters:

"Yeah, Lew!"

"Come on, Deacon. We'll help you sing it!"

Without preliminaries, Grundy lifted his head and poured forth the first line in a deeply mellow baritone.

He forgot the oysters, and his intensity transmitted itself to Carrie. She found her own mature contralto blending in the refrain. The other shuckers paused in surprise at this duet. A low hum cautiously followed the two leaders. Then, like the burst of an organ, all blazed their voices to the rafters as they leapt into the triumphantly hopeful chorus. Wailing minor chords were woven instinctively into the simple melody until a vibrant fullness blotted out the drab interior of the smelly place of toil.

As the last note slipped away and labor was resumed, Grundy beamed on Carrie.

"You sho kin sing, sister!" he exclaimed. His gray-green eyes glowed. "Whyn't you jine de choir?"

Carrie's smile froze abruptly. "Much oblige' fo' shuckin' mah oysters, *Deacon* Grundy!" She snatched the jar and turned to go.

"Hold on!" There was majesty in the boom of his voice. Carrie stopped.

"Wal?" she demanded, impatient at her weakness.

His eyes were wholly green now, and she could not drop hers. His face was expressionless, and so low was his tone it was audible only to Carrie.

"Ah didn't go to say nuffin' to rile you. So you didn't have to be so snappish-like . . . like some spiled young un!"

Carrie whirled away with a toss of her head. His gaze followed her weaving body until she passed through the door. And his hands moved more slowly now.

Chapter 19

I

Hans Newman, one of the first residents of Herdford and long since dead, had been an enterprising young Dutchman. A good provider, he had balked at having his fair English wife walk a quarter of a mile for household water to one of the town pumps on Front Street. So at the back of his house on lower Tilton Street he had dug a well, which was now the source of water for the colored people of the neighborhood. The present owner was gracious about the general use of the well because it gave him a certain prestige. A wooden framework, about the height of a small child's head, built in a square about the mouth of the well, served to prevent dogs, cats, chickens, and children from falling in. But despite this precautionary structure, at times one found the carcasses of careless animals floating on the surface of the water fifteen feet below the ground level. When such accidents occurred, use of the well was suspended until it was drained, or until the villagers tired of going a greater distance for their water.

It was here that Laura Titman and Etta Curley met, as if by prearrangement, the day following Carrie's visit to the oyster-house.

Laura pulled her pail over the top of the well just as Etta creaked around the corner of the Newman house.

"Lawsy, chile!" exclaimed Laura, delightedly. "Ah was jes' studyin' 'bout you!"

Etta adjusted her dust-cap with a reddened hand. "Ah seed you from mah yard," she explained. "Jes' tryin' to finish up the Conklins' wash whilst the weather's mild. Mah rheumaticks sho gits bad when Ah has to hang out clothes in a cold wind. An' Ah knows dis yere warm spell ain't going to last."

Laura could hardly conceal her impatience as Etta went on with her rambling recital apropos the state of her health and the state of the weather.

". . . jes' the way it does every year 'bout this time," Etta was droning on. "Sap ain' riz in the trees yit."

Laura saw a brilliant opportunity and grabbed it.

"No—sap ain' riz in the *trees*," she agreed, with a lift of her eyebrows to indicate that she could tell more if she were urged.

"What you mean?" Etta caught at Laura's sleeve in her eagerness.

"You know, Etta, Ah ain' nobody to carry no tales . . ." Laura hedged, tantalizingly.

"No indeedy! G'on honey."

". . . but from what Ah hears, Deacon Grundy done went an' fell fo' that Carrie Prince woman!"

Etta was spellbound as Laura elaborated on a secondhand account of the incident at the oyster-house. She drank in the words like a thirsty hen at a puddle.

"You means to tell me," she finally exploded, "that *Deacon Grundy* done fell fo' that hussy?" It was too much for Etta. She leaned her ungainly length against the house and raised despairing hands toward an entirely disinterested sky. "An' him wid a wife an' fo' chilluns 'cross the river!"

"It's a shame!"

"It sho is!"

II

Carrie swayed up the street toward the well, a bucket in either hand. She was just in time to see Laura scurrying off, with Etta shuffling at her heels.

"Buzzards!" she commented.

On her return she passed them at Laura's gate. The next instant Grundy's tall figure swung around a bend in the road.

"Good-afternoon, Mis' Prince," he greeted her. "Mought Ah help you wid yo' buckets?"

Without waiting for her reply, he took both of the pails and stood at her side, smiling. Anger and pleasure fought for expression on her face. Then with a little shrug, she fell into step with him.

"Ain't you scared o' bein' seen with me?" she asked, looking straight ahead.

"Scared fo' what?" demanded Grundy.

Carrie glanced pointedly over her shoulder to where Etta and Laura stood open-mouthed, watching.

"Dey *ain't* like oysters," he admitted. But he did not falter in his stride. "Broke both mah knives. Bad luck, too, dey say." He glanced at Carrie meaningfully, and concluded: "But Ah reckons dat ain't true dis time."

"What you mean?"

"Ah runs right into you, didn't Ah?" Grundy chuckled.

They walked along together, both strangely at ease. In another setting, they might have been chieftain and mate, for their straight bodies, swaying easily, were regal. Each head was poised proudly. Each foot had a natural spring. . . .

Carrie unlatched the kitchen door and held it open. Grundy swung the pails upon the shelf opposite the stove and removed his hat.

"Ain't you goin' back to the oyster-house, Mister Grundy?"

"You don't want me to stay—a li'l' while?" he asked, quietly.

"Wal, you see—Ah'm a sinner an' you's a Christian."

Grundy tossed his head impatiently.

"All right. Efn you stays you gots to 'cept what Ah gives you," she warned. "Now—there's the door, an' here's a chair."

Their eyes clashed. He sat down.

Carrie went into the parlor, and Grundy heard her rustling some paper. She returned with a bottle of whisky.

Carrie didn't know why she was acting in this strange fashion. But this man with his green-gray eyes sent an unaccountable glow all through her body.

"Git two glasses from the cupboard there," she directed.

Grundy remained seated for a moment, studying her. Then he did as he was told.

The cork popped. The liquor gurgled.

"To you," Carrie said, lifting her glass.

"To you," repeated the man.

They drank.

Again the liquor gurgled.

"To us."

"To us."

They drank. Their eyes drew nearer. His arm reached out.

III

"Cain't figger what's de matter wid Lew Grundy," Sam answered Bud Saunders.

"D-d-dad b-b-blame it!" spluttered the fat foreman. "Ah c-cain't f-f-figger it mahself. Ain't never knowed him t-t-to l-l-lay off l-l-like he's a-doin' n-n-now. Every d-d-day fo' a-a-a whole w-week!" He blinked disgustedly at the pile of untouched oysters in front of Grundy's stall.

"Wal," opined Sam as he deposited a huge wad of tobacco on his mound of shells, "Ah ain't never seed him mess wid no woman, but Ah'll bet a chew o' tobaccy dey's a woman in dis!"

"What you mean—woman?" said Bud, incredulously, forgetting to stammer.

"Ah ain't sayin' nuffin,'" demurred Sam, and he lapsed into his customary silence.

IV

The object of Bud's concern was, at that very moment, quite oblivious to his defection. He was engrossed in calculating the exact number of hairs that lay in black disorder on Carrie's pillow. Her face smiled serenely up into his. It was a changed face from that with which she confronted the villagers—softer, with a limpid film over the half-closed eyes.

They talked quietly, as if not to break the cocoon of deep contentment that had spun itself about them. And as they talked Carrie fingered curiously an ovular object that was suspended from Lew's neck.

"What you doin' with this ole sack?" she asked, and attempted to slip the brass chain over his head. But he was too swift. He caught her hand and pulled it away.

"Ah ain't never s'posed to take dat off," he said, somberly. "It's a charm."

"Huh!" scoffed Carrie. "You believe in charms?" She sniffed at it mockingly. "Smells like onions to me!"

He disregarded her unbelief. "You knows why Ah wears dis?"

"Don't tell me you bin fixed!" she exclaimed, still mocking.

"Yeah, Ah has," replied Grundy. He waited patiently for her derisive laughter to subside.

"You see mah eyes? Ever seed a black man wid eyes like mine?" He thrust his lean face closer. "Look at 'em good. What dey make you think 'bout? Cat's, eh?"

"Oh, Ah don't care what dey's like!" Carrie pulled playfully at his small, well-set ears. She tried to take her eyes from his, but as at the oyster supper, she could not. Grundy chuckled a bit ruefully.

"You kin say what you wants to, honey, 'bout fixin'. Ah sho wish dey warn't nuffin' in it mahself. But ever since Ah was a young un Ah done had to believe in it, 'cause dat's jes' why mah eyes is like dey is."

His seriousness stifled Carrie's laugh. "Tell me 'bout it, honey," she urged.

It all began with a quarrel between Grundy's mother, Nettie, and Hannah, one of her best friends. The two were young, unmarried belles of Belfort on the northern shore of the Avondale, just opposite Herdford.

Among the newly freed slaves from points south, there came Big Tom, a handsome octoroon. His huge frame and melodious bass voice combined with his blue-eyed moodiness to set the hearts of every girl aflutter, but his fancy was initially attracted to Hannah, much to Nettie's chagrin. However, at church service one moon-ridden night, Nettie's nightingale voice, as she sang at his side, evoked a response in Big Tom. So did her willowy figure and doe-brown eyes.

Then one day Hannah tearfully told her chum that she was with child, and that Big Tom was the cause of her plight. The consternation that crept into Nettie's face was not for her friend alone. Nettie was in the same predicament as Hannah, and Tom again was the cause. The two girls stared at each other mutely until rage took possession of Hannah and she broke into a torrent of blasphemy. Nettie, in a state of hysteria, went home, and that night Big Tom left town to resume his Casanovian adventures elsewhere.

From that day until her confinement Hannah was "queer." In the dead of winter and on the darkest nights, late walkers would see her plodding about, mumbling incoherently to herself. Her aged aunt, with whom she lived, could do nothing to stop her. She grew thin, horribly thin, until her pregnancy made her a creature of grotesque proportions. Her vitriolic hatred and neglect of her physical well-being caused the stillbirth of her child. How she herself survived, no one could understand. Yet, survive she did. And now she was wholly queer. She would sit for hours, rocking back and forth, repeating in a rasping voice that was like a dirge:

"Ah fix you—Ah fix you!"

Two months later, when Nettie's boy was born, Hannah stood before the birthplace shrieking:

"Ah fix you—hee hee—Ah fix you! It's gwine be a boy, an' he gwine have cat eyes! An' he gwine to de gallows when he grows up! Hee hee! Ah fix you!" Able-bodied men had to drag her away.

The baby, Lewis, named for his grandfather, proved to be a healthy young animal—all reddish-brown, presaging that rich, ebon coloring which was his in maturity. But to the anguished fright of his mother, he refused to open his eyes. This fact was remarked about the village, and Hannah crowed in glee:

"Hee hee—Ah fix you!"

She looked for all the world like some famine-racked raven rejoicing over a field of ungarnered grain.

When the child's eyes finally did open, Nettie shrank in horror. The pupils buried in that round, chubby face were green-gray, like a cat's!

In desperation, lest the curse of the gallows also be fulfilled, Nettie stole secretly to the hut of Black Isaac, renowned as a conjurer. Beneath the hanging herbs and other mystical impedimenta swinging from the ceiling, Nettie told her story. Isaac—wrinkled, dried-up, toothless—rocked to and fro in his cross-legged position on the floor. Then when Nettie had concluded he gave a cackle and suggested a bargain. His terms were exorbitant, but the terrified girl agreed eagerly.

After some weird incantations, he produced a small sack and thrust it upon Nettie. "You gots to chain dis to he neck—don't never 'low he to take it off long's he live," he instructed. "Ah cain't change he eyes, but Ah kin stop de hangin'. Make he jine church soon's he kin talk. Make he pray ever' day. . . ."

"An' ever since Ah kin 'member," concluded Grundy, "Ah ain't missed a Sunday in church. An' Ah ain't never fo'got to wear dis yere bag. An' Ah prays ever' day— anyways, up to last week."

"How come you don't pray now?" flared Carrie, angrily. She moved away from him, her brow puckering. "You thinks Ah ain't good, don't you. So you cain't pray no mo'.'"

Grundy's head sank moodily to his chest. Carrie clutched him by both of his hulking shoulders and shook his face upright.

"Ah knows you gots a wife an' chilluns 'cross to Belfort," she said, with less heat, for his dejection caused tenderness to creep back into her voice. "But didn't you tell me as how yo' wife is alius sickly-like? You gives her yo' money an' goes to see her, don't you? You don't treat her mean, nuthah. You thinks it's a sin fo' us to be together when it's like that?" She embraced him hungrily. Not even Jim Prince had awakened the intense feeling she had for Grundy, a feeling that burned and was never quenched.

Her spirit passed quickly to him, and he pressed his face to her bosom. Another impulse prompted her:

"Pray, Lewis—pray now," she whispered.

Grundy lay silent until once more light fingers traced a pattern of warmth upon his face and neck. And then, more softly than he had ever prayed before, a prose-poem flowed from his impassioned lips.

In the middle of a dolefully rhythmical line Grundy broke off with a dry sob.

"Ah cain't keep it up!" he cried, and he swept Carrie violently to him. "An' Ah don't care, nuthah!" he whispered hotly into her ear.

Carrie smiled, and silence, unbroken, descended. . . .

Chapter 20

I

The oyster season flagged toward the end of March, and died during April. The transient oyster-shuckers and their families commenced their trek homeward and the colored census of the town returned to normal. May saw the exodus of Herdfordites to the centers of strawberry-picking. Strange white men, farmers, came to town and selected their foremen, who in turn canvassed the colored residents for workers in the berry-patches of Queen Anne, Caroline, Somerset, and Wicomico counties. Whole families would leave, reducing the population to subnormal until their return in June, a few days before the Independence Day celebration.

With school closed, Martha and Blanche were home during the day, so Grundy and Carrie could not meet in the afternoon. Nights, Jake was a hindrance to their trysts, for most of the men who gambled had left town and Nellie had emigrated to fresher fields, so Jake spent a great deal of time at the house.

Balked on all sides, Carrie and Grundy met in secret—so they thought—at the cove where Grundy was making ready his boat for the crab season. After supper, when the girls were in bed and Jake had perched himself on the front porch with his feet on the railing, Carrie would slip noiselessly out of the back door and down a winding path to the cove's calm pocket of water.

These hours beneath a soft moon or starred sky, with water lapping the sides of the boat, brought Carrie and Grundy together in silence as often as in passion. Sometimes they talked, and their talk ranged widely among things they understood and other things that perplexed them mightily. Grundy's conscience, raised on the strict fare of orthodoxy, was a great burden to him.

"Do you think we's wrong?" he blurted out on one occasion.

"What you mean?" parried Carrie.

"Wal," said the man, uncertainly, "you see—both us is married—an' got chilluns. Ain't dat what de Good Book call a sin—us yere together—jes' same's man an' wife?"

"No! No! 'Tain't no sin!" protested the woman. "Ain't nuthah one o' us wrong!" And she went on pleadingly: "You cain't stop now, honey, 'cause Ah cain't live yere with everybody 'gainst me an' spitin' me 'lessn you's yere!

You make it easy. Ah don't care what they says 'long's Ah has you."

The feel of this woman at his side was enough to shut out everything from the man's consciousness: the codes that were the heritage of his people, other codes that had been instilled in them by their masters in bondage and by a religion imposed upon them for more than two centuries. Grundy turned to Carrie without a word and from that time the subject of their sin was avoided as if by mutual agreement.

II

Then one hot and humid June night Jake eliminated himself as a hindrance to these two.

Denied by Carrie, without the solace of Nellie, and with no gambling to employ his mind, time burdened Jake to distraction. On this night he rummaged about the house until he found Carrie's cache of liquor, and within a short time he succeeded in dulling the edge of his boredom.

Down at the river, Grundy turned an experienced eye to the clouds shadowing the moon.

"Look like we's gwine to have a blow," he stated. "Reckon Ah'd better put out fo' home."

"You better wait 'twell it blows over," said Carrie, anxiously. "You mought meet it halfway 'cross."

"Sho—but Ah gots ileskins," answered Grundy. He began to erect his mast.

"No! Wait!" cried Carrie, a shade of fright in her voice. "You kin come up to the house. Cain't nobody say nothin' 'bout that." She jumped ashore and pulled him after her.

It was one of those electrical tempests that come suddenly out of nowhere. When they were halfway to the house, the heavens broke into ominous rumblings and jagged streaks of lightning cut across the thirsty landscape. They rushed up to the back porch. And just then a terror-filled scream pierced a clap of thunder.

"It's Blanche!" Carrie flew to the door. But Grundy was swifter. With one bound he was through the kitchen and into the parlor.

Almost instantly he reappeared, dragging the drunken, cursing Jake by the collar. Grundy's eyes were emerald flames, his face a frozen mask of fury. Carrie had one shuddering glimpse of him as she hurried into the parlor.

She found Blanche sobbing hysterically.

"Blanche—is you hurt?" Carrie framed the wet face in her hands. "What did he do?"

"He called me downstairs, Mamma—said he wanted me to make him s-some s-sandwiches," sobbed Blanche.

"What did he do?" repeated Carrie.

"Then he grabbed me sudden-like an' commenced to kissin' me. An' I hollered an' scratched, an' bit him—an' then you-all come."

"Is that all?"

"Yes'm," Blanche assured her.

Grundy's light tread halted beside them.

"Ah drove him 'way," he said, quietly.

Carrie looked in relief at his face. The eyes were gray now.

After Carrie had put Blanche back to bed she rejoined Grundy in the kitchen where he sat drumming the table with his finger-tips.

"Ah started to kill 'im," he stated, without emotion. "But Ah reckoned you didn't want no trouble." He looked at his big, right fist from which the skin had been knocked at the knuckles. "Reckon you need a man boarder fo' de summer?" he asked.

"You means yo'self? What'll they say?"

"You mean you don't want me?"

"No, but . . ."

"Den Ah don't care what dey says!" he stated, flatly, and covered her mouth with his to stop further protest.

III

Beneath its dusty white sheet of heat Herdford drowsed through the summer months. But it was not too drowsy to whisper. And the subject of most of its whisperings concerned Grundy and his altered position. Why, asked the town, did he take up residence with that Carrie Prince woman? Why had he stopped attending church?

Why was he seen so seldom? And why had Jake Tillery disappeared?

Then the town knew, for Etta and Laura were diligent. And the town whispered no more, but talked and nodded its head.

By the time autumn had burnished the flat landscape, and the shuckers had made their yearly pilgrimage to the town, the talk had drifted across to Belfort. And it came to the ears of Lettie, Grundy's wife. And she accused him when he went to see her. And they quarreled. And he left her in tears, swearing never to see her again.

IV

Then Crazy Hiram came back to town.

No one knew what had occurred to rob Hiram of his wits, though there were many conjectures. It was only known that he had left the village to try his fortune in Philadelphia two years before Carrie Prince came to Herdford. At that time, he was a gay, stockily built young buck, with a sloping breadth of shoulder and a bullish neck. At work, wheeling smelly barrows of oyster shells to waiting scow-boats, or at leisure, there was always a smile on his jolly face and a song on his lips. For Hiram had a gift of music. He could enliven winter evenings in Ike Thomas's pool-room with his voluntary renditions of popular ballads or old spirituals; and no moon-light excursion up the Chesapeake was complete unless Hiram was there with his smile, his guitar, and his colorful tenor voice.

Now, at the time of the Grundy-Carrie Prince affair, Hiram returned to town, clad in the tattered remnant of a once boisterous checkered suit. No one recognized him at first. It was impossible. His powerful frame had shrunk to the proportions of a sickly stripling. His eyes, that had been so full of zest, stared bloodshot out of the shadow cast by his filthy hat. His lips twisted in a spasmodic grimace, revealing stained fangs of teeth.

When he appeared without warning at the pool-room that September night, a hush fell upon the place, stilling the good-natured banter. He said not a word, but stood for a moment blinking from one to the other. Then he shambled into the back room, to emerge with the guitar that had been stored there during his absence. Hunching himself on an up-ended box, he tuned the instrument, all the while muttering to himself and shaking his head waggishly. Then he played.

At first it was a wild discordant confusion of sound, as if the instrument were complaining of its being rudely awakened after a long rest. But the familiar touch soothed it, for gradually out of its wide belly lazed a rhythmical low-down blues accompaniment to the hum of the ghoulish creature on the box. It was mournful; it tingled up the spine in waves; it brought out goose pimples on flesh that a moment before had been smooth and warm. The men, mesmerized, stayed until Hiram stopped abruptly and shuffled out into the dark. Then they slunk home in pairs.

Carrie came upon Hiram one day when he was being pestered by a band of barefoot boys who fled at her coming. The incident established her as his protector, and on other occasions she had an opportunity to befriend him, for he had no relatives. He proved to be quite harmless. Though he refused to sleep in the house (nobody ever discovered where he slept), he accepted the food Carrie gave him. And in return he would run errands for her and bring wash-water from the well on Mondays. At times he was annoying. Often he would follow her, like a musical fool of an ancient court, strumming his guitar, and measuring the beat to her footfall.

This befriending of the miserable Hiram was not interpreted as a charitable act by the villagers. Superstitious to an amazing degree, they saw in Carrie's association with one "strick by de Lawd fo' his evil doin's" witchcraft pure and simple. It was something else for Carrie to live down.

Chapter 21

I

They said in Shrewsbury that Jim Prince was trying to work himself to death, now that he had no son, nor daughter, nor wife to drive to that fate. As a matter of fact, Prince worked to forget. For he was plagued by the realization that he had lost something which he had not wanted to lose. The night of Carrie's departure he had gone to Amy for solace; but her eager wiles fell upon an unresponsive mood. He had cursed her and left, never to return.

To deaden the longings that attacked him, like insects that pester a haltered horse, he worked as he had worked in the years before his prosperity. He left the store entirely in the hands of the clerk, and went out to his farm. There, throughout the long fall and winter, he labored at the old tasks—harvesting what the greedy sun had left, stable-cleaning, manure-spreading, fence-mending, hog-killing. In the spring he led the hands at the plowing, harrowing, and planting. From dawn to sunset he toiled mercilessly, until the hands protested and he told them that they were not obliged to keep pace with him. Physical tire brought swift sleep, but his dreams were not resting. He grew more lean of body and gaunt of face, until he reminded one of the Jim Prince whom Carrie had known in his youth, except for patches of gray at his temples and that single streak of white up the center of his small head.

II

Jim Prince straightened from the open hill of potatoes over which he had been bending. He pushed back the ragged straw hat from his sweating face and squinted sharply at the man who had addressed him.

"Who be you, stranger?"

It was Jake, but he depended upon the lapse of years to save him from recognition. For two months and more he had wandered from town to town, waiting for the deep gash above his left eye, a product of Grundy's slashing fist, to heal. Now he made himself as affable as possible. This man Prince was a vital cog in his scheme of revenge—a revenge born of a hate that became more poisonous with the rising and setting of each day's sun.

"Ah'm from up to Herdford way, suh—up near Eastland," began Jake, adopting the twangy drawl of the Shoreman. "An' as Ah was a-comin' dis way on business, yo' sister what lives to Herdford told me to stop by an' give 'mongst-you her regards."

"Mah sister?" puzzled Prince.

"Sho—ain't she yo' sister?" asked Jake, innocently. "You know—she got two gals—"

"What kind o' lookin' woman is she?" Jim Prince gripped Jake's arm until that one winced.

"She say you mought'n' know her, 'cause you ain't seed her since 'mongst-you was chilluns."

"Tell me what she look like, man!" Prince was fierce in his eagerness.

"She's tall, wid long black hair like a Injun's, an'—"

"How ole de gals?" interrupted Prince.

"Oh, one 'bout fo'teen or fifteen, an' de li'l' one she 'bout six, Ah reckon."

Joy broke in a torrent over Prince. "Yass!" he cried, "dat's mah sister, an' Ah'm sho glad you stopped by. Come on up to de house an' have a glass o' wine—it's cold."

"Nope—thanks," said Jake, hastily. "Ah gots to be on mah way. Ah hopes you comes to Herdford sometime. Ah knows yo' sister would be glad to see 'mongst-you." He was all the while backing away from Prince. "Ah'm on mah way over to Deerfield so's Ah kin git de first boat out fo' Balt'more tonight."

With that he set out over the field for the road. Prince watched him until he disappeared behind a clump of woods. Where had he seen that face before? It had looked strangely familiar.

Then the thought of seeing Carrie again dismissed Jake from his mind. So she had taken this means of letting him know that she wanted to see him—that she wanted him to bring her home! She must be ready to forget. In his height of feeling, Prince hallooed to one of his hands working in an adjoining field:

"Come on up to de house—we gwine quit fo' de day!"

This was so unprecedented that the announcement had to be repeated. But soon all hands were making eagerly for the cool sanctuary of the farmhouse, because the sun was exceedingly hot. There, they were surprised again. Jim Prince brought out two gallons of wine from the woodshed and told them to drink their fill.

"Lawsy!" was the only comment they could make, so great was their astonishment.

An hour later, washed and shaved, Prince left the care of the farm to Big George and hurried northwards behind the fleetest pair of horses the livery-stable boasted. The steeds felt the lash more than once, for Jim Prince was jubilant. Here he had made numerous trips to Baltimore in search of his woman, and she was right on the Sho' all the time! But that was the way it went. Always look in the least likely place for something lost.

And on the boat that night, Jake Tillery turned his face to the east and grinned.

III

"Carrie!"

Carrie jerked upright from the oven, startled by that lilting, caressing drawl. There was no mistaking the voice. She had known it for eighteen years. Without turning from the stove, she answered him huskily:

"Jim Prince . . ." The words fell flatly on the ear like an object without resilience.

Prince's head sagged, and his partially extended arms dropped to his sides. The muscles at his jaws hunched into hard ridges, then slowly relaxed. Jim Prince had learned to keep himself well in hand. Quietly he moved over to his wife and placed gentle hands on her shoulders, but at the touch the shoulders drew shrinkingly upward. The hands were withdrawn.

"Don't you want to see me, honey?" he asked.

Carrie swung swiftly about and faced him. And sympathy stirred in her at the signs of care and toil which marked him. Except for the change of sudden ageing, here was the Jim Prince who had come to her rescue at A'nt Sue's, who had taken her away to a home of her own. Her eyes lost some of their cloudy blackness. Her face softened perceptibly.

"Whar's de chilluns?" asked Prince.

At this question Carrie's expression froze again.

"What you want to know fo'?" she retaliated. "They ain't yo's, is they?"

The thrust hurt. Prince looked away, out of the window, where the dust-white road sweltered in the afternoon sun.

"Cain't you fo'git dat, honey? Ah knows now Ah was wrong . . ." He paused hopefully, but this strange woman would not help him out. She just looked at him, her black eyes cold, cold. "Cain't you see Ah wants mah chilluns? Cain't you see Ah needs you?" And he ended his plea as erring males have ended similar pleas since time began: "You knows Ah loves you, Carrie. Ah ain't never loved nobody else."

Carrie's derisive smile held incredulity and failed to dispel the bleakness from her face.

"You wants yo' chilluns!" she mocked. "Fo' what? To work 'em to death like you done Jim?"

Prince backed away before her rising voice, but Carrie followed him.

"You loves me!" She laughed harshly. "You didn't love me when you had me, did you?"

"Honey—"

"See that?" She held up a piece of dough.

"See that?" she repeated. "Wal, Ah was jes' like that when Ah was wid you. You could o' done anything wid me you wanted to. But Ah ain't like that no mo'! Now you git outn mah house, 'cause—"

Martha romped onto the porch and through the door, then stopped short when she saw her father. But Blanche, who followed her, ran to him and threw her arms tightly about him.

Since the night that Jake had molested her, a restless dissatisfaction had possessed Blanche. At the supper table, she would sit in moody silence, speaking curtly only when she was spoken to. Any slight criticism brought on a flood of tears which no amount of scolding or coaxing could stem. And there were times when Carrie thought she detected bitter accusation in the girl's face as her look swung from her mother to Grundy.

Her eyes were moist now as Prince held her at arm's-length, a happy little smile brightening his face.

"You glad to see yo' pappy, ain't you, chile?"

Blanche nodded, but in a second she returned to his arms and burst into one of her sudden spells of crying.

Prince turned to Carrie. "Let me take her home wid me?"

"Oh, papa, please! Please take me! Please!" Blanche begged.

"Blanche!" ejaculated Carrie, and she advanced on the two.

But defiance had pulled Prince to his full height and he looked unflinchingly into Carrie's stormy face.

"Ah'm gonna take her! Ah wouldn't want her efn she didn't want to come—but you can't stop me now! Come on, Blanche."

It was defeat, and Carrie knew it. As father and daughter started toward the door, she stopped them.

"Blanche, go git yo' clothes."

"Dat's all right," interposed Prince, "we gwine git a whole new outfit on de way home in Eastland. 'Tain't too late fo' her to git to de Institute, an' Ah calc'lated she mought need some new clothes befo' she goes."

"Institute!"

"Sho, an' you kin take up anything you wants." He stopped beside Carrie, who had sunk wearily into a chair.

"Ah don't know how you bin livin' yere," he said, quietly, "an' Ah don't care. Ah still loves you. Efn you ever want to come home Ah'm waitin' fo' you." There was no answer. Carrie's head had slumped slowly forward against Martha's unruly curls.

IV

Grundy had been called across the river by his wife's illness. Four days later he returned wearing a band of black cloth around his left coat sleeve. He greeted Carrie with a morose quiet and dropped into a chair.

"She was dead befo' Ah got dere," he said, in a voice that seemed to carry a great weight.

"The chilluns?"

"Left 'em wid dey grandmammy."

"Whyn't you bring 'em over yere?"

"Too many chilluns yere now."

"Blanche ain't yere now," Carrie told him. Grundy looked at her without comprehension.

"Her pappy come fo' her," Carrie explained briefly.

Then Grundy emerged from his stupor, rose, and grabbed her roughly by the arm. His eyes were alight with a pale green flame and his features were settled into that bleak immobility Carrie remembered from the night he had dragged Jake from the house.

"You means he come fo' you!" The words scraped out of his throat. "He's goin' to take you away. You're gonna leave me."

"But Ah didn't go, honey!" she cried, trying to free her arms.

"He come fo' you!" the man kept repeating. "He come fo' you!"

"You's hurtin' me, Lew!"

The light faded from his eyes and he pressed his lips to her neck.

"Ah didn't mean to, honey," he whispered, brokenly. "Ah wouldn't hurt you fo' nuffin' in de world! Ah jes' ain't mahself, dat's all."

Because she couldn't help herself, she caressed him soothingly, but the fear lingered.

"You wouldn't leave me, would you, honey?" he asked. It was a mixture of command, question, and plea. And her reassurance, punctuated with kisses, was suspended somewhere between sincerity and diplomatic acquiescence.

It was the beginning of a rift.

Chapter 22

I

Once more autumn brought its chill winds and rains to Herdford. Once more the village's colored population was swollen by the incoming shuckers. It was a prosperous year for Messrs. Gallion and Kirkland, and their prosperity inevitably meant prosperity for Carrie and Big Gussie. Every available space in the Red Brick House was occupied: Carrie even put cots in the parlor. And across the street Gussie's girls were more desirable than ever.

However, Carrie's chief pleasure was not derived from the increased business, but from Blanche's enthusiastic letters from the Institute. She read them over and over, then spent long afternoons composing her replies, to be accompanied by crisp new dollar bills.

"I am going home to see Papa for Thanksgiving and Christmas," Blanche wrote in November. And for the first time, Carrie wished she were back in Shrewsbury.

As Thanksgiving approached, the longing grew and showed itself in her preoccupied manner. Nothing interested her—not even the Good Brothers' dance at which the Bainbridge band would play. At night she lay unresponsive in Grundy's arms until he couldn't fail to notice her detachment.

Only one answer presented itself to her lover, and he became jealous. The jealousy swelled to blind proportions, so that a compliment or a casual admiring glance bent in Carrie's direction while her boarders sat at meals around the kitchen table would enflame him beyond reason. Alone with Carrie, he would air his grievances, but with little satisfaction to himself. He succeeded only in wearing her patience to a shred. Then when she tried to meet the situation by ignoring his inquisitorial complaints, Grundy was infuriated the more.

Affairs were at this pass when the good Reverend Raymond bethought himself to hold a revival and purge the town of its sins. Was not the year of the century's birth a gloriously appointed time for the salvaging of human souls? To that end he imported the Right Reverend Elijah Isaiah Brown, an itinerant evangelist, and he selected Carrie and Grundy as two of the more prominent sinners to be reclaimed from hell fire.

II

The elders of the village remember as if it were yesterday the events of that evangelical harvest at Winters

M. E. Church. Old Cap'n Tom Winters, eighty years old now; Etta Curley, angular as futuristic sculpture; Laura Titman, still plump and smooth-faced—all of them can reach into their packet of memories and recall at a moment's notice a revival that swept the community as no other revival has done before or since.

From the accounts, the Reverend Raymond had in mind five souls he was most anxious to save: Carrie Prince, Deacon Grundy, Cap'n Ham, Tom Bentley, and Hen'y Hooper—in the order of their importance. To the good Reverend these prospects represented all of the Evil One's battle-fronts. Carrie epitomized that ancient iniquity, adultery. Grundy was the stray sheep to be returned to the fold. Cap'n Ham was an incorrigible blasphemer, his vocabulary of profanity would have aroused envy in a seafaring macaw. Tom Bentley was the incarnation of the gambling spirit—(it came to the pastor's ears that Tom had actually wagered a goodly sum that he could sit on the mourner's bench every night of the final week of revival without being converted!) As for Hen'y Hooper, he had been for years the town's ne'er-do-well—a hard worker, hard drinker, hard fighter, hard everything, to whom jail was as familiar as his home.

The petty sinners the Reverend Raymond conceded to be his easy conquest. But these specific five he was determined to have, and the strength of his evangelical attack was directed toward them.

III

On the last Thursday of that three weeks of soul-redeeming a violent blizzard howled over the lowlands, leaving an eight-inch fall of snow and sleet—"a diamond-studded cloak of purity," the Reverend E. I. Brown called it that night in his sermon.

Singly, and in pairs, and in groups, they came to the meeting.

Farmer Bailey's sleek blacks pranced into the churchyard as if they were going to a fair. Two mules jogging cautiously down the slope of Market Street drew behind them a slithering, tinkling sleigh which brought the Johnson family, muffled to the ears in woolen scarves and great-coats. Up the parallel wagon tracks of Shell Street the felt boots and heavy shoes of the townspeople trampled the snow and ice—the whited marsh on one side and the field of icicled brush on the other, both deserts of moon-lit pallor.

So they came, some to renew their spiritual strength, some to find salvation which had hitherto eluded them.

In the company filing up the shelled road was Hen'y Hooper, the ne'er-do-well. At each step he took, a moan escaped his great chest: "Save me, mah Lawd! Save me, mah Lawd!" Over and over again he repeated it. For two days and nights now, Hen'y had been wrestling with his devil. For two days and nights he had been pleading with the Lord. Clearly, Hen'y hungered and thirsted after righteousness. . . .

Inside the church a resonant hum rode the heated atmosphere, and above the hum was heard a voice half chanting, half singing. At intervals the whole congregation, swaying on the hard benches like rows of mechanical dolls, joined in the refrain:

> "Lawd, Ah wants to be a Christian
> In mah heart!"

Finally the sound hushed to a barely audible whisper.

Then up rose Deacon Benlow and strode to the altar, his black skin shining under its sweat. Kneeling with upraised face, he started to pray, and as he prayed he rocked from side to side in an agony of fervor. Now he chanted, now he whispered, now he almost sang.

As an obbligato to his beseechings, the congregation chanted in rhythmical measure: "Yass! Yass! Yass!" And from the mourners' bench Hen'y Hooper implored: "Save me, mah Lawd! Save me, mah Lawd!" But at Hen'y's side Tom Bentley and Cap'n Ham sat imperturbably with legs crossed.

After some more singing, the crusader-against-sin stepped to the pulpit, Bible in hand, prepared to battle Satan in a sermon that ran the gamut of emotions. Now he had the congregation weeping by his descriptions of the suffering damned. Now their eyes shone with visions of a heaven to which their souls would retire if they were faithful unto death. He denounced all the cardinal sins in a trumpeting voice. He pleaded with those bereaved to resolve from that time forward to "meet the loved-ones in the skies on that great gittin'-up morning when Gabriel shall stand with one foot on the sea and one on the land, and sound the trumps for the quick and the dead." This was his climax, and with the congregation reduced to tears, the appropriate time to call for converts.

With shouting and singing, the flock clustered about the mourners' bench. And now Cap'n Ham made a move that went down in the community's unforgotten annals. He rose, pushed his way through the perspiring, hysterical circle, slouched down the aisle and out of the church. There was an instant's silence, for the like had never happened before. Laura Titman wailed, but the sound only served to speed the erring one on his way. Then under the magnetism of the Reverend Brown's voice, the flock resumed the strenuous work of inducting the proclaimed sinners into the fold.

About an hour later, they were rewarded when Henry Hooper's eyes glazed like those of one in a trance, and he toppled off the bench. It is said that he frothed at the mouth. But applications of snow to his temples restored him, and in a minute he leaped crazily to his feet, to rage about the aisles like one possessed.

"Ah'm saved! Praise de Lawd!" he bellowed in his thunderous voice. "Ah'm saved!"

At the height of his frenzy his great strength redoubled itself, and the bear-like embraces he bestowed upon the brothers and sisters terrified those earnest instruments of God. It was cause for relief when he was finally quieted.

Encouraged by Hooper's conversion, the crowd focused its attention on Bentley, who must have taken spark from his seat-mate. He also rose, not in passion, but like the cool gamester he was, and lifted a hand for silence.

"Brothers and sisters," he addressed them, "jes' let me go home to fight dis battle wid mahself. Efn Ah'm a-comin' through, Ah wants to come through right!"

Approving Amens greeted this.

"Ah'm gwine home now an' clean mah house—Ah wants to git dat straight first. Den Ah'm a-comin' back yere tomorrow night an' git mah soul clean!" With that he swung down the aisle and into the cold night.

The following night, true to his word, he came—but not as expected. Into the hot, steaming church he stalked, brandishing triumphantly a broken table leg.

"Ah don't need no singin', brethren an' sisters!" he shouted, whirling about like a dervish in order to face his wide-eyed hearers on all sides. "Ah done bin redeemed! See dat?" He shook the table leg. "Do you see dat, brothers? Do you see dat, sisters?" He was chanting now. "Wal—wal! Wal—wal—wal! Dat's what Ah done to all, brothers—to all, sisters—to all mah gamblin' tables. Oh, yass! Mah soul is clean! Hallelujah! Ah met de sperit—met de sperit out dar—out dar in de snow! Oh, yass! Praise de Lawd!"

When he had raved at some length in this manner, he collapsed suddenly on a bench, a disheveled sodden heap, panting painfully. Tom Bentley had lost his wager to Cap'n Ham.

Through the space between a slightly raised window and its sill, Grundy's gray eyes peered hauntedly at the scene. Something within him strove to respond to the familiar stimulus. But to no purpose. The spirit was dead that would have answered. Grundy turned from the window with bowed head.

Chapter 23

I

A'nt Emma Wiggins was protesting, in that level voice of hers, against the crop of births expected just before Christmas that year. They were in Feuchtman's general merchandise store opposite Newman's yard—A'nt Emma, Gussie, and the stout, florid proprietor.

"Ain't seed so many young uns a-comin' since Ah bin helpin' to bring 'em yere," complained A'nt Emma.

"Vell, who's turned fool now?" questioned the grocer tersely as he puttered about filling Gussie's order.

"Shame on you fo' yo' talk!" retorted A'nt Emma, tossing her shawl. "It's de Lawd's doin's an' you ought'n' to talk like dat!"

"Humph! The Lord's doin's!"

"How many comin', Mis' Emmy?" inquired Gussie. She leaned heavily against the counter, still panting from her walk through the snow.

"Wal, dey's fo' altogedder," answered A'nt Emma, turning her attention to Gussie. "Both dem gals o' Lena's 'spectin' deirs dis week—one o' dem look like hers gwine be twins. An' dere's Cap'n Tom's Julie. . . ." She frowned. "Dat po' woman ain't gwine last long efn she keep on havin' babies near 'bout every year. . . . What's hankerin' me is whether dey's all comin' de same time. Efn Ah jes' knowed somebody to help me!"

"Whyn't you git Carrie Prince?"

"Carrie Prince? Ah didn't know she was no mid-wife!"

"Sho she is. Leas'ways, dat's what she done told me—'lowed as how she used do all de midwifin' down to Shrewsbury way."

"Law-dee!" exclaimed A'nt Emma, in relief. But after a few moments' thought, she shook her head and pursed her lips resignedly. "Nope," she said, "cain't do it."

"Why?" questioned Feuchtman, sharply.

"First place, Lena ain't gwine trust nobody but me. Den, Cap'n Tom ain't gwine want no woman like dat to tech his wife! Nawsuh! Cain't do it!" finished A'nt Emma, decisively.

"Hell!" burst out the grocer, impatiently. *"All' ist der selbe*—a woman ist a woman, ain' id?"

"Sho, but—"

"Look yere," interrupted Gussie, "ain't Cap'n Tom off dredgin'?"

"Yass, but—"

"Wal," continued Gussie, "efn Mis' Julie don't mind, Cap'n Tom ain't got to know nuffin' 'bout it 'twell he come home—an' den de baby'll be yere."

"Wal, Ah don't know," said A'nt Emma. "Ah'll see Julie, anyways."

II

So it happened that Carrie Prince became midwife to Julie Winters. For Julie, long since tired of carrying this eighth child of hers, had turned a weary face to A'nt Emma's questions, saying that it was of no consequence by whose hand the child was delivered.

Carrie in her pride was at first resolved to be coolly distant toward Cap'n Tom's wife, but her resolve melted before the welcoming smile of the frail woman.

"Ah reckon you'll find the place in a kind o' bad way, Mis' Prince," apologized Julie. "Ella does the best she kin, but you cain't 'spect too much from a ten-year-old."

Ella, Julie's oldest daughter twisted her spindly legs in embarrassment until Carrie reached out to pat her kindly. "That's all right, honey," she said to the girl, "We'll set things to rights."

They did. Within a few days the house had undergone a thorough cleaning, and Ella's shyness had given way to friendliness.

Two days before Christmas the baby was born, a girl. Then, relieved of her burden, Julie grew more communicative. During the days of her convalescence, she and Carrie held long conversations that gradually increased in intimacy. Before this woman's sincerity Carrie's bulwark of aloof pride, built up against the town's accusing eyes, slowly crumbled.

"Is it so that you an' Deacon Grundy is livin' together?" asked Julie one day.

"S'pose we is?" demanded Carrie, defensively. "He ain't got no wife now."

"Ah know—but ain't yo' husband livin'?"

In reply Carrie told Julie the whole story.

"But you still gots a husband, Carrie," Julie insisted when she had finished. "Ah married a man, too, an' Tom ain't no better'n yo' Jim. Ah knows—even ef him an' Etta don't know Ah knows." She lifted a hand to stop the remonstrance on Carrie's lips. "Ah knows another thing, too—jes' 'cause a man runs wid a woman don't mean he loves her! 'Sides, look what you doin' to Deacon Grundy. He ain't bin to church in months. You done help him go 'stray, Carrie. Oh, Ah knows it warn't all yo' fault, but jes' the same, 'tain't too late to do the right thing. Den you gots to think 'bout yo' chilluns."

"But Lew is ter'ble jealous, Julie," said Carrie. "He told me he cain't do without me now. He says Ah'm all he's got left—an' he's all Ah got too, now."

"Well . . . you suit yo'self, honey," said Julie.

III

A letter from Blanche in the night mail added further weight to Julie's persuasive talk. It was postmarked "Shrewsbury" and the childishly scrawled first paragraph read:

Dear Mama,

    I am home with Papa for Christmas and New Year's. I wish you and Martha were home with me and Papa. It is so long since we saw you all and we miss you very much. Papa says he wish you would come home just for a day anyway. I would like to see you before I go back to school. I will be here until the ice breaks in the Bay. . . .

Carrie's chin quivered ever so slightly as she refolded the letter and placed it in her bosom.

Chapter 24

I

A bleak rain washed away the few remaining patches of snow and New Year's day dawned brittlely cold. There was no wind, just a stinging frigidity that bit through even the heaviest of woolens and flannels. Herdford's two rivers coagulated into a circle of glazed stillness, and by the next morning the ice was inches thick. No boats could go out for oysters until a path had been cut for them. Even then the catch was small, because all of the oyster-beds could not be reached immediately. And there was no possibility of dredge boats returning. As the holiday rush had emptied the oyster-bins in the packing-houses, a forced furlough was called until the elements turned more favorable. But the icy calm continued, and Messrs. Kirkland and Gallion could do nothing but wring their hands and curse while unfilled orders piled up.

The shuckers, however, taking advantage of this break in the grind, bought or borrowed skates and swarmed onto the ice. Soon the cove, with its icebound boats, was crowded with young and old, white and colored. Everyone at all skilled in skating was there—with the exception of Deacon Grundy.

II

"You ain't goin'!"

From his crouched position at the kitchen table, Grundy shot the words at Carrie in a low, menacing voice. His long black fingers clutched a bottle of whisky so tightly they threatened to crush it. That green fire blazed in his eyes like pale emeralds. His facial muscles never moved.

They were drunk, Grundy and Carrie Prince. For three days now, he had refused Carrie's plea to let her visit Blanche in Shrewsbury. And for three days she had resisted a wild impulse to rebel. She was afraid of this man. He had become a stranger—a huge dark stranger, with peculiar burning eyes; a stranger whose teeth, when they streaked behind the slit of his thinly drawn lips, made her think of the snarl of that black cat she had seen in the road coming from Shrewsbury to Herdford—hateful town! The man's whole attitude reminded her of that cat.

Now, suddenly, there swept over her the same reckless spirit that had urged her more than a year ago to fling herself in mad anger upon Jim Prince. She reached out, wrenched the bottle from Grundy, and tilted it to her mouth. Grundy stared silently as the liquid warmth poured down her throat. The rise and fall of her larynx seemed to fascinate him. When she had finished finally, she staggered back, and an insane laugh tore from her lips. Then she stopped abruptly and swayed toward him, a loose lock of her hair falling across her face.

"You cain't stop me! Ah'm goin'. Ah was comin' back— but now Ah ain't! You think Ah'm scared o' you? Wal, Ah was—but Ah ain't no mo'! You don't care nothin' 'bout me—nothin'!" She broke into that crazy laugh again. "See this bottle? Ah'm a-goin' over to Gussie's an git Marty. An' whilst Ah'm there Ah'm a-goin' to spread joy. 'Cause this is mah last day in this yere town!" She staggered to the door, where she turned, supporting herself drunkenly. "An' with you!" she finished. Her lips writhed about the words. Her face was coarse, ugly.

Grundy sat woodenly, listening to her irregular footfalls on the frozen ground. The retreating sounds fell like lessening blows of a trip-hammer upon his ears. And long after they had ceased, the blood at his temples continued to throb to a measured beat, until a blind impulse sent him careening out of the hot kitchen. Hatless, and with only a ragged, mud-specked sweater between himself and the cold, he struck out aimlessly.

In a few minutes he was at the cove where his boat lay in its frozen fastness. Several skaters were sitting on it, resting themselves. By this time Grundy's swift walk had combined with the liquor to generate an undue amount of warmth. He jerked at the top button of his sweater to loosen it, with a gesture so violent that the button flew off, and following the downward swing of his arm another object struck the ice, then slithered onto a tuft of marsh-grass bordering the shore.

"Hi thar, Deacon!" one of the skaters greeted him as he slid up to the boat. "Thought 'mongst-you warn't a-comin' out dis year, sartin."

Grundy nodded absently, his eyes fixed on Morris' shore, now a barren expanse smudging the eastern horizon.

"Yere," the man offered. He shook off his skates and handed them to Grundy. "Take mah skates. Ah'm hongry as a bear! Bin out since mornin' an' ain't et no dinner yit. You kin keep 'em 'twell tomorrow." And he made for the shore, beating his gloved hands against his sides to warm them.

"C'mon, Deacon," urged another, performing a fancy turn, "Ain't set mahself ag'in you since last year."

"Sho—sho," was Grundy's toneless answer, as he mechanically strapped on the skates.

He was graceful in action. His body slanting at just the correct angle, his long legs cut with rhythmical ease over the shiny surface of the ice. The liquor he had drunk, instead of destroying his sense of balance, added a daring abandonment to his movements. He was a skimming, swooping figure of precision. While the other skaters formed an admiring gallery, he went through his repertoire of grape-vines and figure-eights, finishing his exhibition by streaking a clear piece of ice with the Spencerian capitals of his name.

He might have been alone, for he gave no indication that he heard the applause which greeted him. In a moment he broke through the ring of spectators and coasted to his boat where he took off the skates. Then with them swinging from their straps, he strode off the ice, his great lithe form outlined against the sky, like the trunk of a solitary, branchless pine.

III

Crazy Hiram perched at Gussie's side that afternoon and strummed an accompaniment to Carrie's singing. The light of the sun through dirty windowpanes fell on his grimacing face and brought out the festered pock marks which gave to the skin the appearance of a frog's back. He looked like a horrid gnome, and he played unholy music.

They were in Gussie's parlor. The room was stagnant with the reek of raw whisky and sweating flesh. An obese queen of carnality, Gussie sat surveying her court, her body grooved like a bulging sack against the rounds bracing the bottom and arms of her rocker. And as Carrie sang one after another the songs she had sung years before at Sue's, Martha leaned bright-eyed on the arm of Gussie's chair, as much at ease as another child would have been with mud pies. To her the loose-lipped faces and drink-sodden bodies about her—lounging in chairs, sprawled on the floor against the wall—were familiar and right.

"Let de li'l' un dance," suggested one of Gussie's women, a doll-like creature who was curled, like a sleepy kitten, in the adequate lap of Bud Saunders.

"Sh-sh-sho, C-C-Carrie," Bud struggled to add, "l-l-let 'er c-c-cakewalk!"

"G'on, honey," bade Carrie. "Mought's well give 'em yo' last dance befo' we leaves from yere."

Then just as Martha's eager little legs were about to swing into the first steps, there was a loud, insistent racket at the kitchen door.

"Let 'em in, Carrie," Gussie directed.

Carrie lurched into the littered kitchen, flung wide the door, and swayed against it. There stood Grundy, big, green-eyed, silent. The veins in his neck and temples were like strands of pulsing rope.

"Come on home!" His lips had not moved.

Carrie shrank back, one hand fluttering to her laxed lips. Then she lifted her chin defiantly, and her hand dropped.

"Ah ain't a-comin' nowheres!" she cried. "Ah'll come when Ah gits ready!"

She threw back her head and laughed—an ugly laugh. But as her head came forward again, there was a flash of steel. The laugh gave way to a scream, and the scream in turn was drowned by the single report of a pistol that blazed six inches from her eyes. She collapsed at Grundy's feet across the threshold.

For a fleeting second he stared at the gaping hole that gushed a scarlet stream. Then he wheeled and fled. At the Red Brick House he snatched up the skates he had left before he made for the river.

The sound of the shot had carried far on the still air. Hurrying forms passed him, but he had neither eyes nor thought for them. Through his hot brain ricocheted the single intelligence: "She's dead! She's dead!" It set the beat for his flying feet.

On the ice he bent to fasten his skates, and as he did so his fingers fumbled to his throat and to the chain which hung there.

The charm! It was gone!

His eyes widened with panic. Then the panic closed about him like water about a piece of bait on a crab-line. A dark, oval object on a tuft of grass at his feet! In his eager haste to reach it, he sprawled on his belly and slid.

The charm was in his hands. He fondled it. He babbled incoherently in his joy. But down to the ice-bound shore swarmed a yelling mob. That spoke of no time to lose. He swung to his feet. In a thrice he was a dark streak on the ice blending with the gathering dusk.

And Jake had his revenge.

IV

It was a fitful day of light and shadow that Carrie Prince was borne up Tilton Street and away from Herdford town forever.

Jim Prince was taking her home. And he sat now in the enclosed carriage with his two daughters, his mind extracting bitter and sweet memories from the past to piece with thoughts of the present and the uncertain future.

"Papa . . ." Blanche's voice brushed aside the hush. "Papa, I'm not going back to school. I'm going to stay home with you an' Marty an' the farm."

Jim Prince made no reply. He recognized dimly that a woman, not a child, had spoken; and that she and Martha somehow had in their keeping the future that baffled him.

Behind the little cortège walked Crazy Hiram, a wan, emaciated figure clad in rags. And as he shambled along he addressed himself conversationally to inanimate objects he passed. He followed Carrie the length of Front Street and out onto the pike from Crosley's bridge until they came to the pine woods where the shadows deepened. There the weird creature stopped, but his bloodshot eyes traveled after the funeral carriages until they were no more than swaying specks in the white spine of the road.

Then he made his way back to the town, strumming his guitar and muttering—a somber troubadour playing only wild, eerie blues.

Chapter 25

Jim Prince stood upon a grassy knoll in one of his fields and scanned the level farmland which stretched away from him on all sides.

He had only this farm now. Competition had grown among the merchants of Shrewsbury and had borne down upon him. Debts owing him after that spell of hard times years before had never been paid, and for some reason— possibly because Carrie's death had its mellowing effect— he had been loath to use legal measures against his debtors. (Small good such action would have been anyway, for one cannot exact money where there is none.) So, on Blanche's advice, he had sold the store, the livery-stable, and the town house.

Now the sun lent its last energy to crimsoning the blue above Prince's pine wood. To his right, next the turnpike, Big George still tormented his lazy mules with expert lashes of the reins upon their powerful buttocks as they ripped the plow-blades through the earth. To the left, Josh Williams slouched beside a drag-harrow.

"Hey, George! Josh!" called Prince. "It's time to quit!"

Descending the knoll, Prince followed his men leisurely between the rows of his strawberry patch, examining each vine as he went along, for this long field was his pride.

"Strawberries?" he had scoffed to Blanche three years before. "Humph! They's too much trouble. 'Sides, you don't git nuffin' outn 'em fo' a couple o' seasons."

Yet, here were the strawberries, and the picking season was at hand. It was another indication of the way Prince's elder daughter had bent him to her will since that day years before, in the funeral carriage, when the reassuring clasp of her hand had revealed her in a new womanly rôle.

He pushed through the turnstile, and made his way to the back porch. Here he halted, and grinned at what he saw.

"Put it back, George!" Blanche was saying. "Put it right back!"

She stood at the big oilclothed table, one hand poised in the act of arranging the table ware. There was no anger or annoyance in the low notes of her voice, nor in her facial expression. Her whole bearing suggested an experienced school-teacher repeating a command to an erring pupil for the thousandth time, well aware that it will have to be repeated again—and still again.

Obeying sheepishly, Big George slipped a hot biscuit back onto its serving-dish, and slouched into his chair without a word. He had no retort even when Josh snickered through the suds at the wash-basin. And it struck Jim Prince how easily his daughter exacted obedience from others. Just what was it that made people listen to her? The calm assurance with which she did everything? The determined set of her head? Her long, firm-treaded stride? The carriage of her shoulders, so like Carrie? Jim Prince didn't know. He only recognized the commanding confidence with which she swept everything and everybody before her.

He nodded his head in satisfaction as he watched her, remembering how he had mourned young Jim. For in Blanche he had more than a son. Sons become men and as often as not leave the homes of their fathers, as most daughters do. But Blanche, he was certain, would never leave him. She was as much a part of the homestead as those twin oaks that stretched their gnarled branches protectingly over the front yard and eaves of the house.

His thoughts were interrupted by a halloo from Martha and he turned to watch his younger daughter approach. She was like a sleek, high-strung filly as she swung blithely down the lane. Before the house a sudden notion seized her to leap the stagger rails fencing the lane, and throwing back her two long braids of hair, much as a horse tosses its mane, she charged the barrier. She scaled it, with lanky adolescent legs flying, but her dress caught on one of the splintery rails. For a moment she hung there in mid air, clutching wildly at her rear extremity. Then the cloth gave way and she sprawled in the furrows of the field.

Seeing that she was not injured, Jim Prince burst into guffaws which brought Josh, George, and Blanche in a rush from the kitchen.

Martha, the torn remnant of her dress in her hand, stalked stiffly toward the laughing quartette on the porch. But as she drew nearer, the ridiculous situation was too much for her and she joined their shouts of amusement.

"You-all sho won't have to drag that part of the field, Papa," she laughed. She threw her strapped books carelessly onto the porch. "Lawsy! I sho did hit that dirt!"

"Ain't you kind o' draughty, Marty?" snickered Josh.

"You must think you's a buzzard, honey," boomed Big George.

As always, Martha had a pat answer. "George, you know you ain't never seen no buzzard put his wings where I put my hands when he's a-flyin'." She turned contritely to Blanche. "I'm sorry, sis', 'bout this dress. I'll fix it."

"Oh, that's all right, honey," Blanche answered through her smiles. "Only you hadn't ought to go jumpin' and rippin' like that. You ain't no li'l gal no mo'. You's goin' to put on long dresses next week when you finishes them studies with 'Fessah Johnson."

"Long dresses!" cried Martha in delight. "Honest, sis'? You's really goin' to let me put 'em on? And can I put up my hair, too?"

Blanche nodded assent as she led the way into the kitchen. Martha was her one weak spot and the younger girl knew it. She had only to let her full-bowed lips droop in a certain way and pucker her forehead just so and Blanche inevitably weakened. For ten years now, since the death of their mother, Blanche had watched over her impulsive sister, loving her pixenish ways, supervising her clothes and behavior, offering comforting arms when Martha's childish world went awry.

They were utterly different, these daughters of Jim Prince. Blanche was sure, steady, would always swing evenly within her ordained orbit. Martha, on the other hand, was capricious and flighty. Now she was here, now there. She might in one sudden burst of spontaneity flash to a dizzy height, then, leaving behind a trail of spent vitality, as suddenly drop to oblivion. Her recent attack on the fence, when she left behind the toll of gingham, might be interpreted symbolically. For Martha would always pay the price of her effort.

Chapter 26

It was high noon. The Prince berry-patch lay, a tumult of scarlet and green, in ripe readiness for the short picking season.

"It's about time they was gittin' yere," said Prince to Blanche. They stood expectantly on the back porch, facing the lane.

"Here they come now!" Blanche pointed over the fields to the turnpike where two high farm wagons slowly lurched toward the entrance of the lane.

Prince nodded. "Yep, dat's dem all right. Wonder what dey's like. Will Morris says hisn come from up to Kent County way, and dey's sho a moughty tough-lookin' bunch. Saw some o' 'em yestiddy."

"Well, you went all the way to Belfort to get yo's. Maybe they won't be so bad. Reckon we'll get much fo' the berries this year?"

"'Bout two dollars a crate. We sho gots a mess o' 'em. Maybe you feels like tellin' me how wrong Ah was 'bout 'em, eh?" Jim Prince cocked a humorous eye at his daughter.

Blanche patted his arm affectionately. "You ain't the only one with a head in this family, Mister Jim Prince," she answered.

"Yep, reckon not, gal. You sho knows how to figger ahead, all right. Jes' wish Marty had a hank'rin' the same way."

"Oh, she's all right. Only thing, she's youngish. She'll get over that after she gets to the Institute. 'Fessah Johnson says she's a bright un in her books."

Prince was silent a moment. Then he said, "Sometimes Ah thinks you spiles dat young un."

"Reckon I do," Blanche confessed. "And look like everybody else spiles her, too. She's so purty and—and somep'n. I don't know what 'tis."

"Wal, you's done de best you could, gal." Jim Prince shook his head thoughtfully. "You know, you hadn't ought to turned down 'Fessah Johnson like you done. He'll make a purty fine husband."

"I cain't be his wife and look after you and Marty too," Blanche reminded him. "And I don't know ef I wants to get married. Menfolks is—" She broke off suddenly, seeing the expression on Prince's face. "No, I ain't got enough eddication for him. I kin read and write and count all right, but when it comes to talk I jes' fo'gets 'bout grammar and talks like I been used to doin'. . . . Oh, shucks! I jes' don't love 'im no ways."

II

Before Jim Prince could reply, Martha hailed them from the first wagon. She had taken over the reins from Josh and had whipped the mules into a trot. Now as she drew up her steeds with a flourish before the gate Prince and Blanche examined the newcomers.

There were thirty or forty of them, men and women— even entire families. Like the oyster-shuckers Blanche had known in Herdford, they were dressed fantastically—the men in last winter's over-all jumpers and the pants to their best suits, with exceedingly high-standing collars, yellow "bulldog" brogue shoes, and wide straw sailers setting off the ensembles. The women, in besashed, belaced, bepleated hand-me-downs, were as interesting after their fashion. And the luggage was no less strange and varied. Tattered valises, carpet bags, suitcases, huge blanketed bundles tied with rope, and overflowing pillow-cases gave these laborers the appearance of refugees.

A spare, angular man of burnt-brown complexion strode with outstretched hand toward Prince. At each step he gave a hitch to his pants with long arms which he held close to his body. He had the bearing of an elderly but still game cock.

"Howdy, Mistah Prince," he began, maneuvering his bulging quid from one cheek to the other. "Wal, yere we is, the whole shootin'-match! Hope 'mongst-you's got plenty berries, 'cause dis yere's de pickin'nest gang you ever seed!"

"Oh, we's got a tol'able crop, Jeb," replied Prince. "Dis yere's mah dorter Blanche. Dis yere's Jeb Harmon, honey—de fo'man o' de pickers."

"Ah reckoned dat was her, Prince." Jeb doffed his yellowed straw hat, displaying a cleanly shaven head which reflected the sunlight sifting through an apple tree near by. "Yo sho gots two purty gals, suh—sho is!"

"Yep," agreed Prince proudly. "An' Blanche yere is jes' much boss 'round yere as me."

"Oh, 'mongst-you don't have to tell me dat. Marty done told us dat already. An', Mistah Prince, dat li'l' un sho kin sing! Her and dat Grundy boy what plays de guitar was a-singin' together comin' from de station."

"Grundy?" Prince demanded. "Who's he?"

Blanche moved closer to her father.

"Dar dey go now," said Jeb, pointing.

The pickers were moving slowly across the berry-patch toward the shanties that had been raised for their living-quarters. Martha was with them, walking beside a tall, wide-shouldered youth. The two appeared very engrossed in each other.

"Marty!" called Blanche.

The pair swung about, their faces alight with the keen pleasure they shared. Martha caught the big fellow's hand, and together they returned to the yard.

"This is Jimmy-Lew—Jimmy-Lew Grundy," Martha explained. "And you ought to hear him play and sing, sis'! Lawsy!"

Blanche and Prince hardly noticed her. They were too concerned with the smiling young chap at her side who towered head and shoulders above even Blanche, and her height was that of the average man. . . . There was the same magnificently proportioned stature, she was thinking; the same massive muscularity of sweeping shoulders and arms; the same lithe absence of waist. These details were easily observable because the boy, unlike the other pickers, was clad simply in the rough habit of the farm laborer. He was clean, but much patched.

Blanche, having finished her scrutiny, lifted her eyes slowly until they met Jimmy-Lew's. Then she relaxed, for his eyes were hazel brown. And the roundness of youth still lingered in the smiling dark face beneath his fringy straw hat.

"Who be yo' folks, Jimmy-Lew?" asked Blanche.

He pointed to a white-haired woman in the departing group who ambled beside two strapping girls and a smaller barefoot boy. All three struggled with giant bundles.

"That's mah grandmother an' mah two sisters an' li'l' brother, ma'am," he said.

"Where's yo' father and mother?" Blanche held her breath.

The boy's smile faded. "Mah mother died 'bout ten years ago," he answered, eyes downcast. "Mah father died in jail."

Jim Prince started to speak, but Blanche caught his arm.

"Don't you reckon you better help yo' folks with them bundles, Jimmy-Lew?" she suggested. And as Martha started to follow him, she said quickly: "No, Marty. I want you to help me do some things."

Martha stayed in sulky silence.

"Dat's a fine young un—dat Jimmy-Lew," said Jeb Harmon to Prince. "Ever since he bin old enough he's done a man's work. De chilluns was left wid dey granny when dey mammy died an' dey pappy went to livin' wid a woman over to Herdford, 'cross de river from us. Dey says de boy's pappy killed de woman an' was sent to de cut fo' life. Ah ain't never bin able to git all de story." Having got this piece of gossip off his mind, the foreman suggested that he'd better get down to the shanties and straighten out the crew before a fight started. Then he hitched his way off.

Prince turned to Blanche.

"Reckon we better send 'em on home?"

With the toe of her shoe Blanche traced a wavering pattern in the dirt. "No," she said, finally, "they cain't help it 'cause they's *his* folks. 'Sides, I knows they needs the money."

Prince interrupted impatiently: "But Ah ain't never seed Marty take on 'bout no boy like dis un. He's de only one 'round yere her eekles, an' you knows how Marty likes music. She ain't no li'l' gal no mo', honey," he warned. "An' yo' mammy warn't more'n seventeen or eighteen when Ah married her."

"I know—I know," agreed Blanche, worriedly. "But we jes' cain't send 'em away. Don't worry 'bout Marty. I'll take care o' her—I'll talk to her."

"All right," said Prince, and shook his head. "But dis is one time Ah sho thinks you's *wrong—sartain*!"

"Wait a minute, Papa," said Blanche as a sudden thought struck her. "S'posin' you go over to Will Morris and see ef he needs four mo' pickers?"

Prince snapped eager fingers. "Dog-gone! That's right! He told me no longer'n yestiddy he was short-handed on 'count o' his fo'man didn't bring all de folks he was s'posed to. Ah'll go right over an' see 'im." And he made rapidly for the barn.

His face was beaming when he returned an hour later.

"It's all right!" he exclaimed as he entered the kitchen. "Will says they'll help 'im a lot. Ah'll go down to de shanties wid a wagon an' haul 'em right over."

"That's fine!" Blanche breathed her relief. "I'll go with you."

III

The shanties that prevail in the lowlands of the Eastern Shore of Maryland are flimsy architectural stepchildren hastily conceived and birthed to shelter the help a farmer must import for his harvest. The oblong shed Prince had tossed up to house thirty-odd people was thirty-six feet long by six feet wide; and this was divided into six compartments by planked-wall partitions. Along the back and side walls of each compartment were an upper and a lower bunk. And—touch of luxury—there was a floor of rough boards, laid at the insistence of Blanche.

For the time spent in this crate-like shelter the family unit would lose its identity, for all the men and boys slept together, all the women and girls. If they were an amicable group, the chores—such as supplying wood for the cook-stoves and filling the communal water barrel—would be divided evenly. If it rained, all would be wetted. If it were hot, all would roast. In every sense of the term, this was a share-and-share-alike existence—even to coping with the vermin that infested the straw of the bunks.

Following the wagon tracks that circled from the farmhouse, Prince and Blanche neared the back of the shanties in time to hear a guitar twanging a dance tune. Open palms beat a rhythmical accompaniment and mingled with exclamations of approval. The cause was soon apparent, for there, at the corner of the shanties, in the center of admiring timekeepers, was Martha executing a toe-tangling jig. Her newly acquired long dress raised to her knees, her loosened hair flying wildly about her bobbing head, she was lost completely in the dance. Jimmy-Lew grinned merrily over his instrument from a perch on a stove. As the furious finale ended, and the girl tossed back her shower of hair from a radiant wide-eyed face, Prince would have lunged forward angrily, but Blanche stopped him.

"'Tain't no use to rile yo'self, Papa," she whispered. "Jes' call Jeb." For Blanche knew her sister well. And she knew that no amount of scolding would quiet her restless feet, for those same feet, five years before, had won a dance contest at a Shrewsbury minstrel show. Martha was stagestruck.

When Jeb Harmon heard Prince's orders—that the Grundy family were to be lent to Will Morris—he was frankly disapproving. "You's losin' fo' o' yo' best pickers," he stated, flatly. "But Ah reckons you knows what you's doin'."

As he went off on his distasteful errand, Blanche called to Martha.

Chapter 27

I

Ike Johnson sat facing Martha across his narrow little room in the parsonage, which was, by established precedent, the home of unmarried teachers. A gangling man with pinched, dark features and the deep-set eyes of a scholar, he typified the finest among the first generation of educated freedmen. There was a certain earnest assurance in his bearing that compelled attention, and even the impetuous Martha was listening now.

"You know, Martha," he was saying, "this has been our last lesson together." He paused and smiled slowly. "I suppose you're glad, aren't you?"

Martha sank her head in confusion. "Well—uh—shucks, 'Fessah Johnson, I don't want to go to no school."

"You don't want to go to *any* school," corrected Ike mechanically.

"Well then—*any* school!" repeated Martha. She squirmed a bit and then blurted: "I'd ruthah—I'd ruthah—"

"You'd *rather* dance and sing," finished her teacher, still smiling. "Is that it?"

Martha's head came up with a quick toss, but she said nothing. Ike tapped his fingers thoughtfully on the arms of his chair while he scanned the pretty face opposite his. He said, softly, persuasively:

"It's all right, and natural, also, for you to dance and sing, Martha. You're young, and you like those things. But it's selfish of you to think as you do. You have ability for better things than just dancing and singing. You've a good mind—if you hadn't one, I wouldn't have bothered to help you as I've done. There is a need—and there is going to be an even greater one in the future—for young Negroes who have had training. Right now there is a crying need for trained teachers—"

"I don't want to be a teacher!" cried Martha, sulking away from his gaze.

"You don't have to be a teacher," answered Ike, "but I— it's the best opportunity for a young girl who wants to do a great service for her people—"

"Huh! There's other girls who want to teach," retorted Martha. "I don't! I don't want to be in no countrified town like this all my life—a-lookin' at the same people, and a-doin' the same things all the time! I don't want to!"

"You ought to be ashamed of yourself, Martha," stated Ike without raising his voice. "You know the way your sister and your father have planned for your going to school. If you don't go now, they'll be very disappointed—

and so will I. I can't say anything more. But, believe me, if you throw away this chance, some day you'll be sorry—very sorry. You could at least give it a trial." He got up slowly, and faced the window with his back to the girl. "It's getting late—sun's about ready to set. You'd better hurry home, Martha."

"Fessah—"

Ike turned. Martha was at the half-opened door, her defiance gone.

"I'll g-go . . . ," she choked, and ran from the house, her books trailing behind her.

II

It was sunup. But the pickers had been working for two hours and more. Like kneeling Mohammedans at noontide, they crouched industriously over their assigned rows while snatches of conversation or song shuttled back and forth in the air above them. Inside a shed beside the wagon tracks bordering the field Blanche stood—capable, cool and business-like—to receive from the pickers wooden trays which held two dozen quart measures of berries. It was her duty to inspect each one by partially dumping its contents onto the counter, in order to insure against wily tricksters who might pad the bottoms of their baskets with leaves or purposely pick rotten or unripe fruit. Jim Prince's elder daughter looked well to her father's best interests.

Martha bent moody eyes on the familiar scene. The little pucker at her forehead deepened. She was unaccountably annoyed. She wished she were anywhere but here—say on that turnpike yonder, walking straight ahead with no thought of ever returning. She looked at the road and bit her lip thoughtfully. For the road led to the Morris berry patch. . . .

It was a week now since the Grundy family had moved to the Morris shanties. Each day Martha had awaited eagerly the appearance of Jimmy-Lew. But he had not come. She did not know of an incident that had taken place the evening of the second day after the Grundys' departure.

Coming from an inspection of his land, Jim Prince had encountered the stalwart Jimmy-Lew at the lane entrance, his guitar in hand like some wandering minstrel.

"Whar 'mongst-you a-goin', young un?" Jim Prince's voice was harsh and gave no welcome.

Young Grundy was nonplussed.

"I was jes' aimin' to see some o' the folks from home, suh," he answered.

"Wal, you ain't a-workin' fo' me," stated Jim Prince, coldly, "so efn you wants to see yo' folks, see 'em offn mah grounds. Ah ain't a-wantin' nuffin' to do wid de likes o' you! So git along wid you—befo' Ah makes you!"

"Look here, Mister Jim," the boy protested, a bit nettled, "I ain't done no harm 'round here. I ain't figgered why you sent me and my folks over to Morris', nuthah. Ef you didn't want us, whyn't you tell Jeb Harmon so befo' we come? 'Twarn't right—"

"Is you gwine to git offn mah land?" Prince moved forward, gripping the handle of his hoe menacingly.

The boy held his ground, and did not flinch when the man almost touched him.

"I don't know why you don't want none o' me and mine around," he said, slowly, "but I reckon it's jes' the same to me ef I do stay away!" And with that he turned and walked off.

Martha, frowning discontentedly over her father's berry-patch, did not know all this. She only wondered why she had not seen Jimmy-Lew. And she wondered if he would play with the Morris pickers' baseball team, which had challenged the Prince pickers to a game this very Saturday afternoon. It was to be a prelude to a straw-ride in the evening.

III

Shrewsbury was enjoying itself at the ball ground. Three, four, five, six deep, spectators bordered the field, while others perched on the tops of buggies and the highest rails of hay-wagons. Saturday was "grubbin'-up" day and the town was crowded with shoppers who wanted and expected some sort of diversion before they scattered to their homes.

Martha had left her father and Blanche with the stipulation that she would meet them at the general merchandise store on Main Street. Now she squirmed her way through the tightly packed crowd of men in back of first base. She had sighted the big figure of Jimmy-Lew.

"Jimmy-Lew! Hey, Jimmy-Lew!" she called.

But just then a sharp crack of timber sent that young man in swift pursuit of a grounder. When he had stabbed the ball by a timely lunge and made the put-out that retired the Prince team, his eyes swung on her but he gave no sign of recognition.

This first taste of indifference piqued the girl and called for revenge. She had her chance a moment later when Jimmy-Lew strode confidently to the plate to test the pitching skill of Josh Williams.

"Strike 'im out, Josh!" she shrilled to the lanky, raw-boned hurler. It was during one of those moments of stillness that occur in closely contested games—neither side had made a tally—and her voice carried to the farthest spectator.

Jimmy-Lew lowered his bat and grinned broadly down the first base line at Martha. Seizing upon this laxity, the wily Josh cut the heart of the plate with a quick pitch.

"Strike—one!" boomed Big George.

The crowd howled. Martha, in her excitement, leapt high into the air and squealed her malicious appreciation.

"Aw, do it, Josh! Let 'im have it!"

That pig-headed Jimmy-Lew, instead of shouldering his bat, waved a derisive hand at her. And as he did so, Josh shot another strike across.

The crowd, now fully aroused by the dramatics taking place, jeered viciously. Boos and cat-calls split the air. "Take 'im out! Take 'im out!" The cry became a chant.

But Josh placed too much trust in Jimmy-Lew's seeming unreadiness, for as he sent the next ball to the plate, an amazing thing happened. Without shouldering his bat, Jimmy-Lew leaned forward and swung in an arching, upward swipe from the ground. All of his powerful shoulder muscles were in that quick, rhythmical lunge.

The white pellet sailed higher, higher, out over the center fielder who had been caught lamentably napping, then plunged into the fallow ground beyond the bounds of the field. Jimmy-Lew, in the meantime, had started on the circuit of the bases. Like some blooded stallion with the bit in his teeth, head high, body almost at perpendicular, he shot out in strides that fairly devoured the first base line. By the time he rounded the turn at second, the fielder had retrieved the ball. A beautiful throw relayed it to the left fielder. Then silence smothered the crowd. Would Jimmy-Lew try for a score?

Martha clenched her hands, her bright eyes widened to their capacity. Without knowing what she did, she screamed:

"Run, Jimmy-Lew! Run!"

He may have heard for his legs seemed to draw up a trifle higher at the knees, and his pace quicken. A split second before the ball thudded into the catcher's mitt, he charged across the home plate.

Now the throng, which a few moments before had clamored for his blood, went mad in admiration. But Martha stood wilted and chagrined behind first base, her chin tilted at a disdainful angle.

In the last half of the ninth inning Jimmy-Lew had still made the lone score of the game. The Prince team was at bat and Skinny was pitching for the Morrises. He had hopes of a no-hit, no-run victory.

The first man to face him, a little rabbit-like fellow, pranced and capered exasperatingly before the plate until he was presented with a base on balls. Not content with this, the pirate, aided by a long hook-slide, took possession of second base at the very next pitch. Unnerved at this point, Skinny made a wild throw, which, before it was recovered by the catcher, found the base-runner crowing on third.

Supporters of the Prince team, sensing a last-stand rally, whooped up their chatter, which did nothing to calm the harassed pitcher. He had lost all control of the ball, and now eight wild tosses in rapid succession found the poor chap in an agonizing predicament with all of the bases lodging runners who waited only for the crack of the bat to bolt them scoring over the triangle in front of the catcher.

The din rose deafeningly over the field while the pitcher and the catcher held a hurried consultation. The desperate Skinny poised on the mound in a slow wind-up, but the ball barely reached the batter before it dug into the dirt. The next was no better, for it went wide, outside.

With bases full, no outs, and two balls on a possible pass for a tying run, Skinny dejectedly contemplated the batter before him. It was the same stocky short-stop who had been clouting hot, skidding grounders throughout the game. Skinny knew that the only thing that had saved him from humiliation thus far had been his foe's lack of placement. Granting that he succeeded in achieving a strike-out, which was obviously doubtful, there were two other batters to follow whose long fouls had been a source of considerable worry. Skinny did not relish his position. His nerve was gone—he knew it. And the crowd was unmerciful.

He spat out his flavorless quid, said something to Big George, and dropped the ball.

"Time out!" bawled the umpire over the jeers of the crowd.

Skinny ran over to Jimmy-Lew and tendered his mitt.

"What's the matter?" grinned Jimmy-Lew. "Scared?"

"You's got one ball to lose," said the vanquished pitcher, ignoring the jibe.

Jimmy-Lew's grin widened. "I don't reckon I'll be a-needing of it," he boasted. And as he walked over to the abdicated mound there was a flaunting confidence about the boy's bearing that abruptly hushed the jeering mob.

Shrewsbury lads, for many years to come, were to hear of the feat performed by Jimmy-Lew Grundy that day. Narrators garnish the legend with extravagant hyperbole and quaint simile, but the facts are these: Upon entering the pitcher's box, Jimmy-Lew threw exactly nine strikes—nine ribbons of sizzling white that streamed waist-high over the plate! Three bewildered batsmen faced him, and went down. And when the report of that last strike resounded from the catcher's mitt, the crowd, with customary fickleness, was at Jimmy-Lew's feet.

IV

Martha slunk away, half-provoked, half pleased with Jimmy-Lew's heroics. She had not gone far when a voice stopped her.

"How'd you like the game, Mis' Prince?"

Martha assumed the rôle of coquette.

"Oh . . . it was fair to middlin'," she said.

"You cain't fool me," chuckled Jimmy-Lew. "You wanted me fo' to win that game, didn't you?"

"Oh, did I?"

"Wal—didn't you?"

"Whyn't you speak to me?" countered the girl accusingly. "You heard me callin' to you. And you ain't even been near our place since you left!"

"I ain't used to goin' places whar I ain't wanted," replied the boy.

"What you mean? Where ain't you wanted?" Martha turned angry sloe eyes on him. "You's usin' that fo' a 'scuse, that all!" Young Grundy's arm found its way around her waist.

"Honey," he pleaded, "hope Ah die yo' paw told me to keep offn his land! Don't you know why?"

"No! And I don't care!" the girl smiled coyly. "I didn't tell you to stay away, did I?"

The boy beamed. "Look yere—you goin' on the straw-ride tonight?"

Martha shook her head. "No," she said, her lips in a childish pout. "Blanche said I couldn't go."

"Aw, shucks! Wal—ef you ain't a-goin', I ain't a-goin'!" the boy vowed.

Just then a girl broke away from a group of young people gathered at the bridged ditch leading from the ball grounds.

"Hey, Jimmy-Lew, is you comin'?" she called, making for them.

"Huh!" she said, contemptuously, when she had come closer. "So you's got a new gal?"

"What you mean—new gal?" flared Martha. She resented the newcomer's confident, proprietary manner. She wanted to pull away from Jimmy-Lew's grip. But it was like trying to make one of her father's mules run when the animal wanted to walk.

Jimmy-Lew alone was unruffled. "I ain't never had no gal, Judy," he said. "So you's wrong 'bout that. An' I ain't a-comin' with 'mongst-you. See?"

Judy crumbled before the finality in his tone, and with a sniff of disdain turned away to her companions.

"Who's she?" demanded Martha as they gained the road.

"Oh, shucks! Don't let her bother you," reassured the boy. "She ain't nothin' but a picker from Kent Island way. Been tryin' to take up with me. But I ain't got no time fo' no gal what runs with married men and them that ain't her eekles. 'Sides," he added, softly, "I ain't a-wantin' nobody but you, no ways."

"Well"—Martha was unconvinced but pleased—"she sho acted like she owned you."

"Wal—she don't! An' that's that!"

They took their time walking. The afternoon sun still lingered, and it was pleasant along the shell road with the town just ahead.

Within a few rods of the store where Jim Prince had tied his horse, Martha turned to Jimmy-Lew.

"Papa don't like you, maybe, but—but I do! And—" She halted, looking at the ground. "Jimmy-Lew, do you want me to be on that straw-ride?"

"'Course I do!" cried the boy delightedly. "But you said yo' sister—"

"I'll be on that straw-ride, Jimmy-Lew!"

V

But you can't go out, Martha. Blanche don't want you to.

I don't care! Jimmy-Lew'll be there, and so will Judy, and . . .

But Josh and Big George'll be there, too. They'll tell Papa and Blanche in the morning, sure's you're born!

I don't care! 'Sides, they'll be so drunk they won't know who I am.

But suppose Blanche and Papa hear you going out or coming in?

They won't. I'll climb out on the limb of the big apple tree in front of my window. And I'll come in the same way.

But you hadn't ought to go. Blanche said no.

I don't care! I don't care!

But suppose something happens? You know how much Blanche wants you to go to school. You know how much Blanche loves you.

I don't care! I don't care!

You've never been out without Blanche before. There might be a fight. You know how these pickers carry on when they get to drinking.

Jimmy-Lew'll be there. I ain't scared. Jimmy-Lew'll be there. He's strong!

Here they come now! Hear the horses? Hear them singing? Hear Jimmy-Lew's guitar a-playin'? But don't go out, Martha! Don't!

I will! I will! . . .

Shucks, I knew it would be easy!

VI

"Martha!"

Jimmy-Lew jumped down from the straw and lifted her bodily into the wagon.

"You did come, didn't you?" The boy was highly elated.

"Sho," replied the girl, as if she had done the easiest thing imaginable. "Where's Judy?"

"Now there you go!" chided the boy. "She's in town—down in Gatlin's alley. She didn't come 'cause she was mad with me." He chuckled gleefully. "I told her I warn't a-comin'." He raised up beside her. "Sho glad you's here, honey," he whispered, his lips brushing her ear. It made her shiver a little—a pleasant shiver.

"Strike up that box, boy," coaxed a girl behind them. There were a dozen or more couples lounging intimately in the lurching vehicle. They were young and wanted music.

Out of the curved belly of Jimmy-Lew's guitar came the opening chords of "Sweet Adeline," and soon a chorus of young voices rolled out over the moon-silvered fields of the lowlands until the wagon came to a wood. Then the driver turned off the white road. Let their elders ride on. The young people preferred the woods where fragrant pine needles matted the warm earth. It was quiet there. And one did not have to stay in the wagon. It was nicer two by two. . . .

The guitar hummed a little in the pine wood. The couples hummed a little. Then the guitar was silent, and the couples were silent. And there was no sound except the whisper of needles and the faint rustle of underbrush.

Chapter 28

I

The berries thinned and finally vanished in the lowland patches. The season was over and the pickers were leaving for home. And now the Shrewsbury shopkeepers rubbed elated hands together, for sales were mounting as the scattering pickers indulged in their seasonal spending spree.

The proprietor of the town's clothing store, Heinrich Schroder, was especially gleeful. All the morning of the second Saturday in June, and right up to the shrieking approach of the afternoon train, the Schroders were kept busy.

"Such a loveliness in the feet, lady," Frau Schroder would gush. And the teeth of some splay-footed woman picker would gleam in spite of the agonizing pressure of new leather. (One's shoe could come off in the train.)

"*Ach!* Just like the glove, *mein* friend!" Thus Heinrich, the elder, would convince a new customer who frowned dubiously at a suit. Scratching fingers would rake an itchless head. The garment was sold.

Young Heinrich held forth in the haberdashery department. "Just like they're wearing in New York," he blandly informed the men and boys as he displayed a screaming cravat or a candy-striped shirt.

The money drawers yawned greedily. The pickers' pockets grew lighter. They had made another season.

Martha stared gloomily down the hot, dusty road from the farm wagon in which she and Josh drove the Prince crew to the depot. She wished the wagon's occupants wouldn't chatter so.

"Wonder ef the weeds done growed up in the back yard. . . ."

"You reckon the crabs is much this year?"

"Hope A'nt Lizzie looked to my chickens whilst I was gone."

"Stop bein' so fidgety, Georgie! I'll smack the taste outn you!"

Martha wished they would stop chattering. Didn't they know Jimmy-Lew was going away?

They were jolting by the pine wood where she had stolen every night except the night it rained last week. . . . She wouldn't climb out by the apple tree any more. Jimmy-Lew was leaving. She wouldn't have to wait to hear her father's deep snoring, or to hear Ike Johnson's departing footsteps, before she could go to Jimmy-Lew. Jimmy-Lew was leaving. There would be no more soft strumming on the guitar, no more tender whispering from lips so persuasive against her own. Jimmy-Lew was leaving.

They had passed the pine wood.

II

In town, Martha eluded Blanche and her father to go in search of Jimmy-Lew. She saw him through the window of Schroder's store. My! how nice he looked in his spankin'-new blue serge pants, tan shoes, and white shirt! He saw her and waved for her to come in. No, she shook her head, and signaled that she'd wait for him. He came presently, his discarded clothes in a package under his arm.

"Couldn't git a whole suit," he explained sheepishly, after greeting her. He looked wistfully at the suits displayed in the window. "Had to let Granny have most my money."

"You looks grand, honey!" Martha stood off at a little distance and beamed admiringly. Then dissatisfaction edged her voice. "I bet you'll do some struttin' when you gits home. Bet all yo' sweethearts start to fightin' 'bout you."

"Aw now—there you go!" he reproved her. "Ain't I done told you you's the only gal I ever liked in my whole life?"

Martha smiled up at him happily—pacified.

They turned into a side street where neither Jim Prince nor Blanche would be likely to find them. Then they walked until they found themselves on the white turnpike.

Finally they came to the pine wood. It was just past one o'clock. The train did not come until three. They had time. . . .

Once more they sat under their pine tree and talked. Silly talk. Young talk.

"Sho don't want to leave this place, honey."

"I don't want you to, nuthah."

"I bin thinkin'. Bet you ain't gonna think 'bout me when you's 'way to school."

"I ain't goin' to think 'bout nothin' else!"

The boy made a confession: "I ain't told you nuffin' 'bout it, but I done decided to go to school this winter. They's gonna give night studies to Eastland, an' I figgered I could 'bout make most o' the classes ef the shuckin' ain't so hard or I ain't 'way on a dredge boat."

He glanced at Martha to see how she received this information. She squeezed his hand.

"I warn't noways wantin' my wife to know more'n me," he ended, shyly.

Martha said nothing, only kissed him in awkward, girlish fashion. And in the silence which followed there was complete forgetfulness of the world near by.

III

Jim Prince and Blanche accosted the boy and the girl sternly as they came breathlessly under the shed of the station house.

"Whar you bin?" demanded Prince over the shriek of the approaching train. He seized Martha roughly by the shoulder and spun her around to face him.

Before she could answer, the air was shattered with screams. Then horror clamped down upon the crowd. A child had walked onto the tracks in front of the train, and would have perished before the eyes of the paralyzed, witless onlookers had not a lithe body shot forward. The child was thrust to safety, but Jimmy-Lew was caught beneath the monster engine.

Martha knew nothing after the horrible sound of brakes grinding.

Chapter 29

I

For her father Martha had moody, accusing eyes that said: "Your last words to him were harsh. You were unkind to him always." For Blanche she had only silence.

Day succeeded day, each a meaningless repetition except for a visit, every afternoon, to the pine tree that bore the initials "M. P." and "J. L. G."—hers and Jimmy-Lew's.

"'Tain't no use lettin' it upset you, Papa," said Blanche when Prince complained of the girl's behavior. "Marty'll be gittin' off to school in a few mo' weeks. She's young. She'll get over this."

Then, one sultry morning late in August fear settled on Martha, and grew to panic as the morning progressed. She sat on the porch, tried to calm herself, to think.

If she was pregnant—and there had been cause to worry for a week now—something must be done. She thought of girls she knew "gittin' in trouble." She recalled the sly nods and wagging tongues. She knew what a choice tidbit her own disgrace would be: Blanche's humiliation . . . her father's grief . . . her own unhappy future if she stayed in Shrewsbury or was sent away from the Institute.

If she stayed . . . that was a thought! Suppose she didn't stay? Suppose she ran away? Other girls had run away from Shrewsbury. Minnie Thomas . . . Sofie Lewis . . . plenty of girls. That wasn't such a disgrace.

Martha's head lifted. Her jaw set itself in a stubborn line and her childishly soft lips lost their pout. She glanced at the clock in the kitchen. It was ten. She had an hour to catch the short-line train to Eastland. And from there . . . She didn't care where she went from there.

In furious haste she packed the valise which Blanche had purchased preparatory to her going to the Institute. This she hid in the back of the buggy. Then she went to her father's room, to the bureau where he kept his money. There was forty dollars in all. She thrust twenty-five into the first grown-up pocketbook she had ever had.

When she had scrawled a note to Blanche and her father and washed her face, she ran out into the fields. Blanche was in the potato-patch crushing bugs on the steel of her hoe. Tall and comforting she looked, and Martha wanted to throw herself into her sister's bared arms. Instead she smiled her brightest.

"Well, honey," Blanche greeted her, relieved to see the child apparently so cheerful, "you looks like yo'self fo' sho! Gonna help me git rid o' these here 'tater bugs?"

"Nope, sis'," Martha shook her head. "But I was kind o' thinkin' 'bout school, an' I thought, since I was goin' soon, I better git back to a li'l' history and grammar. So I thought I'd jes' hitch up ole Flossie and git some books from 'Fessah Johnson. Kin I?"

"Sho! Sho, honey. Go right on." Blanche was delighted at this sudden rebirth of interest. "Be sho an' git back befo' dinner time, 'cause Papa wants to go to town on business."

She watched her sister hurry to the farmhouse. She started to call her back, but didn't. She returned to her bug-killing.

II

Martha urged the mare to a gallop, much to that beast's discomfort, for it was hot and dusty on the road. Why were all young uns in such an everlasting hurry?

The fields, the pine woods, Old Ebenezer and its grave-yard on the edge of town—all rolled by. Martha hadn't time for them. She was too busy with her trouble-some thoughts.

You hadn't ought to do this, Marty. You know Blanche and Papa will be worried. Why don't you stay home?

I can't. I can't! I've stayed here too long now. The same thing every day, all your life.

But you were going to school, Marty.

I couldn't go to school and have Jimmy-Lew's baby!

I'd a-had to stay right in Shrewsbury all my life—a-lettin' folks talk 'bout me. I won't do it!

Where you going, Marty?

I don't know. I don't care! Philly, maybe. Maybe New York.

You don't know anybody in Philly or New York, Marty! What'll you do when your money's all gone? Who's going to look after you when . . .

Leave me be! I'll take care o' myself.

There's the train a-blowin' now! You'd better turn back, Marty.

I won't! I won't! I'm goin' 'way from this town! I'll be all right . . . I'll be all right . . .

III

Jim Prince plodded his fields, a tired and very worried man, and thought of his daughters. For a week now there had been no word from Martha. Neither telegrams nor the services of the police had produced a trace of her. Martha had vanished as if by magic. To add to his distraction, Blanche—usually so calm and self-controlled—had given way completely to her emotions. "It's my fault! It's my fault!" she kept repeating. And no words Prince could say would comfort her.

On the other hand, she appeared to derive more than ordinary comfort from the presence of Ike Johnson. And the professor was taking advantage of the crisis in the Prince family life to make himself useful. He dictated telegrams. He fed the chickens. He coaxed Blanche from the brink of hysterics.

Only last night Prince had seen Ike plant a hurried kiss upon the lips of his elder daughter as the two stood at the swinging gate. And Blanche—so her father thought—had not been so sad today. Prince had misgivings. Perhaps Blanche, too, would leave him, now that the responsibility for Martha no longer rested upon her shoulders. Prince couldn't rightfully object. The professor was everything a man could wish for in a son-in-law. He was well able to care for a wife. And if a colored high school was built in Shrewsbury—there was talk of one—Ike's future was pretty well assured. For he was the logical one to be the principal.

But what would Prince do without Blanche?

"Ah ain't gwine to stand in de way," he told himself. But he realized suddenly how necessary this daughter had become to the peaceful conduct of his life.

IV

Ike proceeded with his courtship, not impulsively, but with calm ardor. Then one day in autumn Prince was invited to listen to the plans the young people had hatched.

"An' the school board's made Ike the principal of the new high school, Papa," concluded Blanche. "So I was thinkin' we could live right here on the farm."

One of Jim Prince's rare smiles flitted briefly across his face.

Chapter 30

I

Martha ventured another glance about the car, this time noting more purposefully the faces of her fellow travelers. Their utter impersonality was disheartening. She shrank once more against the sill of her window, not bothering to wipe away the tears that stole down her cheeks and drifted between her quivering, parted lips. She had to admit it— she was frightened.

Then diversion boarded the train at Claybridge, which is a junction point near the boundary of Maryland and Delaware. Tired of watching the bustle at the station, Martha shifted her worried eyes to the seat across the aisle. At the same time its occupant shifted her position, and a pair of hazel eyes met Martha's black ones. It was Judy!

Martha's first impulse was to turn away. But she was too relieved at seeing any familiar face, whether it belonged to enemy or friend. So she returned Judy's gaze with one of curious surprise.

Judy spoke first. "You-all goin' far?"

"Philly," replied Martha, shortening the name in an effort at nonchalance. But nonchalance fled before Judy's incredulous grin as her eyes traveled critically over Martha's gingham dress. Martha bit her lip and looked away in hot embarrassment. She felt Judy slip into the seat beside her.

"What's the matter?" Judy laid a persuasive hand on Martha's shoulder.

Martha dropped her head and Judy smiled knowingly —a one-sided smile.

"Who was it—Jimmy-Lew?" she asked.

Martha made no answer.

"Aw, 'tain't yo' fault, honey," soothed Judy. "What yo' folks do—put you out?"

"No!" Martha's head shot up defiantly. "I jes' come on 'way befo' they found out."

"Oh . . ." Judy's freckled brow contracted, puzzled. And again: "Oh . . ." Then: "Well, what in hell you goin' away fo'?"

Martha shook her head dumbly.

"Come on—betcha hongry—let's eat," Judy said, brusquely, and reached for a shoe-box from the seat she had vacated.

"I don't want none," said Martha.

"Don't be no fool—you gots to eat," answered Judy, practically.

Martha took the fried chicken leg proffered her and at the first bite she knew how hungry she was. She almost snatched a biscuit from Judy.

"Naw, you ain't hongry—much!" mocked Judy.

When they had made away with the contents of the box, Martha asked Judy where she was going.

"Philly. Got a a'nt there," replied the girl. "Says she got a job fo' me. Ef you wants to, you kin stay with us."

To Martha this was equivalent to an invitation to heaven, the solution to her most pressing problem. Then her face fell.

"No, I can't go with you," she said, gloomily. "Yo' a'nt might not like it when she finds out 'bout me."

"Huh!" Judy scoffed. "You must think you's the only gal what ever had a baby without bein' married! I gots one— year old—home with my folks. Shucks! 'Tain't yo' fault Jimmy-Lew got killed. Wouldn't a-mind havin' one o' hisn myself." Her smile made Martha feel easier. She added: "A'nt Liddy ain't been no angel herself! What's yo' name?"

Martha told her.

"All right, Marty—it's a go. 'Course, now, don't let me make you do nothin' you don't want to do."

"Oh, I'll go with you!" exclaimed Martha, eagerly. "I can pay yo' a'nt until I get a job."

"Don't let that worry you," said Judy, magnanimously. Then she looked Martha over critically. "Reckon you better change yo' dress ef you got a better one," she suggested. She smoothed the mail-order garment she wore, and adjusted her hat at a cockier angle. The suit was of gray serge, and she carried it to attractive advantage. Judy had that something called "style."

When Martha returned to her seat, she had on a blue serge outfit selected, with Blanche's help, from *Markson's Magazine.* It set off her slim figure and soft beauty perfectly.

"Sho look kind o' good, gal," said Judy, with relief in her voice. She had a horror of appearing countrified, and hadn't relished the thought of being seen with one who fitted that description. To her dying day Judy was to stand firmly for what she later termed "class."

The train paused at Wilmington and then took up the rattling journey. Twilight gathered and the girls grew silent. Suddenly Martha asked:

"Why'd you pay any attention to me? I thought you didn't like me on 'count o'—"

"Jimmy-Lew?" finished Judy. "I don't hold no hard feelin's long. 'Sides, he was just a notion, anyways, to me. That's the way I am. I ain't lovin' no man no mo'—never!" Her laugh had a hard edge to it that was unpleasant. "Guess I felt sorry fo' you." She shrugged.

II

Broad Street station, with its bustling crowds, made Martha glad that she was with Judy.

"Porter, sir?"

"Porter, ma'am?"

"Kin Ah help you, suh?"

Martha started to relinquish her valise to one of the porters who glided skillfully among the disembarking travelers, but Judy pinched her arm.

"You ain't got no money to waste on no red-cap, gal," she stated, out of the wisdom of practical experience. "They spots you ef they thinks you's from the country, 'cause country bucks always tips big so's to make folks think they's what they ain't."

Having made this pronouncement on conduct in a big city, Judy adjusted her hat on her sandy hair, seized her bag, and weaved ahead, followed meekly by Martha.

They had hardly passed through the big iron gate when a stoutish woman swooped down on Judy and gathered girl, bag, and all into her capacious arms.

"A'nt Liddy!" gasped Judy.

"Lawdy, gal, you's a woman, sho enough!" A'nt Liddy stood off at a little distance to look over her niece.

Martha felt immediately at ease with this broad-beamed, capable-appearing woman. She liked the pleasant cheerfulness of her freckled mulatto face, the amiability of her laugh. Fiery wisps of hair that showed under A'nt Liddy's umbrella-brimmed hat gave a clue to the origin of Judy's sandy thatch.

A'nt Liddy shifted her attention to Martha. "Who's this here, Judy?" There was a friendly twinkle in her gray eyes.

"She's my best friend, A'nt Liddy," answered Judy, easily. "She's come to Philly lookin' fo' work, too."

"Well now, that's sho nice," beamed A'nt Liddy. "You got folks here, honey?"

Judy didn't give Martha a chance to reply. "Oh, I told her she could stay with us, A'nt Liddy."

"Sho, gal, that's right. I gots a room what'll be jes' right fo' you young uns."

"An' I thought," Judy rushed on, "seein's how you got a employment office, it'd be easier fo' her to git a job—"

"Sho—sho," agreed A'nt Liddy. "Don't you worry, chile, I'll be a-lookin' out fo' both you-all." She patted Martha on the shoulder. "Come on, let's git goin'. I gots supper all ready."

She led the way through the station and out the Broad Street entrance. Martha had never seen so many people in one street before in all her life. And the buildings appeared huge. She was silent with amazement and not a little thrilled by the crowds, the noise, and the brilliant lights. She'd heard tales of the wonders of remote "Philly." Now she was actually there!

They boarded a crowded street car and rode until A'nt Liddy said, "Here we is, gals." Then they got off.

To Martha South Street fairly swarmed with colored people—more than she'd ever seen at a fair, or at camp-meetings, or in town grubbin'-up on Saturday nights. And there were kitchen smells in abundance, for it was a neighborhood of restaurants.

Halfway up the block A'nt Liddy turned into a door beside a big window which bore the legend: LYDIA

WILLIAMS—EMPLOYMENT BUREAU. She flung the door wide in a gesture of welcome.

"Here you is. We's home!"

When A'nt Liddy had touched a match to a gas jet, Martha could see that the place was the essence of cleanliness and order. In one corner to the left stood a roll-top desk with a comfortable armchair designed especially for the accommodation of A'nt Liddy's bulk. Flanking the walls ran benches, and down the middle of the room were three rows of chairs. The linoleumed floor gleamed. And not a smear marred the surface of the curtained show window. On the wall near the desk was a small box-like contraption with a crank to it. Martha guessed it to be a telephone.

"Sho is got a nice office, A'nt Liddy," commented Judy.

"Yep—ain't so bad," agreed the proprietor, complacently. "But come on out in the kitchen." And she bustled through the back door of the office, with the girls close at her heels.

In the kitchen Martha again witnessed the wonder of light leaping out of a thin pipe.

"Yeah," A'nt Liddy said, seeing the direction of Martha's gaze, "things is a whole lot easier here than they is down home. No water to tote, no lamp chimneys to clean, an' "— her eyes twinkled—"you-all kin take a bath every day, 'stead o' jes' on Sat'days."

She liked these two. She liked their youthfulness and their eagerness. She had been like that years ago—full of "git up." But she wondered what was worrying the new young un. She had an idea, but she hoped it wasn't that. Well, she wouldn't worry her with too many questions yet-a-while.

III

Martha lay between the cool, sweet-smelling sheets, enjoying the effects of a bath and vigorous rub-down. How clean she felt! It certainly was different from stooping and standing in one of the wooden washtubs at home. She had been able actually to lie down in Mis' Liddy's gleaming-white tub. Above Mis' Liddy's hum in the adjoining room she could hear Judy splashing.

A train whistle blew, and turned her thoughts to Jimmy-Lew and the folks back home. She hoped they weren't too upset by her disappearance. She still thought she had taken the best step.

Judy came in, her hair twisted in little sandy tufts about her head, and slipped into bed. Through the ceiling above them drifted strains from a piano that had never known an expert tuner. Nevertheless, there was a catchy rhythm to the music.

Mis' Liddy thrust her head into the doorway from her room. "That's them theater people up there," she informed them, almost apologetically. "They mought keep up that rumpus right smart o' the night. Hope they don't bother you much." Then she vanished.

The girls lay listening to the discordant sounds from above. Now a soprano was singing and Judy started to hum:

> "Tell me, long tall papa,
> Where did you stay las' night?
> Tell me, long tall papa,
> Where did you stay las' night?
> Now, yo' hair's all nappy
> An' yo' clo'es doan' fit you right!"

Judy's sinuous body was weaving in the bed as she snapped her fingers toward the ceiling: "Aw, sing it, gal!" The voice obligingly continued:

> "Look yere, long tall papa,
> Ef you ain' home to stay,
> Look yere, long tall papa,
> Ef you ain' home to stay,
> Ah's gonna pack mah suitcase
> An' make mah git-away!"

Now Martha's contralto joined in:

> "Look yere, long tall papa,
> Dis ain' gonna do a-tall!
> Look yere, long tall papa,
> Dis ain' gonna do a-tall!

An' ef you keeps on a-doin' it
Ah got 'nothah mule fo' yo' stall!"

When the piano and voice above had moaned to a stop, Judy looked at Martha in surprise.

"They told me you could sing, gal!" she exclaimed. "You gots a alto what *is* a alto, sho 'nuf!"

Martha smiled. "You don't sound like no crow yo-self."

"You know," said Judy, looking at Martha speculatively, "we mought git a job with some show." Her hazel eyes glowed at the prospect. It was the first time Martha had seen her animated. For if Judy had any feelings, she seldom showed them. Everything she did, even walking, was stamped by a pronounced lack of interest. Cat-like— the adjective suited her. She moved like a cat and she had about as much emotional verve. It was this very quality that was to catch the fancy of theater-goers a few years later.

"Kin you dance any?" she asked.

"Sho, a little," was Martha's conservative reply. Could she dance, indeed!

Judy was jubilant. But she immediately sobered. "Aw, hell!" she groaned. "I clean fo'got."

Martha knew what Judy had forgotten.

"Well, it won't be too late afterwards."

"Yeah," came Judy's muffled reply from under the sheets. "Yeah—ef you don't git too fat!" Her voice was tart.

"You ain't fat, is you?" Martha flung back. And she returned the sly pinch that Judy gave her.

Chapter 31

I

"Git up! Git up from there, you lazy scamps! What in 'ell you tryin' to do? Sleep 'twell Gab'el blows? Git up!"

Martha and Judy sat up in sleepy confusion to stare stupidly and a bit frightened at Mis' Liddy. One look at her face, though, was enough to start them giggling. Her freckles mingled and separated as great gusts of laughter shook her. She leaned against the wall, clutching the covers she had snatched from them.

"You-all—you-all," she gasped, "must o' thought I was the devil!"

Judy assumed a frown.

"What kind of a way is this to treat yo' niece what's come to stay with you? I'll fix you." And she flung a pillow at her aunt that caught Mis' Liddy flush in the face and gave off a shower of feathers. In reply, Mis' Liddy charged the bed, seized both girls in her strong, freckled arms, and rolled them tightly in the bottom sheet. Then she reeled laughing into the kitchen, where breakfast had been noiselessly prepared.

After the merry meal was finished, Martha took her courage in both hands.

"Mis' Liddy, I—I want to tell you somep'n—"

Mis' Liddy interrupted: "I know what you gonna say, honey." Her smile seemed to Martha to rival the bright softness of a single sunbeam slanting through the kitchen window across the sink's white enamel. "I knows. I reckon I kin jes' 'bout guess why you come 'way from home. I reckon you don't want to go back, nuthah. I ain't tellin' you to go back, and I ain't tellin' you to stay. But I is tellin' you you kin stay here with us long's you wants—an' there ain't gone be no charge. Only thing—you gots to do as I says. I'm gonna look to you same's you was my own chile." Then, after a moment: "Well, what you say, gal?"

"Yes'm—I mean, thank you, Mis' Liddy!" Martha was tearfully grateful.

"Well"—Mis' Liddy's freckles clashed—"that's 'bout that! An' I'll smack the water outn you ef you don't mind me—see?"

Now she turned and pounced upon Judy.

"Yo' maw writ an' told me 'bout how you was runnin' with married men!"

"Why, A'nt Liddy!" Judy's assumption of injured surprise was perfect.

"Don't you 'why, A'nt Liddy' me!" stormed the big woman. "You's too much like me—I knows you! Now you listen to me. You ain't gonna do no messin' 'round here. You gonna take this job I gots fo' you—an' you gonna keep it, too! You hear me?"

Without warning, Judy burst into giggles. It was too much for Mis' Liddy; she, too, began to chuckle. Soon all three were laughing.

"I ain't promisin' 'bout the men folks, A'nt Liddy," said Judy. "I jes' can't do so good without 'em. I is promisin' I'll do all right by the job."

"Huh!" Mis' Liddy's grunt was noncommittal. "All right. You starts out day after tomorrow—Monday." She turned to Martha. "I ain't lettin' you go on no job, 'twell after. You ought be able to help me in the office and 'round the house here."

Not able to say a word, Martha threw her arms about the big woman, who seemed the personification of all kindness.

"Huh!" grunted Mis' Liddy again, well pleased. "Now you scamps clean up these dishes whilst I go open up my office." And she left the kitchen briskly, all business and energy.

Judy eyed Martha impishly. "What'd I tell you?"

Martha pinched her. "Git a towel," she ordered, imitating Mis' Liddy's tone.

II

It was Monday morning.

Judy dressed and ate, her hazel eyes half-draped by sleepy lids, while Mis' Liddy tried to pierce the armor of her nonchalance with last-minute counseling.

"An' don't you git sassy with Mis' Smedley, nuthah. 'Member you's workin' fo' her." It was Mis' Liddy's parting shot, and in order to deliver it she had to trail Judy from the kitchen table to the front door.

Judy gave a final yawn.

"I needs a winter coat, A'nt Liddy. I'm waitin' 'twell I gits that befo' I do any sassin'." She winked at Martha. "Don't let A'nt Liddy kill you with work, gal!" And she was off.

"Lazy, red-headed heifer!"

But Martha was not deceived. She knew that the exclamation was really a blessing.

Left to herself, Martha went about the business of putting the bedrooms and kitchen to order. Then, as soon as she could, she joined Mis' Liddy in the office.

It was crowded, for Monday was a busy day. The benches along the walls were occupied by the men; the chairs down the center of the room, by the women. There was every indication that Mis' Liddy was an extremely popular and well-patronized agent.

Now she looked up from the ledger in which she was making an entry and beckoned Martha to the chair beside the desk. She was engaged with a sloppily dressed woman who slouched at her elbow.

"Ah'm a-lookin' fo' a sleep-in job, Mis' Williams," the woman was saying. "Somep'n what ain't so hard . . . you know. . . . Ah ain't bin so well yere lately, Mis' Williams. . . ." Her voice took on a wheedling tone.

Martha noted the sudden hardening of Mis' Liddy's jaw as she leaned over the corner of her desk and in a voice that was barely audible said:

"You listen to me, Nanny Johnson! I sent you on a job two weeks ago—an' what did you do? You kin cook all right. But Mis' Laney called me up and give me the devil fo' sendin' you to her! You know why?" Mis' Liddy's ears looked like slices of beets to Martha. "I'll tell you why! It's 'cause you don't keep yo'self neat an' clean! I wouldn't send you on another job to save you, 'twell you kin show me you means to do better! Now you git outn here, an' ef you don't like the way I talks to you, you kin try somebody else's agency! Git!" And before the fiery eyes of Mis' Liddy there was nothing for Nanny to do but "git."

Mis' Liddy turned to Martha with a snort and shoved the ledger toward her.

"Take this down," she ordered. "'Nanny Johnson, 212 Elmsley Alley—no job 'twell she gits clean'!" She scowled at Martha. "An' there ain't nothin' to grin 'bout!" she added vehemently.

So it went all day. The applicants were of every kind and class: dirty laborers in overalls, primly dressed women who spoke in soft tones and inquired about positions as housekeepers, nurses, and day-workers. Time and again Mis' Liddy proved her judgment of human nature by a terse phrase which summed up her opinion of a person's capabilities, character, and appearance: "lazy-lookin'"—"smart, but looks like she might be flip with the madam"—"neat as a pin, suit anybody—" These and other little notes Martha scribbled beside the names she entered alphabetically in the big, blue-backed book.

Early in the afternoon there was a breathing-spell for sandwiches and tea.

"You mustn't take on 'bout how I talks to you sometimes," said Mis' Liddy between bites, "but some o' these no-'counts makes me mad'n blazes! There's that Nanny Johnson—one o' the best cooks in the city—but she ain't got gumption or sense enough to keep clean. When I sends Nanny out on a job an' the madam ain't pleased with her, that makes it hard fo' me to send another colored woman on that same job. White folks is funny. Ef one colored man or woman do somep'n wrong, they takes all colored folks to be the same way. There ain't no sense in it, but they does, an' that's why these furriners is takin' house jobs 'way from us. Use to be a time when nothin' but colored had butler an' cook jobs. But ef it keeps on like this we ain't gonna have no kind o' jobs. Booker Washington says we gotta beat everybody else doin' things ef we wants a chance to do 'em. An' that's right!"

Martha could not help but believe that there was wisdom in what the big woman said. She had often heard Jim Prince talk in the same fashion.

III

While they were eating supper, Judy arrived, and stood scowling in the kitchen doorway.

"So!" she blazed. "So you had a nice, easy job fo' me, did you? Nothin' hard a-tall! Nothin' to do but wash, an' cook, an' serve tea, an'—" A gust of laughter from her aunt interrupted the eloquent sarcasm.

"What's so funny 'bout it?" demanded Judy.

"Oh, shet up!" chuckled Mis' Liddy. "Come on an' set down efn you's so tired."

The truth was that Judy appeared as fresh as she had been that morning. She flopped into a chair at the table. "Here," she said, placing a parcel before Martha. "Some nice rice puddin' fo' dessert. Ef you wants to give her some"—she jerked her head in the general direction of her aunt—"suit yo'self."

"Look out, Marty," warned Mis' Liddy, laughingly, "she mought o' tried to pizen Mis' Smedley."

Judy wrinkled her nose disdainfully.

"Now, no foolin', you young heifer," ordered Mis' Liddy, "tell me how you likes yo' job. I know it ain't hard 'cause I done worked fo' Mis' Smedley myself."

"Oh, it's all right," said Judy. "Tell you the truth I wouldn't mind workin' fo' her ef it was hard work, 'cause Mis' Smedley's real nice—an' that baby's cute's he kin be."

"Well, Monday's hardest day on 'count o' washin'," said Mis' Liddy. "But there ain't but three o' them to cook fo'. Ten dollars a week an' board ain't bad. You gits every Sunday afternoon off, too, an' every other Thursday after breakfast. Huh! When I first come to Philly, I got ten dollars a month—an' was glad to git it!"

Mis' Liddy leaned back in her chair and started on her reminiscences. When she got to her favorite passage, "All I had time fo', seem like, was eat, sleep, an' work," Judy winked at Martha.

"I saw you wink!" Mis' Liddy exclaimed. "You thinks I'm jokin', but it's the gospel truth! That's why I skimped an' saved so's to have a li'l' somep'n laid up fo' a rainy day. An' that's why I was able to git a part-time job an' go to school at night so's to—"

"Have some puddin', A'nt Liddy," interrupted Judy, and she shoved the bowl across the table.

Mis' Liddy caught the hint. "All right, drat you!" she laughed. "Guess it ain't no use preachin' to you, noways. You alius done what you wanted, even when you was a li'l' un—an' you growed no better."

"No, A'ntie," was Judy's candid reply, "yo' niece ain't believin' in no kind o' work no time! Some o' these days yo' niece ain't gonna do too much work, neither—an' she ain't gonna be dead, neither!"

And, somehow, neither Mis' Liddy nor Martha doubted her. There was a light in her eyes that told of a spirit that usually got what it wanted.

"Nope," she continued, "I can't see this housework, an' never will. The first chance I gits to do somep'n easier fo' bigger money—I'm gone! I jes' warn't made to wait on nobody. I'm gonna have somebody wait on me one o' these days!"

"An' lose yo' soul, too!" exploded Mis' Liddy.

"I mought," agreed Judy, slowly, as if pondering the possibility. Then she made a characteristic addition, "But won't I have a good time a-doin' it!"

"Shet yo' mouth, gal!" ejaculated her aunt. "The Lawd'll smack you down. Don't listen to her, Marty—she's a no-good li'l' hussy!"

Chapter 32

Thanksgiving came and went, Christmas and New Year. Then one blustery February day job-seekers who came to Mis' Liddy's agency had a surprise. For the first time in the-Lord-knew-when there was a sign hanging at the door which read: "Closed Until Further Notice." No amount of ringing at the bell brought a response. And, since it was uncommonly cold, the disappointed ones did not linger, but slushed on their various ways through the stinging sleet.

The next day the sign had been removed. There was an unusual brightness about Mis' Liddy's freckled face. And the lusty wails of an infant sounded through the back wall of the office.

Young Jimmy-Lew had come.

II

One week after the birth of Martha's son, Judy received a letter which sent her rushing home. Her own son was sick. When she returned, eight days later, she was hollow-eyed and shrouded in black and her breath reeked of whisky. She was sobbing out details of her recent experience when her eye was caught by Jimmy-Lew and she picked him up.

"He's mine, now, too!" she told Martha, almost fiercely.

So from the very beginning Jimmy-Lew had two women to spoil him.

"He'll be so dern sp'iled he'll be rotten," Mis' Liddy warned Martha. But this sage advice was lost. Martha was a young mother.

Martha was working now, as well as Judy. This left Jimmy-Lew to the care of Mis' Liddy a great part of the day, and that lady saw to it that her spare hours were profitably spent in "unsp'ilin'" him. She had some degree of success. But when night brought the girls home, all disciplinary rules were tossed aside.

Jimmy-Lew grew rapidly into a sturdy, intelligent child whose black eyes and chuckling laugh could captivate even Mis' Liddy to the point of sparing the rod on occasion. He knew better than to invade her office during business hours, for several experiments in that direction had brought painful results from Mis' Liddy's broad palm. But in the kitchen he could do much as he pleased, and he spent happy hours dissecting the toys with which Martha and Judy provided him.

When he was three years old he asserted himself and passed from the first to the second phase of male life. This was when he objected to aprons.

"Wanna wear pants! Wanna wear pants!" he howled. And not even Mis' Liddy could force his squirming body into one of the objectionable feminine garments.

He wore pants after that, like the boys in the apartment above Mis' Liddy's. And his fond women, seeing him stand swayed back on his stout legs, hands in pockets, and expectancy on his pinkish-brown face, called him their "li'l' man."

Chapter 33

I

When Jimmy-Lew was four, Martha and Judy had
their first chance before the footlights. For years they'd
danced and sung together in the kitchen for Mis' Liddy's
disinterested and the baby's gleeful inspection. Now the
Ruby Theater, a vaudeville house around the corner which
they frequented with Sam Jenkins and his friends, was
having an amateur prize program. Sam, who was a waiter
and Judy's beau and fancied himself a judge of the dance,
had persuaded them to do a number.

The Ruby was under the management of a genial, florid
Irishman, one Patsy O'Keefe by name. Patsy was an old-
timer to the boards. His oft-repeated assertion was that he
knew all the headliners among Negroes of the theater—the
Coleman brothers, who'd taken New York by storm with
their song-hits and musical comedies; their co-worker,
Ross; and even the great black-face comedian, Bill Wilson.
And, faith, since he'd come to make his living among these

people, his boast was that he knew them better than they knew themselves. He patronized their restaurants, their saloons, even their bawd-houses.

On this evening—which was Thursday and the domestics' night off—Patsy strutted from the wings and doffed his brown derby, baring a bald dome of a head as he waved the eager audience to silence.

"Lad-eeez an' gen'man," he began, importantly.

There was a round of applause, punctuated by whistles. "The management is anxious to uncover new talent that must be among so large an' enthusiastic an audience. So we have set aside cash prizes from the box-office to reward the winnahs—who will be picked by you—an' you—an' you." Here Patsy pointed dramatically to different sections of the theater.

After the hand-clapping had died down, Patsy finished his speech: "An' now, will the contestants come up to the stage an' pick for the order of their appearance in the contest? Come one! Come all! Strike up the band!"

The ill-trained orchestra blared forth, and to Patsy's coaxing the ambitious ones straggled shyly to the stage to receive a hearty handclasp from the manager and cheers from the audience.

"Let's go—huh?" whispered Judy to Martha. They were seated in the middle section of the orchestra.

"Bet you ain't got nerve 'nuf!" jibed Sam.

"Dare you," chimed in his friend, who had escorted Martha.

Martha rose abruptly and moved toward the aisle.

"Hey—wait a minute—I'm coming," called Judy.

The orchestra finished its number and Patsy motioned the ten contestants to him with the request that they draw slips of paper from his derby. Judy drew fourth position.

Now Patsy pushed them off to the wings to wait their turns.

Maggie Hanks was the first to perform. She waddled out to the front of the stage, a huge ungainly figure whose rolls of fat rebelled at the confining services of cloth and stays. But she had not sung more than half a dozen bars of "The Curse of an Aching Heart" when catcalls and whistles drowned her screech.

"Git the hook! Git the hook!"

A huge hook attached to a stout pole shot from the wings and poor Maggie was hauled ignominiously out of earshot of her ungrateful public.

Judy was the only contestant who had the temerity to laugh at this episode. Martha and the other aspirants for honors found themselves suddenly very weak in the knees.

Next came an elocutionist, a timid-appearing youth who looked as if he had just donned long trousers. He managed to stumble through "The Face on the Barroom Floor" despite torrents of perspiration which poured off his closely sheared head and seriously threatened a celluloid collar bearing a diminutive black bow tie. But unfortunately he ended upon a too-dramatic note. When the vagabond of the piece succumbed finally to alcohol and exposure, the young reader suited actions to words, and pitched himself onto the stage. Alas! His trousers were meant for gentler motions, and the seams gave in various humiliating places. To the accompaniment of delighted howls from the audience, the hapless one escaped to secluded regions, and with him went the skinny girl who had drawn third place.

"Here we go!" said Judy to Martha. Patsy had just introduced them as "two charmin' young exponents of the song an' dance."

"Come on. You ain't scared, is you?" urged the impatient Judy.

"Y-y-y-yes!" Martha fumbled with her handkerchief and looked at Judy with frightened eyes.

"Aw—fo'git it!" and Judy almost dragged Martha on-stage.

The orchestra, at Judy's direction, swung into the number the girls had sung their first night at Mis' Liddy's. They knew it well. So did the orchestra. This was their kind of music! Soon Martha forgot her nervousness and her husky alto joined Judy's vivacious soprano. Seized by the rhythm of a tune familiar to them, the audience began to hum, and feet all over the house took up the beat.

But it was when Judy caught Martha's hand and they glided into their dance that the enthusiasm of the audience reached its height. They began with an easy shuffle, the beat of their feet being as the whisk of a broom across a floor in measured time. Then the taps became more intricate and pronounced. From two-four time they shifted to a triple beat, followed by four and five taps of heel and toe to the musical bar. Each tap was brought out with precision and clearness.

"Aw, knock them boards, gals!" and "G'on, now!" could be heard from all sections of the house.

There was nothing extraordinary about the girls' routine. They had acquired a few of the regular steps known to all tap-dancers. But their performance was a miracle of cooperation—it was as if one brain dictated every movement of the two lithe bodies.

As they took their hurried, breathless bows and scampered off-stage, the house broke into a roar. For this crowd knew good tap-dancing when they saw it.

"We got it, gal!" said Judy, jubilantly.

Martha nodded, her eyes shining.

Later Patsy came up to congratulate them, and stayed to talk. "Say," he said, after surveying them critically, "you two ain't bad-lookin', neither! How'd ye like a job in a show?"

"Show!" gasped Martha.

Judy arched her brows at Patsy, and then turned half-closed eyes on her partner. "'Course he said show, honey—don't you think we's good enough? You thinks so, don't you, Mister Patsy?" Her accents dripped syrup. Patsy's eyes narrowed speculatively and he grinned.

"Shure now an' we kin talk it over sometime. . . ."

"Tonight—after the show?" Judy asked insinuatingly.

When Patsy had returned to his duties Martha demanded, sharply:

"What you goin' to do, Judy?"

"Git us jobs in a show," was the laconic answer.

"But you knows what he wants."

"Baby," interrupted Judy, "I knows *jes'* what he wants!" She faced Martha with that crooked smile of hers. "Listen—ef you thinks I'm gonna sling vittals an' wash an' scrub all my life, you's crazy! You mought think you's made fo' that, an' you kin have it, ef you wants to. Me? I'm tired of it!"

II

About four o'clock in the morning, after a disgruntled Sam had taken her home, Martha bolted from bed and stole into the kitchen. Judy was fumbling at the back door.

"Sh-sh!" cautioned Martha as Judy came reeling in. "Don't wake up Jimmy. An' fo' God's sake don't let Mis' Liddy hear you!"

"Wha' I care 'bout A'nt Liddy? Wha' I care?" Judy grinned drunkenly and waved a hand in a broad gesture of disdain. "You's in a show, gal! Hic! In a show!" And she immediately fell dead asleep in the chair where Martha had placed her.

This was fortunate, for Martha had no trouble in getting the girl to bed. At six o'clock she began to apply restoratives. A towel soaked with water made icy by the biting October cold brought a muffled howl from the sleeper.

"Sh-sh-sh, you fool!" whispered Martha, and pointed to Mis' Liddy's door. This effectively sobered Judy and she sat up, blinking.

"What'd you do last night?" Martha demanded, sternly.

Judy's grin was sickly but triumphant. "Got us jobs in a show an' told Patsy what a nice man he was." She swayed languidly to the kitchen, her cotton kimono caught tightly about her waist so that the curving line of her hip was more prominent.

"But, Judy, you hadn't ought to done that," protested Martha, following her.

"Done what, honey?"

"You know!" snapped Martha, irritated.

"Oh, you mean *that?* Don't worry none, honey. Li'l' Judy kin take care o' herself, an' don't you fo'git it! 'Sides," she added, spluttering over the washbowl, "I don't ever pay fo' nothin' 'twell I gits it—ef I pays then!" And she winked solemnly.

Martha brightened. "Well, when do we git the jobs?"

"You know this Sol Batey we been readin' 'bout, the one that puts on all these colored shows? Well, he's gonna open in Philly next week fo' a try-out. Patsy says he been knowin' him—fact is, they's friends. So Patsy says he's gonna see that Sol puts a spot in fo' our dance."

"Wonder what Mis' Liddy'll say?" speculated Martha, uneasily.

Judy's shrug was indifferent. "We's both grown, ain't we?"

"An' then there's Jimmy-Lew, too," continued Martha. "I can't leave him."

"Oh, you kin leave him with A'nt Liddy," said Judy, confidently. "She'll take care o' him, all right. He ain't no baby now."

"Maybe so. . . ." Martha's voice was doubtful.

Martha was silent most of the way to the trolley line.

"Aw, come on," urged Judy, "we ain't gone yit. Ef I kin grin with this headache I got, you ought to be able to laugh out loud."

"I know," said Martha, "but I can't leave 'im—I can't! He's too young."

Suddenly Judy had an idea.

"I got it! Martha, you ain't been home in a time. Whyn't you go home an' take Jimmy-Lew to see yo' folks? You kin leave 'im down on the farm—be better fo' 'im, too. City ain't no place to raise chilluns, nohow."

Home! Martha turned to Judy, suddenly radiant. Blanche—Papa—Big George—Josh—the farm—the pine wood. All these had faded from her somehow. She'd had so many other things to think about.

"Maybe so!" she answered. "But what'll I tell em, Judy?"

"Tell 'em the truth. You's yo' own woman now." And Judy waved a blithe hand as the girls separated.

III

Mis' Liddy met them at the door.

"Now don't you git all up in the air, gal," she said, hastily, to Martha. "Jimmy-Lew's sick. He ain't sick bad, but doctor says 'twas best fo' 'im to be in the hospital. Jes' a tech o' diphtheria with a li'l' fever."

This was unpromising comfort, and when Mis' Liddy suggested that they go to the hospital immediately it was with difficulty that Martha's legs carried her to the street. Judy was crying openly, though she made a show of brave talk.

"Oh shucks! That li'l' devil's too healthy fo' somep'n like this to keep 'im sick. He'll be a-tearin' up things in a couple o' days, you see!"

"Mercy Hospital in a hurry," Mis' Liddy told the hack-driver. "But I ain't wantin' to stay there—you git me?"

IV

Mis' Liddy's optimism was well founded. For Jimmy-Lew was home in no time at all. And what a stormy, rebellious convalescent he was! He kicked and squirmed when his throat had to be swabbed. He refused outright the watery foods that were specified on his diet. He cried to be allowed to join Isaiah and Amos Thomas in the alley—which had never looked so alluring before.

Now and then Martha's gentle disciplinary measures failed completely and Mis' Liddy had to take a hand.

"Shet yo' mouth, you sassy scamp, you!" Mis' Liddy would command, and then remind him: "Ef you'd a-put on that sweater like I told you, you wouldn't a-got sick. Out there in the alley a-playin' with them li'l' Thomas devils with nothin' on but a shirt! You's so lickety-split you ain't got time to do no thinkin'.'"

But one day the lure of the alley was too great, and Martha returned from shopping to find Jimmy-Lew— without sweater or coat—playing in the alley, and reasserting his authority over the two Thomas boys.

"Jimmy! Oh, Jimmy-Lew!" she wailed.

When they were in the kitchen she tried to scold him but the words wouldn't come. She gave up and, surrendering to the strain of the past weeks, put her head on the table and sobbed. Jimmy-Lew was at her side in an instant, his small arms around her neck.

"Please, Mamma, don't cry no mo'. I gonna be a good boy. Please, Mamma, don't cry no mo'."

But he had defeated her temporarily. That night when Judy came in late to whisper that Patsy had made all arrangements for their spot in the new show just come to town, Martha shook her head firmly. She couldn't leave Jimmy-Lew.

V

Judy left with the show two weeks later.

"You ain't comin' to no good, gal," her A'nt Liddy stated. Then, shoving a crisp banknote into her niece's hand: "But jes' in case you don't—here's yo' way back home."

"Don't you worry 'bout me, honey." Judy pecked Mis' Liddy's cheek gratefully. And to Martha she said, "Tell Patsy I'll pay 'im when I git back—maybe!"

Chapter 34

I

The war, that began so inauspiciously with the assassination of an Austrian nobleman, reached across the seas and stirred the sluggish stream of American industry.

A number of the girls Martha knew quit their jobs. There was better money to be made in the munitions factories. But Martha stayed with the Spearmans. She liked it there well enough with fluttery Mrs. Spearman and her viking stockbroker husband who was confident that some day he would put across a really big deal and retire. In any case, the only other job she wanted was on the stage.

Mrs. Spearman, apparently, was worried lest the prevailing fever of unrest rob her of a good maid, for one day when she gave Martha her pay she added an extra bill.

"I just wanted to tell you," she said in her nervous, hesitant manner, "that you've been very satisfactory and that I wouldn't like to lose you. The children have become so attached to you. And Mr. Spearman praises your cooking all the time. He suggested that I raise your wages—if you decide to stay with us—beginning this week."

"But, Mrs. Spearman—," Martha began. She had never expected this.

"Now, I hope you're not going to tell me that you were thinking of leaving, Martha," Mrs. Spearman interrupted, hastily. "You see, I—I don't like hiring new girls. It upsets me so. Really, if the two dollars isn't enough, I'll see that your salary is advanced right along with salaries in general. I do hope you'll stay!"

Martha decided that it was the part of wisdom to encourage Mrs. Spearman in her generous humor. So she said cautiously, "Well, Mrs. Spearman, I'm satisfied— if I'm giving good service and you are going to give me more wages." That, she felt, left the matter open for further adjustment.

II

So Martha remained with the Spearmans. And Jimmy-Lew grew out of babyhood. And the war came closer.

For a long time nothing of importance happened. Then Judy paid a comet visit home—a Judy who was a genuine trouper, a stylish Judy who wore diamonds she explained with a knowing wink, a Judy who talked in an unintelligible lingo of the theater and the gay places that made up her world.

When she arrived without warning on Easter Saturday night, Martha and A'nt Liddy were too surprised for immediate speech. The gray suit with mannish shoulders and daring split skirt, the jaunty blue straw hat and pearl-buttoned shoes, were outside the experience of Philadelphia, and they were frankly dazzled. Judy had to come across the room and kiss them soundly. Then speech was restored to A'nt Liddy.

"Well!" she said. "You sho look like you done took care o' yo'self, all right."

"Thought I wasn't comin' to no good," Judy reminded her.

"I takes it back," said her aunt, generously.

After that the three of them—four, when Jimmy-Lew was routed from bed—settled to a babble of questions and answers. How was the show business? Did she like it? Where had she been?

The show business was swell and she liked it fine. She had been to Pittsburgh, Chicago, New York . . .

On and on they talked, that night and the next week. Then she left. She had accomplished two things. She had succeeded in stirring Martha to discontent with her own humdrum life. And she had given Jimmy-Lew such a dose of pampering that Mis' Liddy despaired of ever bringing him around to normal. "He's so sp'ilt he stinks!" she was heard to complain. But castor oil for an upset stomach and a day in bed worked wonders.

Outside the windows the Thomas brothers laid up trouble for themselves by singing:

> "Jimmy's gotta bellyache! Bellyache!
> Jimmy's gotta bellyache! Bellyache!"

Chapter 35

I

Overnight, it seemed, the war engulfed America. For Jimmy-Lew, who was going on eight, it was the most wonderful thing that ever happened. He memorized all the military phrases he heard, questioned everyone he met—even soldiers on the street—respecting military tactics, and organized a half dozen neighbor boys into an army. He was commander-in-chief, field marshal and general—and no one dared question his leadership. For quite apart from his ability to organize and dictate, he had the handiest pair of fists on the street. The rank of captain he bestowed upon Isaiah Thomas, but this was the single concession he made toward a division of authority.

Puffed up with importance, he was drilling his troops on the alley parade-ground one day in spring when a sharp masculine voice rasped at his back:

"Halt!"

Jimmy-Lew's shoulders flinched upwards—not in fear, but in anger at this unprecedented interruption.

"Comp'ny—aaa—teez!" he hissed, then wheeled slowly to face the cause of the interruption.

Hardened campaigner that he was, Jimmy-Lew was guilty this once of knowing awe. He'd seen colored soldiers—heaps of 'em—but this resplendently booted, spurred, braided, and chevroned figure was too much even for the field marshal! His eyes grew round with amazement and he returned the newcomer's snappy salute in a daze.

"Attention!" the man barked.

From the field marshal down to the lowest buck private, little Amos, brother of Isaiah, there was a stiffening of spines, while roughly-fashioned wooden guns clicked smartly against clamped heels.

"Shoulder—arms!"

The voice acted as a galvanic current; there was an immediate commotion as boyish arms and legs sought to respond. But the action was ragged.

"Halt!"

To the relieved surprise of the company and its commander, the face of their self-appointed officer lost its sternness and the man broke into a howl of laughter. Discipline took sudden wings.

"Who showed you kids how to shoulder arms?" he asked, when he could get his breath.

"I did. Why?" Jimmy's voice bristled. His lips shot out in an ugly pout. The generalissimo did not relish ridicule or criticism.

"Oh, nothing," the man said in a pacifying tone. "Only—here, give me one of your guns, please."

Jimmy presented one snappily. His frown remained, however.

"Now—look," directed the soldier. With brisk, smooth motions he executed the "shoulder arms," to the great admiration of his small audience. "You got it?" he asked as he repeated the motions more slowly, counting.

Jimmy-Lew watched the performance through sulkily narrowed eyelids, but no one lent him any attention, for his company was too occupied with its teacher.

At this moment Martha turned into the alley. And the first object to catch her eye was not her moody son but the broad-shouldered figured in khaki. Something—the back, the carriage, the voice—was strangely reminiscent.

"Jimmy-Lew! Jimmy-Lew!" she whispered, ever so softly.

The man turned, and was the first to speak.

"Lieutenant John C. Carlton, U. S. Army, ma'am—at your service." A smart salute finished the introduction. "And who are you?"

"Martha Prince, sir, off for the day, Lieutenant, from cookin', cleanin', an' general housework—at yo' service!" and Martha imitated his salute. They both laughed.

"And what's your relation to this army?" asked the lieutenant.

"I'm the general's mother."

"You?" John Carlton was clearly astonished.

"Well, can't I be a mother?" demanded Martha, amused.

"But you look like a high-school girl!"

"All right, we'll see. Jimmy! Jimmy-Lew!"

Jimmy-Lew sulked over to them, his hands jammed into his pockets, his head downcast.

"What's the matter, honey?" Martha asked.

"Nuffin' . . ." came the flat reply.

"I think I know the answer," Carlton put in. He squatted in front of the boy. "Listen, Jimmy, I didn't mean to hurt your feelings. But you want your army to be first-class, don't you?"

Jimmy-Lew nodded without looking up.

"Well then, I only helped you out a little. You don't mind, do you? Now, you take your army and forget all about a second lieutenant who doesn't know half as much as you do! But remember this. You've got to be a good general. Understand?"

"Y-yes sir," answered Jimmy-Lew. It was the first time in his short life he'd felt completely overwhelmed, and he hadn't had time to decide whether or not he liked it. But he did return the lieutenant's salute before reassuming command of his troops.

Carlton turned to Martha. "You mind if I stick around?" he asked. "I came to see Mis' Liddy, but she's busy now."

"Come in," Martha suggested, and led the way into the house.

In no time at all it seemed to Martha that she had known John Carlton forever. She talked to him as she had talked to Jimmy-Lew years ago, and John in return told her about himself. He would soon be twenty-five. He had been studying law at the university in Washington, and was in the National Guard down there, when war was declared. Now he was worrying how to tell his mother that he would soon be going overseas.

From Mis' Liddy, who had been John's Sunday-school teacher, Martha got the rest of his story. John's father had been a big caterer in Philadelphia, and prosperous, before the foreigners came in with their chefs and fancy foods. He died leaving his wife, a daughter, and John very well off. The daughter, Nina, who was younger than John, started running around and soon got herself into trouble. She went to a quack doctor. And died. Since then Mrs. Carlton, who was an invalid from partial paralysis, had clung to John. There was good reason why the boy hesitated to break his news.

"If you come with me," he suggested to Martha, one afternoon, "I bet I could tell her."

Martha hesitated, then gave in, and in a short while the two of them were leaving the smell and bustle of South Street for Christian Street and a section where no children or gossiping housewives broke the genteel quiet.

For the Carltons were among the colored Four Hundred of Philadelphia.

"Here we are," announced Carlton at last.

They stood before a three-story red-brick house, flat-roofed. Similar houses lined both sides of the street. At the top of the broad marble steps, John swept low before Martha in an exaggerated bow.

"Welcome to the ancestral hall, fair lady!"

To his delight, Martha executed a demure curtsy and tripped mincingly over the door sill.

He led the way up carpeted stairs to a door opening off a balcony; knocked and a faint voice answered. Inside the room near a window a patch of white topped the back of a rocker that swayed ever so gently.

"That you, son?" The query was low-pitched, but firm, and the voice struck pleasantly on Martha's ears. "Who's that with you?"

"I've brought a friend of Mis' Liddy's to see you, Mom," answered her son, cheerfully. "Wait until I turn your chair around." He did so carefully.

"Well—how do you like her?" he asked, stepping to Martha's side.

Martha felt the patient eyes upon her, but did not mind. They were friendly, in keeping with the whole of the calm brown face. She saw the lips part in a smile of welcome, while wistfulness settled on the broad features. A faint nod of approval ended the brief scrutiny.

"She's real purty," said the mother. "What's yo' name, chile? You 'mind me o' my Nina now, sho 'nuf. Don't she, son?"

"Her name's Martha, Moms—Martha Prince—and she lives over with Mis' Liddy Williams."

"Martha," repeated the older woman. "Sho that's a good name, now, 'cordin' to the Good Book. Draw up a chair an' make yo'self comf'table."

"You two get along fine," said Johnny. "I'm going down to see what Nellie's got for supper. Hope she has corn bread. Be back in a minute."

"So, you's with Mis' Liddy," began Mrs. Carlton. "Liddy's a case! I 'member when she first started that job office o' her'n—nigh on fifteen years ago. Used to git waiters fo' my husband. Fine woman, Liddy—ef she do try to make everybody think she's gwine to bite they heads off." She laughed softly, and went on to recall anecdotes of Mis' Liddy and her strong-mindedness.

Martha hadn't expected to find Johnny's mother so cheerful. As she listened, she let her eyes wander about the room. It held the usual clutter of nineteenth-century furniture and bric-à-brac that denoted financial security but not the best of taste—a grand piano with yellowed keys and gold-green fringed coverlet, a black mohair spindle-legged sofa, and on the mantelpiece of a mock fireplace, a brown plaster-of-Paris lad eternally tempting himself with a cluster of grapes. From the walls, smiling or stern gray countenances looked down with disturbing fixedness. One held Martha's attention, the tinted likeness of a young girl which bore a strong resemblance to Johnny. There was the same high, broad forehead, the same widely set eyes, and straight, low-bridged nose above gay lips.

"That's my Nina," Mrs. Carlton said, seeing Martha's interest. "Jes' like her picter, she was—alius laffin' an' ready fo' a good time. Come day, go day." The old lady sighed and finished half to herself: "That's why she's in her grave today, I reckon. Take after her pappy's brother, Jethro—reg'lar ladies' man, he was—gamblin' an' drinkin' his life 'way." She seemed to have forgotten her listener. "Ain't none o' us left now 'cep'n Johnny and me, an' now he's tryin' to keep from tellin' me he's got to go fight in this war."

"You knows that?" exclaimed Martha before she could check herself.

The old woman bent her wise, maternal eyes upon the younger woman and nodded.

"'Course I knows, chile. A mammy alius knows 'bout her chilluns! An' me here par'lized with nobody to be with me cep'n a girl I hires with the money my man left me." For the first time she grew impatient. "Money! Hadn't been fo' money my Nina mought still be livin'. She wouldn't o' had no time to go foolin' 'round ef she'd o' had to work. An' ef it warn't fo' that money, my son wouldn't have to go to no war. He'd have to stay here an' take care o' his mammy. I prays the Lawd'll let 'im come back, honey. But it don't seem like a man's got much chance, the way they fights nowadays. Well—the Lawd gives an' the Lawd takes away. Jes' hope, ef you ever has a son, he don't have to go to no war."

"Who's that talking about war?" demanded Johnny from the doorway.

"Yo' mother an' me was just talkin' 'bout yo' goin' to war," said Martha. Seeing John's face fall, she continued hurriedly: "I was tellin' her you'd be back all right. Ain't that so?"

"Sure—sure, Moms—that's right," he followed the lead. "Why, they say in camp that the war can't last long now. They're just sending us over to discourage the Germans, that's all. Shucks, Moms, don't you worry, I can—"

"Let's not talk 'bout it no mo', son." His mother lifted a pleading hand.

Casting about for a change of subject, John wandered over to the piano.

"Yes, son—play that music you made up fo' 'Steal Away,'" his mother urged.

"The queen shall have her wish." He bowed, and beckoned to Martha. "Come here, young lady."

Martha snapped to attention and saluted as she had seen Jimmy-Lew do. "Yes, sir!" she said.

"Now, what voice do you sing?"

"Play an' see, sir!"

"A-ha! Insubordination!" Johnny frowned sternly. "Young lady, if you do not perform most proficiently, you shall be court-martialed. Attention!"

His fingers flexed over the keys, and descended skillfully. Then, when he had played a few preliminary measures, Martha's contralto picked up the rich minor melody. And, gaining confidence, she sang as she had never sung before. It was Blanche's voice and Carrie's voice and the voice of all her ancestors who had known the slave-ship's stench and the auction block; untrained, but with a beauty of quality and expression that needed no conservatory.

When the last "I ain't got long to stay yere" had faded into the shadows of the room, Johnny turned to face her.

"What's the matter?" asked Martha, not quite sure of the meaning of his expression. "Do I get a court-martial?"

"It was lovely, honey—," began Mrs. Carlton, but Johnny interrupted.

"My God, girl! Do you know what you're doing? You're throwing away a voice! You're hiding a candle under a bushel! You're committing sin every day, keeping that voice to yourself! Why—the whole world ought to hear it!"

Martha laughed, partly from pleasure, partly from incredulity.

"Don't laugh!"

"Now, Johnny, don't take on so," said his mother. "Don't you mind him, honey," she said to Martha. "He alius liked music—wanted to take it up, but his pappy's wish was he'd be a lawyer or a doctor."

"Oh, I don't mind," said Martha.

"But you should mind about a voice like yours," persisted Johnny. And he worried the subject through supper until Mrs. Carlton shooed the two of them out of the house for a walk in the park.

III

Martha was on her knees, scrubbing the kitchen floor and feeling that nothing was worth while because nothing could matter any more. It is easy to feel that way when you've tried to slice half your finger off first thing in the morning, and you've burnt the toast to a crisp, and you've answered a commanding buzzer more times than you can count, and you've faced a fretful woman at her bedside with a trayful of food which she declares is unfit for a pig, and you've got two quarelling girls off to school, and the night before you've loved your man for the last time in a don't-know-how-long. For Johnny's leave was over and he was off to France.

"Martha! Martha!"

Martha flinched at the impatience in the voice, but did not lift her head. "Ma'am?" she answered, dully.

Fussy, fluttery Mrs. Spearman stood in the doorway.

"Martha, when *are* you going to finish that floor? Have you forgotten I'm entertaining the Volunteer Patriot Workers this afternoon at tea? I don't know what's come over you today. I—"

She got no further, for Martha had risen, and the expression on her face suggested that she had put on a mask. All the girl's gentleness and smiling good humor had fled.

"Gimme my pay!" It was a hoarse whisper. "You hear me? Gimme my pay!"

"Why, Martha—"

"Gimme my pay, I said. I don't want to hear nothin'. Just gimme my pay." The voice was dull and flat and implacable.

"What *is* the matter?"

"Sick an' tired o' scrubbin' an' cookin' an' washin'. Sick an' tired o' waitin' on folks all day. Sick an' tired! Every day somep'n's wrong." Martha spoke as if she had given long thought to her grievances. Actually, she had never considered them before. "Ef it ain't this, it's that. The clothes ain't clean after I wash 'em. The eggs ain't fried right. The livin' room ain't been dusted. I ain't never gonna work in no service no mo'. Gimme my money."

When Mrs. Spearman returned with a hastily scribbled check, Martha was huddled over the table, sobbing hysterically.

Mrs. Spearman nodded her head knowingly. Nerves!

"Listen, Martha," she said, "suppose we forget all that's happened."

But Martha had gone too far to retreat. "Gimme my money." Then she reached her hat down from its peg and walked out.

IV

So eight years after she had left home, Martha returned, to find her father older, Blanche larger in girth and more mature. Ike had been drafted into the war, but there were his two boys, Booker and Paul, who were just the right age for Jimmy-Lew.

It was fun coming home to people who loved you, but when two weeks had passed, Martha knew that she could not stay here. In two weeks all experiences had been exchanged. She knew which seasons had been fat for her father, which lean. She had a report of the deaths and marriages, the current and stale gossip of the town. There was nothing more to be discovered.

Consequently, when a letter arrived from Judy, Martha was prepared with an answer.

"Why don't you come to New York?" Judy wrote. "I can get you a job in the show I'm going to be in this fall. . . ."

Martha had had a taste of freedom and a wider life. She wanted more. Jimmy-Lew could stay here and grow up on the farm. So, just as suddenly as she had returned, Martha went away again.

Chapter 36

I

When he first came to his grandfather's, Jimmy-Lew enjoyed the prestige of a guest. His cousins treated him with deference and listened breathlessly to tales of his life in the city—tales highly spiced with imagination. Even his grandfather and aunt gave him a certain special consideration. Jimmy-Lew was still cock-o'-the-walk.

With the departure of his mother, however, he became a permanent member of the family. Booker and Paul, growing more familiar, accepted him now as an equal rather than a superior. Jimmy-Lew was no longer a being from a wonder-world, but their cousin. And Jimmy-Lew did not like this shrunken interest.

An incident occurred to fix his status very firmly.

It was a hot, sultry morning after a hot, sultry night. Paul was already up and at his chores in the chicken-yard. But Booker and Jimmy-Lew—laggards always—were trying to snatch an extra ten winks of sleep.

"Hey, up there!" Blanche's voice rose above the kitchen noises. "You boys git up now! Them pigs is got to be fed, an I needs mo' kindlin'-wood! Come on!"

Rebellion frowned up Jimmy-Lew's face as he sulked out of bed and pulled on his overalls. His mother's small mouth settled in a pout, the lower lip hanging. And Booker's mood, as he also moved sluggishly in the direction of duty, was companion to his cousin's. For no particular reason, hostility sprang up between them. The very silence was charged with it.

It so happened that both boys possessed blue denim shirts of the same size. Now, as ill luck would have it, they grabbed for the same shirt, the only one visible.

"Hey! that's mine!" growled Booker, giving the garment a vicious jerk.

"'Tain't yo's. Leggo!" snarled Jimmy-Lew.

There was a brief tug-o'-war until Jimmy-Lew's patience reached its short limit. In another moment the battle had begun. Though not as tall as his cousin, Booker's body and limbs held no small amount of strength. Jimmy-Lew, on the other hand, had the advantage of a formidable technique which was the result of greater experience in holding his own against opponents who were his superior. By side-stepping and feinting he would have thrashed Booker thoroughly at long range, but Booker kept boring in like some enraged bull calf. Finally the two closed, and now Booker had the distinct advantage. For he knew nothing of polite city codes which outlawed rough-and-tumble wrestling. Gaining a strategic position astride Jimmy-Lew's chest, he let his fists fly.

"Git up, you coward, an' fight fair!" howled Jimmy-Lew.

Blanche, arriving at this moment to investigate the wild commotion, took matters into her own hands.

"Git up from there, you scamps!" she ordered, and with one back-hand stroke sent her son hurtling against a wall, the print of her floured hand stamped on his cheek. Jimmy-Lew shot to his feet, blood streaming from his bruised nose. Before Blanche could stop him, he was snarling over Booker like some infuriated cat. His boxing finesse had fled.

"I'll kill you! I'll kill you!" he screamed.

Blanche stood between them and shook them violently at arm's length. "Stop it! You ought to be 'shamed o' yo'selves—two cousins a-fightin' like cats an' dogs!" She shoved Booker toward the stairs. "You git me Pa's strap. I'll larn you to fight one another!"

"An' you, Jimmy-Lew. I promised yo' mother I'd look to you, an' I'm a-goin' to do it, takin' Lord to be my helper! You's jes' sp'iled as you kin be, that's all. But I'll have you know I ain't a-goin' to put up with none o' yo' foolishness. Now, you-all git on yo' knees at that bed. G'on!"

Then began Jimmy-Lew's unwelcome, but beneficial, intimacy with his grandfather's razor strap. The last vestige of his prestige was shattered. He was now indeed a member of the Prince family.

II

The advent of Jimmy-Lew to the grammar department of the Shrewsbury Colored Grammar and High School did not lighten the burden of the two young women in charge. Far ahead of his class by virtue of his superior training in city schools, he found time a hundredweight on his hands while pinioned in his seat with Booker. There was time to carve notches and initials into the desk, time to torment everyone around him with paper wads shot from an elastic band. And for this last diversion Ellen Miles was his favorite target.

Ellen was the color of maple leaves in autumn, with auburn pigtails that stuck out stiffly from her head—a challenge to impolite little boys. Unfortunately, Ellen had shown her liking for Jimmy-Lew, and Jimmy-Lew was at that age when a woman's devotion is a handicap to the male ego. He took every opportunity to pay her back for the jibes he suffered on her account.

Ellen tolerated his persecution just so long. Then one gloomy day prior to the Christmas holidays, her patience reached an end. For the better part of the afternoon Jimmy-Lew had been ingeniously improvising misery for her. He jerked her hair (she sat directly in front of him); he drew frayed paper across her bare neck. Not content with that, he must pinch her as she arose to recite.

This last was too much. Her eyes aflame, she whirled upon him and clawed his surprised face before little Miss

Winston, the teacher, could intervene. Booker sprang away from the seat, and retired to watch the fray at a safe distance. The room was in an uproar.

"Ellen! Jimmy!" shrieked Miss Winston.

"He kept botherin' me!" sobbed Ellen, scowling at her late hero, who stood beside his cousin and sheepishly wiped his bleeding face with his shirt sleeve; Jimmy-Lew, who could lick the spots off'n any boy his size!

"What have you to say for yourself, young man?" demanded Miss Winston, as severely as she could. For this was the principal's nephew.

"He hasn't anything to say!" It was Miss Warner, assistant principal, a woman of adamantine qualities. She didn't care whose nephew Jimmy-Lew was! And Jimmy-Lew, seeing her frowning mahogany countenance, had an excusable qualm. "I saw it all, Miss Winston. This young fellow thinks he can do as he pleases around here. But, believe me, he can't. Come here, young man!"

On the platform, where the two teachers' desks stood like thrones in an audience chamber, Jimmy-Lew felt the stings of a willow branch vigorously applied. To the disappointment of the other pupils, not a cry escaped him. When Miss Warner stopped at last, he stood there like a carven image, his black eyes dull spots of slate beneath sweaty curls, his lips a thin taut line.

It was the first time Miss Warner had met with response of this sort. What kind of a boy was it who refused to be beaten into submission? She was annoyed, and at the same time immensely intrigued. That night after school, she faced a sullen Jimmy-Lew across her desk and tried a different approach.

"What makes you do wrong things, Jimmy-Lew?"

The boy lowered long-lashed eyes and bowed his curly head. Nice-looking youngster, thought Miss Warner. What was it they said about his mother . . . ?

"Don't you know," she continued in her most persuasive manner, "that you can't do mean things and get along with people. What's your aunt Blanche going to say when she hears how you're acting? You ought to be ashamed of yourself—bullying a girl!"

Where the rod had failed, her scorn succeeded. Jimmy-Lew was ashamed of himself for one of the few times in his young life.

"You may go now," she said.

Outdoors, he crossed the tracks to the road, his despondent head sunk in meditation of his sins. If A'nt Blanche wrote an' told Moms what had happened, then it wouldn't do any good to say in his weekly letter that he'd been a good boy. . . . Shucks!

"Jimmy! Jimmy-Lew!"

A timid voice just behind him interrupted his somber thoughts. He knew the voice, but he didn't turn.

"Jimmy, I-I didn't mean to get you kept after school—honest, Jimmy. Let me walk home with you?"

"'Smatter? 'Fraid o' the dark?" he demanded, gruffly.

"Y-yes!" she lied eagerly. Ellen wasn't afraid of anything—not even the big rats in the old warehouse.

"Well . . . come on, then."

Ellen drew up to his side and peered cautiously at him. "I didn't go to scratch you, Jimmy."

"Aw, shet up!"

The girl meekly obeyed. But when they came to the first patch of woods on the pike out of town, it was getting dusk, and she placed her hand shyly in the boy's. He let it stay.

III

But Jimmy-Lew was not wholly a tribulation to his teachers. He could outspell anyone in the room. On one occasion he saved the timorous Miss Winston from humiliation by spelling correctly every tricky word in the vocabulary of Joshua Damon, county supervisor of schools, who had come on a periodic visit of inspection. One by one the rest of the school went down to defeat, leaving Jimmy-Lew to face the supervisor alone. At that moment Miss Winston forgave the boy all the grief he had caused her, for Joshua Damon—yam hued, shifty eyed—was a cross to be borne by every teacher who served under him.

Not only could Jimmy-Lew spell. As an athlete he was an asset to any school. All the Prince boys could run—Paul with a scampering jack-rabbit gait; Booker with a driving headlong stride. But Jimmy-Lew on the track course was like some wild thing in flight. On that first field day in May, when he won the relay race for Shrewsbury against the Deerfield team, Jimmy-Lew was elevated definitely to a place in the sun.

IV

Six years went by on the farm, and they were good years for all three boys. At the end of that time, each one gave clear indication of the mold he would take in maturity. Jimmy-Lew was brilliant, mercurial, quick of temper, good-looking. Above a stubborn chin and willful lips his nose was losing its youthful snubness for the aquiline curves that were Lew Grundy's. Paul was like his father, serious and scholarly and more poised and sagacious at twelve than either Jimmy-Lew or Booker. It was always Paul who at the end of the week had a remnant left of his twenty-five-cent allowance. Booker for his part held only a forced toleration for the stuff contained in books. He had the kind of mother wit that coins quips and catchy sayings, and this gift was enhanced by a lazy drawling voice and a slow white smile that would break across the ginger brown of his square-cut face. Booker belonged to the earth and the earth would hold him. Every movement of his powerful young body attested this fact.

The war was long since over and Ike Johnson was back among his beloved books when Martha sent for Jimmy-Lew. She could afford to have him with her now, for she had prospered. The Negro weekly journals carried full-length semi-nude pictures of the new song-and-dance team of Judy and Marty—the Maryland Song-Birds. And all Shrewsbury was agog at the dazzling rise to stage fame of Jim Prince's younger daughter.

V

They were down at the station seeing Jimmy-Lew off—Jim Prince, Blanche, and her two boys—when a mule-drawn farm wagon pulled up beside the platform and a big red-headed mulatto descended.

"There's Ellen," said Booker, and stuck a sly tongue in his cheek as he nudged Paul and rolled his eyes in the direction of their cousin.

Ellen ran over to them and shyly held out a package to Jimmy-Lew.

"I—I baked a cake fo' you last night," she explained. "Thought you mought want to eat it on the train." Her voice trailed off in confusion.

Much as he liked cake, Jimmy-Lew would have disdained the gift but for A'nt Blanche and Grandpa looking on. Since there was no help for it, he accepted the package with surly thanks. Girls were a fool nuisance.

Jess Miles came up at this point adjusting a fresh chew of tobacco. He was full of talk, as usual.

"Hi thar, Jim Prince," he boomed. "My Ellen yere kept a-pesterin' me fo' to fetch 'er to the depot. Was a-messin' 'round the kitchen all last night. But, boy," he turned to Jimmy-Lew, "I dunno how you gwine to make out with that cake. Likely it ain't fit to eat." And he roared with laughter at his wit.

Ellen's temper flared. "You alius eat my cake, don't you?" But when her father only roared the louder, her eyes filled with tears and she fled to the station house.

To his own surprise, Jimmy-Lew ran after her. It was the first time. And when he had cornered her he could think of nothing adequate to say. A desire to comfort her stirred him vaguely, but he would not for worlds be soft.

"Aw, what you cryin' 'bout?" he managed, finally. "Don't be such a baby!"

Where was his customary gruffness? In spite of himself, the edge was gone from his voice. Ellen leaned against him and gave way to her grief and humiliation.

"I s-stayed up late last night to make you a cake—an' Paw h-he makes fun of it—an' you don't like it—an' now Booker an' Paul'll tell all the rest the boys an' girls—an'— Oh, I wish I was dead!"

Jimmy-Lew's hand went up in an awkward, sheepish gesture and patted her shoulder. There was a mournful howl from the approaching train. Then, as they separated, the girl reached sudden lips to the boy's. A clumsy, hasty caress, but it widened the boy's dark eyes and set him tingling. A door had opened a crack to a new avenue of experience.

"Hey, Jimmy-Lew!" Booker stood grinning at them, impish glee stamped on his face. He'd seen!

Jimmy-Lew made a belligerent move toward the tormentor but Blanche interrupted.

"Come on, Jimmy-Lew! Don't fo'git to change where I told you—an' keep a watch out fo' yo' mother when you git to the station in New York." She pulled him after her, talking above her usual calm. "I told the conductor to mind out fo' you. Be a good boy, now. An' don't fo'git to write. Here's yo' suitcase. Tell Marty I'll send yo' things by parcel post."

Then they were waving to him from the station shed and the train was puffing under him, gathering speed. His throat closed unpleasantly as the familiar green lowlands slid behind him.

Chapter 37

I

The huge crowd clung tenaciously to their stadium seats in spite of the rain and drew furs and woolens a bit tighter. Not for many seasons had there been a gridiron battle to equal this one.

Down in the bowl, one forward line of the opposite teams crouched, tense as leashed animals, feet gripping the soggy earth, legs braced. Behind them a voice barked. Three players snapped in unison, unhurriedly, ignoring the lifted pistol of the time-keeper.

The crowd leaned forward. Something was about to happen. That Tony Sarnocco took chances no other quarterback would think of taking . . . born gambler, that little Italian.

Huddled on the Staunton bench, following each maneuver, was coach Jock Hanlon. He was talking to a keen-faced man at his side who made swift jottings on a damp pad.

"Now! Watch that boy on this end if you want to see some running. It's a pass."

"Pass?" scoffed the other. "How in the devil's a prep-school kid going to throw that wet ball? It's hard to find a guy doing that in the Big Ten. . . . My Gawd!"

His exclamation stopped conversation for the time being.

A big Hebrew lad had whipped the ball to the bantam quarterback. There was a clash of young bodies meeting and locking. Even from the stands one could see the white teeth of the quarterback as he crept back slowly, sure-footedly, like a wary cat at bay. He had no nerves. The charging line of Holbrook fought desperately to break through his blocking team-mates, while their backfield spread in a four-pointed fan to protect the territory assigned to it.

Tony was on his goal line now. There was no more time to lose. He knew where to throw. There was a spot thirty yards away. . . . His arm went back, then snapped forward. The ball bulleted in a high arc over the tangled bodies in front of him. Then he went down, and a wild roar rolled over the field.

Elusive as a buck deer, the bronzed giant on the end had slipped through the scramble at the scrimmage line. Without so much as a backward glance he sped a straight course down the middle of the field, a Holbrook backfield man at his heels. The time-keeper's gun barked, and as if this were a signal, the runner peered over his shoulder. The ball was about to pass above his head!

With a leap that did not break his long, rhythmical stride, he reached out and clutched the oval in the long fingers of his right hand, juggled it a moment, then tucked it in the crook of his arm and continued on his weaving way. Ten . . . twenty . . . thirty . . . forty . . . fifty . . . sixty . . . The chalked stripes fled behind him. But his pursuer would not be shaken; in a final lunge he flung his tired body into space and his arms encircled the waist of the ball-carrier. But it was too late. Bending forward, and with his legs churning the ground, the bronze boy dragged his tackier over the final line. Then both collapsed in a puddle of mud.

Over the tumult of spectators swarming the field, the man at Hanlon's side yelled:

"Say! Who *is* that Indian-looking kid? I'll get him a scholarship to—"

"Save your breath, Whitby," advised the coach. "He's colored, and he's going to some college down South—in Maryland, I think he said."

"But he don't wanta go there, man! Why, I'll fix it so he won't have to worry about anything! Boy! Can he step! Does he go in for anything else?"

They were making for the locker-rooms.

"Yeah—yeah," answered Jock, wearily, "he's one of the best guards I've seen on a basketball court in many a year. But it's track and football that're his main interests. Runs all the dashes, and pretty good broad jumper, too. But you're wasting your time, Whitby. I tell you this kid's dead set on going South to college. Has some crazy notion about working with his people. Good student, too. Graduates this spring."

"Boy-o-boy! Is he a find! Wait'll I talk to him."

"Yeah—wait!"

The Staunton dressing-room was a hubbub, with everyone talking above the noise of showers. And permeating it all was the odor of young sweating bodies. The Negro boy stood apart from the others—a great-shouldered lean-flanked figure in bronze, toweling his almost hairless skin to a reddish glow.

"Atta boy, Jimmy!" "Great goin', kid!" "Swell catch, boy!" Compliments showered on him as one, then another, passed by.

The swarthy little quarterback came up to him, stopped, and broke suddenly into a torrent of speech punctuated by Latin gesticulations. Without a word the big bronze boy picked him up under one arm and started to walk off. "Hey, Nick," he called to a black-haired linesman, "turn on that cold shower."

"Wait—wait a minute, Jimmy!" howled the Italian. "Nick! Don't turn it on! Aw, ya big bullies—takin' 'vantage of a little guy! I'll tell me big brother!"

The room filled with great gusts of heartless laughter, and poor Tony had no rescuer. Jimmy-Lew ruthlessly shoved his captive under the icy water and held him there. Tony, however, was not to be subdued. When he was free and rubbing his chilled body briskly with a rough towel, he persisted doggedly, "Just the same, it was a helluva catch!"

"Well, you threw it, didncha?" answered Jimmy. "S'posin' it'd been intercepted? Good thing it's the last game—coach'd give you hell!"

"Here he comes now," whispered Tony. "He don't look so hot, either."

The coach came up with Whitby.

"Sarnocco! What'd I tell you about passing in your own territory? Think you're smart, don't you?" Hanlon's gray eyes bore into his prize quarterback, then turned on Jimmy-Lew. "Fine catch there, Prince. Didn't think you could make it—but you did. I don't like such chances, but—Well, the game's won and it took nerve. We still have basketball and track ahead, though, so you two see that you stay in training. I know I don't have to tell you, Prince. But—*no wine,* Tony!"

An aggrieved expression came over Tony's face. "Aw, coach—Tony, he don't drink-a . . ."

"Yeah? Not-a much-a!" mocked Hanlon. He motioned to his companion. "Fellows, this is Bill Whitby, from the mid-West. He's here scouting for material. Might mean a chance for scholarships."

"How're ya?" The scout gave each a professionally warm handshake, talking rapidly all the while. "Great game! Great pass, Tony—and a fine catch, Prince. Heard a lot about you two. You both ought to go great out our way. How'd you like to go to State in the fall? Fix it so you'd get scholarships and nice jobs on the side. No proselyting, understand. Just a big alumnus has established a scholarship fund for good athletes same as they have for good students.... What say?" He looked expectantly from one to the other.

"That's on the level?" asked Tony, all eagerness.

"Sure! Sure, boy! Here." Whitby pulled a sheaf of papers from his inside coat pocket. "Here y'are—look 'em over. How about you, Prince?"

"Nope." Jimmy's voice was as final as it was soft. Whitby opened his mouth, but changed his mind.

"Aw, come on, Jimmy," put in Tony. "It's a great chance."

"I said no." Jimmy's voice was impatient as he bent to lace his shoes. "I told you I was going back to Maryland to college. I'm going to be a teacher, and I want to know something about my people down there. Besides, I don't need any scholarship."

Coach Hanlon nudged Whitby and the two walked off together.

"No use," said Hanlon. "Just like I told you. You're not the only one. Plenty colleges right here in the East have been angling for him. But he always gives the same answer. Seems as if he has an uncle teaching down there in Maryland somewhere. Wants to follow in his footsteps. In a way, I think he's right. Don't really need a scholarship, either. His mother's this singer and dancer, Marty Prince."

"Oh yeah?" exclaimed Whitby. "Say, she's good! And some looker! Saw her in Chicago. And did the Johnnies go for her!"

"Yeah, I know. But don't ever let him hear you talking about her! One of the kids came into the gym one day last year when she was playing the Capitol with that big colored band. He started raving about her shape—you know how these kids are. Well, Jimmy pulled him into the locker-room and before I could get to them he'd nearly slapped the kid silly. He's got an awful temper. And when he gets mad his damn face freezes."

Hanlon shrugged. "Life's going to do a lot of hard things to that boy. He's a curious mixture. Bright as they come. Idealistic. Bad temper. I've seen him go berserk because someone called him nigger. Yet I've heard Jimmy and Johnson, that other colored boy, call each other nigger just as they'd use any other nickname. Of course, they didn't know I was listening. You figure it out."

Whitby's face took on an expression that indicated he was about to arrive at a profound truth. "Say, you know, I've never thought about this racial thing much. Way I see it is, let time take care of it."

II

Jimmy-Lew, Tony, and Dave thrust their way through the disembarking subway passengers and bounded up the steps to Lenox Avenue. Gaining the wet pavement, they sprinted to a little provision store on the corner of 136th Street. Across one of the crowded display windows glinted the gilded caption, "TONY'S MARKET."

"Hi, Pop!" Tony greeted a florid little Sicilian with twinkling black eyes and mustachios which bristled proudly.

"Ha—Tonee!" the elder Sarnocco cried. "I hear you ween-a da champeenship—no? Good-a boy!" Catching Dave and Jimmy-Lew by the hands, he beamed in turn on them. "Ha—Jeemee an' Davee! Good-a boys! I tell Mike Senici—I tell heem, I say: 'Mike, your bambino's team, she no beat-a my bambino's team!' An' wotta you t'ink? I ween-a da five dollars from Mike on da game! Ha!" And he flourished the green-back triumphantly.

"Atta boy, Pop! Where's Mom?"

"Ma-ma? She's in da back. I tell her to make da nize, beeg-a pot da spaghett'—weeth a lotta hot sausage! I tell her, I say: 'Tonee he bring-a Jeemee an' Davee home for sup.' Ha! We celebrate—no?"

The Sarnocco kitchen back of the store was spotlessly clean, and smelled deliciously of spaghetti. Stout, cheery Mrs. Sarnocco sat at one end of the table opposite her husband and near the gas-range, where she could promptly replenish any dish that ran low. On either side of the table, distributed between the guests and Tony, were pretty olive-skinned Angelina and the three younger Sarnoccos—Maria, Rosa, and Peter, who ranged in age from three to eight.

Jimmy-Lew had a comfortable sense of well-being as he sat, silent for the most part, amid the clatter of voices and silverware, for at the Sarnoccos' eating did not interfere with talk and everyone talked at once. These dinners were a custom after every athletic victory, and a relief from the apartment on 141st Street where Judy and his mother were endlessly entertaining a lot of chattering stage people. At the Sarnoccos' Jimmy-Lew felt that he was among friends. It was like being at home with Aunt Blanche, Uncle Ike, Grandpa, and the boys.

Tony and Dave, both Harlem-born, had been pals since grammar-school days. When Jimmy-Lew entered Staunton, they were the first to make friendly advances and persuade him to try out for the athletic teams. It happened, also, that they were the first to bring him into contact with the white people's world. At home in Shrewsbury, white boys were to be passed on the street with little notice. Here in New York you met them in mental and physical competition, and the best man won. They were Jack and Joe and Mike and Nick and Bill to you. You caught the baton from them at the Penn Relays and ran your guts out while they cheered you. You threw your body in the path of an opponent on the gridiron so that these fellows might make touchdowns, and they did the same for you. And when you had your squabbles you went into the gym and fought it out, and shook hands after it was over.

While they were still at the table the evening paper came, and there was a rush to see what the sports writers had to comment on the day's dramatics. It was the same old story . . . but even heroes never tire of their own praise.

While Papa Sarnocco and Angelina exclaimed and took on, Jimmy-Lew, Tony, and Dave tried to appear indifferent.

Dave had made the All-Scholastic for the first time. His air of boredom indicated that the achievement was of no moment, that except for the stupidity of the judges he would have been recognized long since. But Jimmy-Lew wouldn't have it that way.

"Yeah, you been overlooked for three years—not! A tackle hasn't any business being lazy like you were before this season. Told you to get mean."

"Oh, well—once is enough," said Dave, off-handedly.

Soon Jimmy-Lew got up to go and motioned Dave to come along.

"Thanks, Mrs. Sarnocco, for the feed," he said. "It was swell. We'll be seeing you-all after Thanksgiving. And, Tony—no wine! Don't let him have any, Mr. Sarnocco."

"I no let-a heem," promised the father. But the visitors were hardly beyond the door when he pulled a big jug from under the table.

"Angelina! Get-a da glasses. No wine! Sacre Virgino! How you celebrate an' no wine?"

Chapter 38

I

"Turn out that damn light!"

Martha giggled as Judy sat up in bed and scowled. Her reddish hair, lighter now than formerly (thanks to a bleaching agent), was a disheveled mass. Her lips, still rouged from the night before, curled in their old way. She was as angry as a disturbed setting hen.

"That's the sun," Martha informed her.

"Yeah? Well turn it out! What you doing up so early? Your old flame must be righteous. What'd he have to say?"

"Wouldn't you like to know! What'd you do—show the 'fay the spots?"

"Yeah." Judy crawled unwillingly from under the covers and sat on the side of the bed. She held her head and groaned.

"Oooo—wotta man! Tried to drink all the lush in Harlem. And every dive we went in he kept talkin' about how he liked up-town, and the laughing jigs, and—Aw, he made me sick! Come to find out, he's a shoe salesman. And me thinkin' I'd hooked a big-timer! Spends his dough, though. . . . C'mon, break down! What'd the sweet man have to say?"

"He's coming around this afternoon."

"Oh-ho! So that's why you're up so bright and early! Don't blame you much, gal—I could go for him myself. Looks kind o' prosperous."

"Anybody with any brains has dough nowdays."

"Everybody but us! I swear, I don't know where the money goes. Do you?"

"Easy come, easy go," shrugged Martha. "What're you kickin' about? Ain't we still in the money?"

"Yeah. But sometimes I get to thinkin' . . ."

"Oh, well . . . I wish Jimmy'd be a doctor, though, 'stead of a teacher. They make all the money, from the looks of the cars they ride around in."

"Humph!" Judy lit a cigarette and made for the hall.

After breakfast, she suggested a pick-me-up.

"Ought to be some o' that bad gin o' Mike's in the living-room," Martha said. "Let's see. I could stand a shot myself."

The living-room, like the rest of the apartment, spoke of an easy-going, careless existence. It was large enough to hold the necessary furniture and no larger: a divan, several easy chairs, a radio, an upright piano bearing autographed photographs of stage and screen celebrities. The place was not shabby, but liquor stains and cigarette burns bore witness to hard usage.

"Hope none of the bunch come bustin' around today," said Judy from the comfortable depths of a chair. "Seems like they can't find no other place to go when there ain't no rehearsal."

"Maybe the rain'll keep 'em away," suggested Martha.

She was curled on the divan, looking very small and childish in her blue pajamas. For at thirty-three Jim Prince's younger daughter still had something of the sprite in her. Success in a career that is hard on youth had not robbed her of her little-girlishness. She was more knowing than the child who hung herself on her father's fence, but there were freshness and softness in her beauty still. Not like Judy. Judy was all hard sophistication touched with satirical humor. It was the explanation of their comet-rise to public favor. Martha—slim, feminine, wide-eyed, graceful in silver or jade green—was one thing in entertainment. Judy—playing the male in tails and high hat, with a cigarette drooping from her mouth and a so-tired-of-it-all expression on her face—was something quite different. Together they were everything. They were "tops."

Judy was opening the mail. "Here's a letter from A'nt Liddy," she said, and started reading aloud:

"My Dear Niece, I take my pen in hand to write these few lines to you and Marty. I hope they will find you well. You write so little to your old aunt I have to learn about you from the papers. I see you and Marty are still doing all right. I hope you are saving your money because times are not going to be good like this all the time. You might think this sounds crazy but I am older than you all. I have been through hard times and good times and you have both of them in life. I still wish you and Marty would give up that life and come home to your old aunt because I am feeling my age all the time now. If you all ever hit up against hard times just remember I am here. I feel more like a mother to you girls and I hope you feel the same about me. Tell Marty Johnny Carlton is somewhere in New York now. He was around to see me last week and I told him where you all work. I do not see much of him now because he do not go to church no more since he come back from the war and they cheated him out of the money his father left. I hope you girls go to church because you ought to remember the Lord and be thankful for what he done for you. If you can I wish you and Marty would come home some Sunday and bring little Jimmy with you. I guess he is a big boy now all right because I saw in the paper about him playing in some games. He come round to see me last year when he come down here with his running team but I was to a convention of the lodge. Please write your old aunt soon. I am trying to keep up. Hoping you are well and doing fine.

"Your loving aunt Liddy."

"Well," said Judy, "that ought to make us good girls! So that's how the old flame come to the club."

"You know," she continued after a moment's thought, "maybe A'nt Liddy's right . . . about saving money. Ever notice these old, broke-down women walking the streets when we come home in the morning? None o' that for me!"

"Have we any money in the bank?" Martha did a little lightning calculation. "Seems like we put some in about two years ago. . . . Fifty dollars, wasn't it?"

"Yeah! That's right. What say we start putting some more in? You know, we ain't got no renewal on this contract. And I swear—them three-a-day shows kill me! Must be gettin' old."

"Good ole A'nt Liddy!" said Martha, fondly. "We ought to run down there some Sunday, just as she says."

Just then the door bell rang briskly.

It was Johnny Carlton at the door—an older, slightly gray edition of the Johnny Carlton who had gone overseas with the famous Fifteenth. He had come to the Plantation Club the night before and Martha's eyes had caught him during her solo number. Later, at his table, they had talked eagerly, trying to exchange in an hour all that had happened to them since their last meeting. And they had arranged to see each other again today.

Judy let him in, then turned to announce him to Martha in her best burlesque manner.

"Mr. John Carlton of The Philadelphia Carltons, lately of the A.E.F.!"

Gravely, Johnny handed her his hat and overcoat. Then, reaching into his pocket, he produced a quarter.

"Here, my good woman," he said, "buy yourself some little knick-knack."

With a grimace that acknowledged herself beaten, Judy stalked haughtily from the room and left John and Martha, laughing, to themselves. In a minute they were absorbed in a conversation that began where they had left off last night.

How was Johnny's mother? What had happened to cause the deep scar jagging across his neck under his right ear? And the two fingers missing from his left hand? What was he doing now, or planning to do?

"I'm bootlegging," Johnny explained in reply to her flood of questions. "Mother died while I was in France and the money just disappeared. The lawyer Dad named as executor of his will had made the most of my absence. But I couldn't pin a thing on him. He was too slick. I came back from France after six years in a hospital to find a couple of thousand left and no ground to fight on. Probably wouldn't have been able to scrap much, anyway. I was sick as a dog even then. Once that gas gets into you there's no getting it out. I have spells and lapses aplenty now. So not wanting to start from scratch in law, I just took a chance. Got in with a few guys in the know, and here I am—sitting on dynamite, but, hell! I got used to fireworks over there."

He grinned and shrugged. Life wasn't to be taken too seriously.

"By the way," he said, "where can I get a nice room? Boss wants me to work on this and the north Jersey districts."

"How'd you like to stay right here?" Martha's eyes were half cloaked as she raised them to his. And he smiled. It made him look incredibly young.

II

Jimmy-Lew accepted the new lodger without comment. In a way it was a relief to have a man about the apartment, some one older who took him and his problems seriously. As the months passed, a warm friendship sprang up between the boy and and his mother's lover. He was not deceived about Carlton's position in the household. A magnificent diamond which Carlton gave Martha for Christmas, Martha's concern when Carlton suffered his chronic bronchial trouble during damp weather, the note of affection which underlay their simplest gestures toward each other—these and countless other signs gave them away. But Jimmy-Lew found nothing to condemn in the relationship. Carlton was a person of genuinely fine quality, and the influence he exercised over Martha was wholly beneficial.

Martha was drinking and smoking less and taking more time for rest. As a consequence, a certain nervousness disappeared from her manner and a zest returned to her work. She was no longer bothered by a cough which kept her periodically under doctor's orders. Even the *Chatter* and the *Harlem News,* in their gossip columns, found it worth while to comment upon the new liveliness that had been injected into the routine of the Maryland Song-Birds. Particularly, they found much to praise in Marty's torch-song numbers.

For Jimmy-Lew, the peak of his senior year at high school was reached the week before Easter when he returned from the Penn Relays bearing proudly a gold disc with the figures of four runners in bas-relief. Spurred on by Carlton to make some unusual gesture in celebration of the victory, everyone went to church Easter morning— Judy protesting until the last minute that she would do no such thing . . . what did they think she was? . . . she needed sleep more than she needed religion . . . and further remarks to the same effect. But go she did.

Never had there been a lovelier Easter Sunday. Never had Harlem's three main avenues presented such a picturesque riot of color. Times were good, everyone was in money and disposed to spend it on finery—whether it was finery bought on 125th Street or finery bought downtown, it was finery just the same—and Easter was the traditional time to show it off. Laborers and domestics, stage folk and bootleggers, students and colored "quality" poured into the churches of their choice, emptied their pockets into the collection-boxes in return for the best religious show of the year, then drifted out and home, satisfied that the time had been, if not profitable, at least well spent.

Martha and Judy—still protesting at the unwarranted exertion—got dinner. Carlton and Jimmy-Lew cleaned up.

Over the sink, industriously swabbing dishes, Carlton returned to the table conversation.

"So you're really set on this teaching idea, Jimmy?"

"I think so, J. C."

"You've a lot of fine ideals locked up in your head, kid. I hope they stay." John smiled wryly. "Had a few myself, once, but . . . Oh, well! Try to keep as many as you can. You'll find it not so easy. Life at its best isn't so good, you'll find. . . . You're going home to teach, you say?"

"Yes. I was talking to Uncle Ike—he's superintendent in our county now—and he says that as soon as I finish my course he'll get me right into the system. And Ellen says that she's going to teach down there—"

"Oh-ho!" John's brows heightened and he looked quizzically at the boy. "So there's an Ellen?"

Jimmy-Lew grinned sheepishly. "Yes," he confided. "She's the girl whose hair I used to pull in school."

"And you've decided that you don't want to pull her hair any more?"

Jimmy-Lew grinned again. "She's swell! I saw her last summer when I was home. She's going to the Institute.

Gee! I felt right funny meeting her after all these years. Felt like a kid beside her—listening to her talk about things I never even had a thought about. They teach 'em a lot of things down there that they don't get in school up here— about Negroes, I mean. Gee! She makes these girls up here look like—"

"She's swell, eh?" finished John. "If I remember rightly, Booker T. had his Ellen, too. . . . Go to it, boy!"

Chapter 39

I

Jimmy-Lew was to learn that a fixed goal was an excellent thing to have during four years of college. He entered Bolden at the peak of the prosperous 'twenties, when youth had a right to confidence in the future. When he graduated, the country was plunged in a financial depression, and a college degree had lost all its power to impress. In the interval between, old attitudes gave way to new ones more seasoned by experience, and death altered emotional ties. With all these changes to contend with, it was good to know exactly what he wanted to do with his life.

Arriving in Baltimore gave him a sense of returning home. New York and its hurrying, breathless crowds belonged to Tony and Dave, but not to Jimmy-Lew. Even when he was enjoying himself he had felt an alien. Baltimore—Queen City of Maryland, busy with its steel mills and markets, famed for its hospitality, boasting a modest tower or two in its skyline—was a metropolis, also, but a metropolis with an old-fashioned air and a slower tempo. This was an atmosphere Jimmy-Lew knew. This was a corner of the world he was used to.

II

College for Jimmy-Lew, like many major events, had an ignominious beginning. He had had word from the athletic director to report to the coach for football practice and he was making his way up a gravel driveway toward a building that had evidently been the manor house on the original grant of land. Like all the other college buildings, it had an appearance of great respectability tempered by long neglect.

Three youths stared from the porch, arrogance fairly spouting from them. Each wore a blue sweater bearing an orange letter B. A rawboned giant, who seemed too large for his clothes at every point, was the first to speak:

"Where you going, feller?" he asked.

Jimmy-Lew resented the tone. "I'm looking for the coach." His voice was a dull monotone, his face stony.

"You a freshy?" the giant planted himself firmly in front of Jimmy-Lew, and his companions ranged themselves on either side. One was slightly shorter than Jimmy, but stockily built like Booker. The other was slender, lithe, with an intelligent, blunt-featured brown face and eyes that twinkled merrily.

"Yes, I'm a freshman," replied Jimmy-Lew. "Why?" He dropped his bag and took the tall one's measure.

"Well, you'll have to use the back door. We don't allow dogs to come in the same door as upper classmen!"

"And who might you be?" demanded the nettled Jimmy.

"I happen to be an upper classman—'Lord' to you, dog! And you're a *dog*—get me?"

"Oh! And supposing I don't want to be a dog? And supposing I don't want to use the back door?"

"Oh, yeah? Wise guy, eh? Smart dog! Take that!"

"That" was a slap in the face too swift for Jimmy-Lew to dodge. His anger flooded. With one dart of his hand he grabbed the "Lord," yanked him from the steps, and planted a neat upper-cut squarely on his chin. But now the reserves rushed in and bore Jimmy-Lew to the ground. In a minute, with the most impartial good spirits, they were taking turns thrashing the newcomer with their belts. Jimmy-Lew put up no struggle but lay low pending the moment of his release. The lousy bullies! He'd show 'em!

"All right—that's enough," the giant called a halt.

Jimmy-Lew slowly gained his feet and faced them, his jaw at a jutting angle. Without a word he sprang at the giant, but again the three bore him to the gravel. And again they applied themselves to strapping him lustily.

"You got enough, dog?" the stocky boy asked, finally. "We don't want to have to kill you!"

"You better call it quits, freshman," advised the third boy with the merry eyes. His voice held no animosity.

Jimmy-Lew weighed the situation, giving due consideration to the two-hundred-pound chap astride his chest, and decided in favor of discretion.

"Lemme up," he said, sullenly, through bruised lips.

When he was free this time, the hero of Staunton took his bag without further ado and made for the back of the house, while his three tormentors nursed minor evidences of the conflict and speculated on the newcomer's qualities as football material.

III

These three—Moose Johnson, Bull Spears, and Chip Taylor—were Jimmy-Lew's closest friends for the next three years, so contrarily are friendships established. Bull lived in town and his home was open at all times to hungry invaders tired of dormitory fare. Mrs. Spears, broad of beam, hospitable, cheery, did laundering to put Bull through school, confident that when he got his degree and became a preacher she could have her turn of leisure.

The other three boys shared the large top-floor room in Belham Hall—their palace, they called it. Except on Saturdays and Sundays, when the dormitories held open house and bedspreads and bureau scarves and trunk covers were miraculously unearthed, an elegant compliment to feminine visitors, the place was shabby enough, with sweaty athletic gear decorating the radiators and obstructing corners. But the boys liked it. It was a symbol of freedom from family dominance, an amphitheater for study or the sessions of argument that are as equally important a factor in student life.

Moose was headed for the law, Chip for medicine. They differed from Jimmy-Lew in temperament as they differed in habits of study. But these differences were as much a part of his college training as any course on the academic schedule. Through intimate living with Moose and Chip, Jimmy-Lew learned to accommodate himself to others and admit the justification of alien points of view. Moose and Chip were specialists. In their particular fields they excelled. But they had no patience to bestow on subjects in which they were not interested. They, with their sporadic efforts, were a liberal education to Jimmy-Lew, the prospective teacher, who had need of a thorough grounding in every branch of learning.

IV

Just before the Christmas recess of his freshman year Judy telephoned—a very excited Judy.

"Catch the first train, Jimmy. Your mother's very sick with pneumonia. You'll get a telegraphic money order in about an hour. Don't waste any time!"

But Martha had hurdled her last fence and sung her last torch song. She was dead when Jimmy-Lew arrived in New York.

He grieved, for there had been genuine affection and companionship between the youthful Marty and this child of her first love—circumstances had made their relationship that of friendly contemporaries rather than mother and son. Her death left him with a sense of deep loss, but outwardly his life went on unchanged. John Carlton and Judy between them kept him in college, and Jimmy-Lew helped with the expenses by taking a bellman's job in Asbury Park during his summer vacations.

This arrangement continued for two years—until a renewal of the old lung infection sent John Carlton to the Veterans' Hospital, where he died. This was when Jimmy-Lew was a junior. There was already being felt the pinch of hard times. Judy, after Martha's death, had been forced back into chorus work. Then, tiring of the uncertainties of stage life, she went to live with the aging A'nt Liddy and take over the management of the employment agency.

"No more four-a-day shows for me!" she said. And she meant it. Life was chastening even the indomitable Judy.

V

Gladys Parker belonged to Jimmy-Lew's senior year. Until then she had been Chip's girl, and it took Chip to describe her:

"Marble front, man—that's what she is. Always looks like she'd stepped out of a milk-and-roses bath. Tall—not *too* tall—with the curves where they're supposed to be. And that hair!"

He could go on for hours to the same effect. But when he graduated and left town—medicine was out of the question with times as hard as they were—and saw Jimmy-Lew succeed him in Gladys' affections, he held no animosity. Gladys had beauty and she was clever, but she was no one-man woman. Chip knew it and was the first to offer Jimmy-Lew his blessing.

"Don't let your conscience bother you," he wrote. "Half a year out in the world has shown me that if I'm going through med. school, I'll have to get help from other hands than Dad's. So if you hear of my marrying some homely, well-to-do gal, you'll know that li'l Chip has made the supreme sacrifice to the profession. Gladys is a lovely thing. But I know what she's looking for—and I haven't got it."

Jimmy-Lew wasn't sure that he had what she wanted, either. They disagreed quite as often as they agreed. And one argument, shortly before graduation, brought them perilously near an open quarrel.

Jimmy-Lew, wanting to escape the campus turmoil, had struck off up Old York Road. He was walking rapidly and trying to give some thought to his valedictory address when the saucy toot of a horn broke the country quiet. Gladys pulled her low-slung roadster to a stop beside him and motioned him to get in.

"They told me you'd taken this road, Hamlet," she explained. "Come on. Riding's better than walking any day." Gladys was teaching and the roadster was a symbol of her prosperous independence.

"What're you thinking about?" she asked, since he showed no inclination to talk.

"How lovely you are," lied Jimmy-Lew, though she was lovely in a blue knitted outfit he hadn't seen before.

"Oh no!" she declared. "Tasted fruit ceases to be food for thought. You can't fool me. You don't love me." She pouted. "If you did, you'd have taken the city examination for a teaching job here, instead of insisting on going over on the Shore. What do you want to teach down there for? You get real money here. Look at me. You don't hear me complaining about the depression, do you?"

"Yes—you have your car, and money in the bank, and nothing to worry about," Jimmy-Lew summed up tartly. "It's you that don't love me! You don't love anyone but yourself, anyhow! You don't care anything about the kids you teach. All you care about is the money you get for it."

"Yes, and you're an impractical dreamer!" retorted Gladys, sharply, then softened. "I do love you, Jimmy," she said. She stopped the car by a clump of woods.

"Then why don't you marry me and share my life with me?"

"Because, regardless of your silly notions to the contrary, life isn't what you think it. You have to pay bills—wear clothes, eat food, sleep in houses that you either buy or rent! I know that all sounds unromantic, but it's true, nevertheless. Now, if you would take this job I can pull for you, and forget about your little dream of *service* on the Shore, we could get married and make it. If it were five years ago I could do as you say, because Dad could have helped us then. But now—why, it's good I do make my own money. It's all Dad can do to provide for himself and mother."

"I've told you I don't intend just to teach."

"Yes, I know—you intend to write, don't you?" Gladys' voice was ironical, her carefully rouged lips curled as she quoted him: "You intend to 'tap the untouched literary material offered by that little-known-section of the American scene, the Eastern Shore of Maryland.' Humph! You talk as if writing a book is something to be done overnight. Besides, publishers aren't interested in Negro writers. Anything they want concerning Negroes they can get from their own writers."

"That isn't true."

"Oh, I know about the few Negro scribblers," scoffed Gladys, impatiently. "How much of a success are their works compared with their white contemporaries? Do you see any of them getting their stories in the movies? White folks know what they want to read about Negroes—and the stuff you'd write wouldn't be what they want!"

"How do you know what I'd write?" Jimmy-Lew was angry now.

"Didn't you tell me once that you'd like to put into novel form the life of your family—all about your grandmother and grandfather, and their parents, a sort of a Saga of Achievement, I think you called it? Their lives might be glorious and interesting to you, Jimmy-Lew, and you might see it all as a part of the great American Scene. But try and do it without the good old Uncle Tom stuff and see how far you get with it."

"You're just like a lot of other college-bred Negroes!" growled Jimmy-Lew. "You're so puffed up with your pseudo-knowledge, complexes, and cynicisms that you can't see yourself as just another American. You've always got to remind yourself that you're an American Negro, and that there's nothing glorious in your past, and nothing hopeful in your future. You never think in terms of coming generations."

"I'm living *now*!" stated Gladys, flatly. "And there's no use in my kidding myself about how I have to *live* now! What Negroes do after I'm gone won't mean a thing to me. I'll be dead! I want to get something out of life *now*! And I can't do it worrying about what's going to be. The others can take care of that when they get here. That's the trouble with Negroes today—"

"There you go!" cried Jimmy-Lew, bitterly. "Always talking about 'what's the trouble' like the rest of us—and doing nothing about it! You're just selfish."

"Oh, let's cut it out, Jimmy!" Gladys laughed and slid

over against him. "We've only a few more days until you graduate. Let's forget it. Let's just be us."

All of the hard crust of fact and reality was gone from her now. She had softened all over. Like this she was irresistible—with her face lifted to his and her left hand slowly creeping about his shoulder.

"Let's go home," she whispered after a long embrace. And Jimmy-Lew nodded his assent.

VI

". . . to live so, that when our last deeds shall have been recorded upon the books of our lives, we shall be able to voice a more valiant and a prouder farewell than it is our privilege to speak to you today. Dr. Leander, members of the faculty and trustee board, fellow students, parents and friends—the class of 1931 bids you good-by, with a firm resolve that your kindly guidance, well wishes, and sacrifices shall not have been made in vain."

Jimmy's-Lew's earnest voice floated over the audience of upturned faces and found a hiding-place in the deep, creek-cut glen beyond. It was the brave voice of Youth expressing its premature convictions, hopes, and determination. Some who heard him shared his faith and expectation. Others were inclined to skepticism. For the day was past when a Negro with a college degree was a unique representative of his race, an intellectual oasis in the cultural desert. Today he was simply one in thousands.

"Five thousand of 'em this year," one middle-aged skeptic remarked to his companion as they rose to go at the conclusion of the exercises.

"Yeah, I know," answered the other. "Wonder how many of them'll do their post-grad' work in a railroad station carrying bags."

Chapter 40

I

"How do you like it?" asked Ellen.

She had come upstairs from her primary department—the same room where she and Jimmy-Lew had studied under the Misses Warner and Winston. Jimmy-Lew turned at his desk in the small, box-like cubicle, his face aglow.

"It's great!" he exclaimed. "When I see these kids sitting before me I feel as if all those old slaves were sitting right here with them and watching to see if I'm making a good job of what they prayed for."

"You have a great dream, haven't you, Jimmy-Lew?" Ellen's calm voice was quizzical.

"Surely!" The boy fixed intense eyes upon her. "Certainly I have a dream! I see generations unborn—"

"Why not just see these for the present, Jimmy-Lew?" Ellen tempered her practicality with a soft laugh. "I'm going now. Are you going with me? It's after four o'clock."

"Is it? Gee! the time flies! Be right with you."

As they left the building, Jimmy-Lew studied this new Ellen. Three years at the Institute had done things for the fiery girl he'd known in childhood. She had ease and restraint now. Her voice was low-pitched, but clearly audible, her carriage erect, her gaze as level and steady as Blanche's. In fact, she reminded Jimmy-Lew very much of his aunt. And that thought was twin to another: How unlike the sophisticated Gladys Parker she was. Gladys was like froth one sipped from sodas. Ellen was more like the potatoes one ate with steak—substantial and a source of nourishment.

As if she had divined his mind, Ellen asked, "When have you heard from the beautiful Gladys?" They were getting into her coupé.

"That's right—rub it in!" Jimmy-Lew answered, good-naturedly. "Absence made her heart grow yonder, that's all. I hope she's happy with her big-shot doctor husband."

"You mean you're not jealous?" Ellen drove with her eyes on the road ahead and quoted from the recent issue of the *Home Journal*: "'The autumn season opened auspiciously with the brilliant Wellington-Parker nuptials which were solemnized by the Reverend J. Norman Hollis at the home of the bride. The bride was given in marriage by her father, William D. Parker, prominent city barrister and of an old Baltimore family. She wore a gown of pale—'"

"Oh, for cryin' out *loud*!" Jimmy-Lew jammed his foot on the brake.

"'Why so pale and wan, fond lover? Prithee, why so pale?'" Ellen's merry voice was tinged with malice. She turned off the switch and faced him.

"I'm neither pale nor wan," said Jimmy-Lew, gruffly. He added more softly: "If you had any sense at all, you'd know I'm rather glad."

Ellen bent serious, level eyes on her frowning companion. "I suppose," she said, not without sarcasm, "you're going to tell me that it's for me your heart's been pining. Really, you want me to be the balm for your bruised ego."

"But—"

"You needn't think I'm going to play Comforting Katy."

Since there seemed nothing to say, Jimmy-Lew kissed her—fiercely, hungrily, a little angrily. She struggled for a minute, then gave up. When he released her she sank back weakly against the door of the coupé.

"Now will you listen?"

"Yes," said Ellen, her face flaming. Only, don't kiss me like that again, Jimmy-Lew. It's been so lonely down here ... and if you don't mean it ..."

"It was you I was thinking about when I went to Bolden, Ellen," he answered her. "I didn't know then ... exactly. But you talked to me that summer when I came home. I guess it must have been you all along—sort of unconsciously. Love's funny like that, isn't it? Guess this was what I wanted to do that day in the station when you kissed me good-by and ran away."

"I thought you'd forgotten that," murmured Ellen. And in a minute: "Jimmy-Lew, don't fool me. Don't tell me this now, then change." All of her woman's practicality was gone. Again she was the girl who had waited to walk home with the boy in the dusk of a winter's day.

His answer was to draw her gently to him.

II

Hard times had made themselves felt in Shrewsbury as elsewhere. To Jim Prince, whom the years had given patience, one more period of depression meant little. He had weathered storms before. He could weather this one. And with his customary stubbornness he refused to part with even an acre of land. Sit tight until times were better, was his advice to any who sought it. More and more, now, he was coming to depend upon Booker, home from the Institute and full of book knowledge of ecnomics and farm management. Booker belonged to the land and would stay here in the Low Grounds. Paul, who had never held with farming, was off to New York, to invest his Institute learning and small capital of savings in a business of his own.

Yes, Jim Prince felt secure in the present, and confident of a future which he intrusted gladly to his three grandsons. But his neighbor and friend, Jess Miles, had not reasoned with the same foresight. When Ellen needed money to complete her education, Jess sold every foot of land he owned with the exception of the lot on which his house stood—not realizing until the transaction was irrevocably concluded that in selling the land he had yielded up his heart and soul. Not long afterward, he was stricken with paralysis, and added to his brooding grief over the lost acres was a terror that he would become a burden to Ellen. Within a month after the beginning of school, he dragged himself laboriously out of his wheel chair and up the stairs to the bureau which held his pistol. Ellen found his great sprawled body when she returned that evening.

III

Now Ellen turned instinctively to Jimmy-Lew for comfort. And Jimmy-Lew gave back to her a wealth of tenderness that had never until now found complete expression. They planned to be married in June, before the opening of summer school.

In the meanwhile, as they came closer to each other in sympathy, they came closer also in their work. Ellen helped Jimmy-Lew with his lesson plans, for she had the advantage of a year's teaching experience. He helped her from his richer store of academic learning, for he had had four years of college to her three years of normal-school training.

Out of their collaboration there emerged gradually a scheme for a consolidated school which would serve all the colored children of the county. There would be a modern teaching plant centrally located at Shrewsbury, with adequate bus service to insure the attendance of students living in the outlying districts.

The plan grew slowly but steadily. At one moment it leapt ahead, urged by Jimmy-Lew's impetuous vision. The next moment it submitted to the rein of Ellen's common sense. Ellen could dream as well as Jimmy-Lew, but her dreams were as a cautious bark following the surging stream of his thought. She was a true product of the Institute, with a mind guided by the orderly hand of discipline.

When the plan was perfected to the point where it seemed to them workable, they presented it to Ike as superintendent of the county. Then for two days they anxiously awaited his verdict. On the third, he called them into his office.

They stood breathlessly at his desk.

"You two seem to have something worth while here," he said, smiling at their eagerness. "I've been thinking about the same thing for a number of years, but I never sat down to figure it out like this." He ran through their points briefly. "I believe it can be worked, and I'm going to present it to the state supervisor. Wait," he cautioned as they joyfully turned to each other. "I can't promise you what his reaction will be. You see—these hard times have caused a howl among the taxpayers, and the cost of education is one of the biggest bones of contention."

"But they built a new school for the white children over in Deerfield this year—"

"I know," interrupted Ike, with a patient smile, "but that's a horse of another color."

"You mean a *child* of another color!" exclaimed Jimmy-Lew, bitterly. He broke off as he felt the pressure of Ellen's fingers on his arm.

"I realize that, too, son," said Ike. "But that's the way things are. I've learned that there are more ways of picking a chicken than scalding it. You have to learn those things in life—especially when you're in a position like mine. Now you two let me handle this in my own way. I can't promise you that you'll get your plan through this year. But"—Ike smiled again—"there are other years ahead."

"Well—," began Jimmy-Lew, but Ellen broke in:

"Thank you very much, Mr. Johnson," she said, quietly. "I'm sure you'll do all you can. We can wait—can't we, Jimmy-Lew?" And she pressed his arm once more. Jimmy-Lew murmured something inaudible and they withdrew.

Ike sat staring at the door through which they'd passed, his long body slumped into his favorite thinking position. This boy of Martha's was a problem. There was no question but that he was a "natural" as a teacher. That was obvious to anyone who had watched him conduct a class. He had a gift for attracting and holding the interest of students. Boys especially idolized him. They knew of his athletic exploits, and because of them were more willing to respect his scholarship. Even Piggy Wright, of the fightin', cuttin', shootin' Wrights, held Jimmy in awe—and no other Wright in Ike's remembrance had submitted to a teacher's authority. They were a surly, unruly clan, the Wrights; all of them, with the exception of Piggy's father, Ham, had ended their careers in prison.

But Jimmy had other qualities, Ike realized, that were less desirable in a teacher. He had Martha's impetuosity, and he had that forthrightness which bears the stamp of virtue but is too often the cause of embarrassment. If Jimmy took a dislike to some one, he scorned to stoop to polite deceit. At the county teachers' meeting, for instance, it had been very apparent that he had avoided the unpleasant, fishy-eyed, pallid little man who was state supervisor of Negro education. And this would never do if he was to get on in the profession. No one knew better than Ike Johnson the value of diplomacy in the academic life. Jimmy, he feared, needed discipline. . . .

Had Ike only known it, Jimmy-Lew was being disciplined that very moment. Over at the parsonage, where Ellen lived now, he was listening to a piece of calm and reasonable advice.

"You know, honey," Ellen was saying, "you must learn to control your feelings more than you do." Her eyes were soft with love of this great moody man who was still so much the child.

"I guess you're right," he grinned, ruefully. "But—I don't know why it is—when a thing is wrong, to me, it's wrong! And I just say so, if it's a concern of mine."

"But you can't do that, Jimmy-Lew—not in life. That's all well and good in school—sometimes not even there—but when you're dealing with human beings in life, it's different. A straight line *isn't* always the shortest distance between two points—and two and two *doesn't* always make four. I'm not saying that wrong is ever right, nor that justice does not finally triumph. But I *am* saying that the way to what is right is often round about. Do you see what I mean, dear? There wasn't any need for you to get angry with your uncle because he doubted whether the state board would adopt our scheme. He's been dealing with them longer than either of us. Those things take time. Time, Jimmy-Lew. So you mustn't let your uncle see you sulk as you did. It might make him feel that you want to take advantage of your relationship. And he might even believe that you think he's a 'handkerchief head,' when he really isn't. He simply knows when he must bide his time to get what he wants. It's the important *getting* that he's interested in. You see, dear?"

"All right, little teacher!" Jimmy-Lew laughed. "I'll be good." He kissed her forehead lightly. "And shake off those wrinkles! You frown worse than I do when I'm thinking!" A sudden thought struck him. "By the way, do you know that Bolden and Institute play tomorrow in Baltimore?"

"Do they?" Ellen was instantly all excitement, and Jimmy-Lew took his cue.

"Let's drive over! It'll give us a change. We'll take Booker along and maybe we'll see some of the old gang. How about it?"

"All right," agreed Ellen. "We'll leave about six."

IV

In the gray light of the following morning Jimmy-Lew nosed the coupé down Main Street. Ellen sat beside him, looking her best—so he thought—in a green swagger suit and a sliver of a brown felt hat. Beyond her was Booker.

"Old Shrewsbury's getting to be a big town," Jimmy-Lew remarked, his mind running back to grammar-school days and the athletic events that were a part of the Saturday grubbing-up program.

"Yep," agreed Booker lazily, "but she's going to stand still awhile now. Old Man Depression's got her. The same," he added after a moment's consideration, "as Institute's got Bolden today." Booker had been an athlete of no mean reputation himself, and Jimmy-Lew's antagonist on the gridiron. It pleased him to keep the feud alive.

"One more crack like that and you'll get out and walk," Jimmy-Lew promised him.

"One more crack from either of you," Ellen put in, her voice calm as always, "and you'll both walk."

Booker retired to his corner of the seat with a great show of meekness. But it wasn't in him to be quiet for long.

"Did you hear about the trouble at the box factory yesterday?"

"No," said Jimmy-Lew. "What was it?"

They were circling the court-house plaza in the middle of the town, from which several streets radiated like spokes from a hub. The courthouse, a white, Pantheon-like structure with six Tuscan columns fronting wide, concrete steps, was the pride of Shrewsbury. It stood, symbol of justice, guarded by three ancient oaks.

"Well," said Booker, settling back with a yawn—a sure sign that he was about to indulge in some comedy—"Ole man Parsons decided he wasn't making enough profit or somep'n, so he ups and knocks off all the gentlemen of color in his employ, and sort o' kind o' forgot to pay 'em in full. This oversight one Ham Wright thought was unpardonable. Hence, the said Wright bethought himself to make right the wrong done to one of *the* Wrights. Forthwith, the wronged Wright stalked into the box magnate's office and demanded, in no uncertain terms, that the wrong done the Wright be righted. The upshot of the affair was that Ole Parsons had three of his trusty lads from Virginia, whom he has hired in the place of the native gentlemen, to cast Wright out on his—Well, ejected forcibly, I suppose, is the phrase pedagogues would use. Finally, it is said that Wright picked his outraged anatomy from the ground, shook his fist at his shortchanging boss, and bellowed vengeance for this indignity to the clan of Wright. It is further rumored that at eleven o'clock last evening Ham was sitting in his palatial residence, in that delightful little thoroughfare known as Gatlin's Alley, and imbibing heavily of a stimulant known as White Mule— which is noted for its power to stir the wrath of the Wright clan. And, moreover, it is said that he was singing a particularly wild variety of blues songs."

If Booker was doing any thinking throughout this long recital, it was not apparent, for not a muscle altered the expression of his face. He was master of the "dead pan."

When he had finished, Jimmy-Lew was sober. "I can't blame Ham much," he said, slowly. "It's a shame, the way Parsons has thrown all his colored employees out of work, and hired that bunch of scum from the Virginia side of the line. After all, our people have to live somehow—and they've worked and built his factory up to what it is."

"And the Lord knows Ham can't afford to be out of work with that family of his," put in Ellen. "It gets under my skin to see those ragged Wright children. Little Maggie and Raymond—Lord. They look as if they hadn't had a bath in years! But you can't say anything to their mother about it. I tried it last year, and the cussin' I got was an education. She's proud as a princess. So I have to be satisfied with having them wash their faces and hands every day at recess time. It's a pity, too. Those two kids have just about the highest I. Q. in the primary department."

"And I haven't had any trouble with Piggy so far," said Jimmy-Lew. "He says he's going to be the best forward on the Eastern Shore this year. He even washes that one khaki shirt he has at night, so's to be clean when he comes to school. I'm going to give him three when I get my first pay."

"Ah—the inspired young pedagogue! Another Booker T. come to his people," sighed the irrepressible cousin. "I, a poor son of the soil, must content myself with the lot of Cain—to reap not where I have sown. Yea—even harvest not where I have planted!"

"Oh, shut up!" growled Jimmy-Lew. "Pinch him for me, will you, Ellen?"

And these three latter-day children of Maryland's lowlands bowled on—laughing, care free—through the mounting warmth of an autumn sun, through fields and woods that flamed in beauty before their annual submission to Death.

Chapter 41

I

Gatlin's Alley, crooked, like a dusty serpent, slumbered late this Saturday morning. The box factory's whistle held no meaning for the alley residents. There'd be no pay envelopes to bring home today. Blue Dobson wouldn't sell as much White Mule as he usually did. And the boys from the other side of Main Street would have to pay a little more tonight for brown bodies.

But there was one who didn't sleep. Inside the dilapidated Wright shack, which slouched amid a junk pile of a yard like a king hobo in his favorite camp, sat Ham Wright. All night long he had sat there, a great hulk of a man with reddened eyes that the white liquid in a half-empty jug had kindled to twin fires of anger. Incongruously, he twanged at a stringed box on his knees, paying no attention to a faint female voice that called to him from the room above. Nor did he look up as his son Piggy came in and stole upstairs.

Moanin' . . . moanin' . . . moanin' guitar . . . Black, thick, labor-roughened fingers ripping the strings into savage harmonies. . . . Black, liquor-crazed minstrel . . . Black, poverty-ridden creature . . .

Hard times . . . out o' work . . . gittin' cold . . . an' dey ain' no mo' wood in de shed . . . chilluns ain' got no shoes . . . nuttin' to eat . . . credit gone . . . what I gone do? . . . what I gone do? . . .

Went to the railroad—
Laid mah head on the track!
Went to the railroad—
Laid mah head on the track!
Got to thinkin' 'bout mah baby—
Snatched mah dev'lish head back!
Cryin' how long—is Ah got to wait?
Lawd—Lawd—'spect Ah bes' hes-a-tate!

What I gone do? . . . Ain' no mo' work yere in town . . . What I gone do? . . . Goddam 'im! . . .

Now come yere purty mamma—
Set on yo' daddy's knee!
Now come yere purty mamma—
Set on yo' daddy's knee!
Won't you tell me dat you lovin'
Nobody else but me?

> Cryin' how long—is Ah got to wait?
> Lawd—Lawd—'spect Ah bes' hes-a-tate!

'Nothah baby comin' . . . How's I gone feed 'im? . . . I *gots* to have mah money now! . . . *Gots* to have it! . . . Goddam 'im! . . .

> Um—um—some mean black snake
> Bin suckin' mah rider's tongue!
> Um—um—some mean black snake
> Bin suckin' mah rider's tongue!
> Ah's gwine down an' git me
> A grea' big Gatlin' gun!
> > Cryin' how long—is Ah got to wait?
> > Lawd—Lawd—'spect Ah bes' hes-a-tate!

What I gone do? . . . What I gone do? . . . I *gots* to have dat money now! *Gots* to have it! . . . Goddam 'im! . . . I gone go git mah money! . . .

It was noon when Ham Wright staggered from his shanty and went lurching along Gatlin's Alley. His hulking, bow-legged figure cast an ominous shadow before it as he reeled southward on Main Street toward the solitary smokestack that belched its soot into the tangy air. And those who saw him go shook their heads, for he spoke to no one, nor did he stop at the poolroom. Big Dick Wright had acted just like that before he cut Slim Turner to death. . . .

II

A portentous stillness had crept over the town. It was a strange quiet for Shrewsbury on a Saturday night. There should have been more noise, because Main Street was thronged as usual with its out-of-town crowds come to do their weekly "grubbin'-up." But there was a certain tight-lipped grimness about the men who gathered in little knots outside the barber shops after they'd had their week-end shave and hair-cut, or leaned against dusty, ramshackle Fords while they waited for their women-folk to bargain with the merchants. There was not a black, brown, or yellow face to be seen in all the crowd. And the eyes under slouched hats were steely and the voices were low.

". . . Tell me old man Parsons' dyin', Jeb."

"They say he ain't come to sence that nigger shot 'im."

"Sho orter be somep'n done 'bout it—damn niggers is gittin' so they thinks they's much as us."

"How come they ain't nobody done got together an' strung 'at nigger up, noways?"

"They says he's dyin', too—damn 'is black hide!"

"Wal, it's a damn shame to let 'at nigger die in a nice white bed—'at's all I got to say!"

"The mayor sent fo' the state troopers to guard the hospital. 'Bout twenty of 'em strung 'round it. They say he even sent fo' the militia. Reckon they'll be yere in the mornin'."

"How'd he shoot ole man Parsons anyways?"

"Went out to the mill 'bout twelve 'clock an' broke in on 'im. They says 'twas 'bout some money Parsons owed the nigger. Ole Parsons drawed a gun an' shot 'im. But the nigger snatched it an' shot Parsons in the chest—lung, they says. Then the nigger staggers back to his house an' 'is boy an' gal took 'im to the hospital bleedin' like a hog. All happened so quick didn't nobody know 'bout it till they finds old Parsons stretched out in 'is office 'bout twenty minutes after. . . ."

"Wal, wait'll them boys from over Virginny Sho' gits yere. They's a bunch of 'em comin' up in cars, they says. Things'll start poppin' then. . . ."

III

Dr. Stevens, superintendent and chief surgeon of Shrewsbury's newly built hospital, watched with anxious eyes the mob that milled in front of the window. For two hours now these madmen had been heckling the group of two dozen troopers stationed at the entrance. He shuddered, reminded of that night when, as a boy, he had watched his father rush off with frantic Jim Prince, and he had crept trembling into his mother's arms. God! He hoped the governor would hurry those troops.

Damn depression! It put these people in an ugly frame of mind. There'd been slight clashes already between those laborers from Virginia Shore and the lower element of Negroes here in Shrewsbury. Parsons had been a bigoted old fool to throw those men out of work. Damn it! When would these people come to their senses about their Problem! Same thing in the school board. They robbed those colored kids and their teachers of the money appropriated for them. Then if you said anything about it, you were a nigger-lover! Jesus! Give them a lousy deal all around and then expect them to grow up to be nice, intelligent, law-abiding citizens! Dr. Will Stevens smiled ironically, even while he watched the example of mob mania there before him. Hell! Half of these men had hated old Parsons—called him skinflint and miser! And now look at them! Look at them in the glare of the torches they bore! Women and children, too . . . God!

"Think they'll be able to hold them off, sir?"

Dr. Will turned, startled by the tremulous voice at his side. It was the new nurse, just graduated from training-school. What was her name? Ramsey? Yes, Ramsey. She was white-lipped, and in her starched uniform looked like a frightened blonde child at a masquerade.

"I don't know," he answered, slowly. "That mob's in a nasty mood. How's Mr. Parsons?"

"He's sinking faster—no hope, I'm afraid . . . And it's only a matter of minutes now for that man who shot him. But he certainly has vitality—Look, Doctor!"

The harried man jerked around to the window and stood fixed in dismay. The mob had charged! It swarmed around the grouped troopers, until it finally hid them from sight.

When he could gather his wits to act, the doctor rushed into the corridor, but the foremost of the frenzied pack completely submerged him before the horrified eyes of Nurse Ramsey. Amid screams of the sick, with the attendants scurrying for cover, the pack surged onward to the ward marked "Colored," which was at the far end of the passageway. A moment later and the benumbed nurse, who had pulled the unconscious superintendent back into his office, saw them drag a nude, inert, black body past the door. An unearthly cry roared through the window and down the corridors, like the hungry voice of some great-throated wild thing. . . . Nurse Ramsey groped blindly for support, then sank limply to the floor beside her superior.

IV

It is done.

The streets of Shrewsbury town are silent once more. The muddy automobiles have rattled away from the curbs, and the shop windows are darkened. The guardians of the state law rest on cots in the hospital.

Down in Gatlin's Alley shutters are tightly closed. There is no light at any window, neither is there a sound to be heard on the street. But inside one hovel a black woman, large with child, moans her anguish to a silent, brooding boy at her side. And in their miserably filthy bed five younger Wrights whimper like a litter without its mother.

Chapter 42

I

In Baltimore, Gardner's neat little restaurant was jammed with post-game patrons. At one table Jimmy-Lew and Booker were continuing the verbal feud that had been going on all day.

"Well, I'll say this much: Bolden was plenty lucky."

"Says you! You mean Institute had a rabbit's foot somewhere! Why—"

"Oh, hush up, both of you!" laughed Ellen. "You sound like two freshmen."

"Hi, Hoss!"

The people at the other tables turned curiously to watch as two apparently wild men charged the trio.

"Moose! Chip!" Jimmy-Lew leapt from his seat and was enveloped in what seemed to be a cloud of arms. Then followed much intricate handshaking as the three solemnly exchanged the grip of their fraternity.

Ellen was introduced to the newcomers.

"Ah-ha!" exclaimed Chip, fingering the wisp of a mustache he had at last coaxed to grow. "The boy's an eye for beauty! And who might this be?" He indicated Booker.

"I," replied Booker, with drawling good humor, "am the doughty knight who, on two occasions, unhorsed you when you were galloping for touchdowns. Remember?"

"Yes," answered Chip, wryly. "If I'm not mistaken, yours is about the hardest shoulder I ever had the misfortune to come in contact with!"

"Sit down—sit down!" ordered Jimmy-Lew.

"Sorry—can't," said Chip. "You see, Gladys—"

"Wuxtry! Wuxtry!" A newsboy broke into the clatter of voices. "All about the shootin' in Shrewsbury! Wuxtry! Wuxtry! Negro threatened by lynch mob! Guv'ner orders troops to Eastern Sho' town! Wuxtry! Wuxtry!"

The buzz in the dining-room ceased abruptly as men dug for their loose change. The little brown urchin distributed his wares feverishly. What a sale! He'd be able to see the conclusion of "The Masked Rider" tonight.

"Say, isn't that your town?" asked Moose.

"Yes!" answered Jimmy-Lew, shortly. "Here, boy!" He extended a quarter and snatched a handful of the papers.

They were all quiet as they read the glaring headlines. Booker was the first to break the silence.

"It seems as if ole Parsons is about to be gathered to his illustrious ancestors."

"It seems as if there's about to be a human barbecue!" retorted Jimmy-Lew. He sprang to his feet. "Come on! See you, Moose and Chip."

Booker shrugged to his former opponents, then followed his cousin and Ellen to the coupé.

Chip looked at Moose.

"I feel like a heel sitting here," muttered Moose.

"Let's get a drink," suggested Chip.

II

"Be careful, Jimmy-Lew!" Ellen glanced hastily at the speedometer. The clock read "sixty."

They were careening around the curves of the Philadelphia pike, and each pressure of Jimmy-Lew's impatient foot shot them forward more recklessly. Once or twice they barely avoided head-on collisions. Booker looked askance at Ellen. But there was no word from the driver. Finally Booker asked:

"Just why are you in such a rush to get home?"

"You ask me that?" snapped Jimmy-Lew. "If there are any *men* in Shrewsbury, and we can get there in time, there's not going to be any lynching!"

"Oh . . ." Booker slumped in his seat. "Well, cuz, if that's your mood, all I can say is, *pour it in 'er.* I'll kind o' sort o' be around." His voice was quietly determined.

"You mean you're going to try to stop it?" asked Ellen. Her heart skipped a beat when Jimmy-Lew nodded. "All right—*pour it in 'er!*" Her lips drew thinly over her set teeth, and she tore her eyes from the speedometer.

They had fled past Elkton and were on the lonely stretch from there to Eastland when the motor stuttered and coughed. In vain Jimmy-Lew pressed on the accelerator. All of the pull was gone from the overstrained mechanism.

"She's missing," said Booker. "Spark's shot."

"The mechanic at the garage at home said that the spark plugs needed cleaning," said Ellen.

They had slowed to a snail's pace. Jimmy-Lew fretted and fumed. But there was nothing to do but drift until they sighted a garage. The mechanic there took one look and shook his head.

"Needs cleaning bad," he said. "I can do the job in about two hours."

"Two hours!" stormed Jimmy-Lew. "We'll try to make it like this."

"Yes, it's seven-thirty now," said Booker. Some of Jimmy-Lew's impatience had crept into his voice. There was a strange light flaring in his narrowed eyes. Ellen looked from one to the other of these silent, taut-faced men between whom she was wedged, and tried to still a sudden terror that gripped her. Jimmy-Lew's taciturnity she was used to. But she had never seen Booker like this. . . .

Four hours later they sputtered into the silent town, the coupé lurching like some drunken thing. Booker was the first to mark the peculiar pall that hovered in the very air. The infrequent street lights were powerless to dispel it. Then, as they rounded the half-circle of the court-house plaza, Ellen applied the foot brake and pointed. The men's eyes followed her trembling finger to the grimly silent, awful thing that swung in the horror-shrouded dark.

III

"It's no use, Ellen. . . ."

It was the Friday of the following week. Jimmy-Lew slumped at the desk in his room, glumly staring at the cracked, worn floor. Outside a drizzly rain heightened the gloom of the day. A train crew cursed and called to one another on the siding as a puffing locomotive maneuvered to connect a string of freight-cars. Chalk-dusted erasers lay around the borders of the blackboards where they had been carelessly dropped by pupils eager to be gone from this place of discipline. And the atmosphere hung with that peculiar odor which overcrowded, poorly ventilated schoolrooms carry at the close of the day. Every outward indication proclaimed this Friday like all other Fridays.

Ellen stood at the door, her tender, troubled gaze fixed on the figure of utter defeat that was Jimmy-Lew. All week he had avoided meeting her in the building, and at the end of each day he had vanished. Now she moved over to his side.

"What's no use, dear?" she asked.

"I'm going to leave this town," he said, slowly, his eyes averted. "There's no use in my staying. Every time I look at Piggy I see the court-house and the trees. . . . Yes, I'm leaving!"

He shot to his feet, to rage about the room while Ellen watched as one observing the tantrum of a child.

"I saw what kind of men there are in this town at the meeting Monday night! Every one of 'em scared to breathe—except Thornton and Reverend Williams! Two out of over two hundred men—only *two*—who were willing to sign a petition to the governor! Hell! I feel less than a man! I'm going where I can act and feel like a man among people who don't make me ashamed of being an American Negro!"

He whirled on Ellen. His face was a stony mask that held no color. And the black eyes had become slate.

"Why should I teach children of men who aren't willing to make one step for the future welfare of those same children? Why should I give a damn about the whole nigger race? Yes, that's what I said—Nigger! It's a damn good name for all of us! One of us is lynched—and what do we do? We write letters to the *Home Journal,* and send telegrams to governors and to Congress! Damn it! That isn't going to stop lynching! Niggers! All they want to do is exist. No wonder they can survive! Hell—they haven't got the guts to die!"

He paused in his pacing, dropped into a chair, and buried his face in his hands.

"Won't you walk home with me, Jimmy-Lew?" Ellen's voice held no hint of her agitation.

"Sure." Listlessly he took his overcoat from its hook on the door.

They were silent most of the way to the parsonage while he kept his moody mask-like countenance bent on the damp, red-brick pavement.

"The car's all fixed," Ellen said as she let them in the door. "Had a general overhauling instead of just the spark plugs cleaned. Heavens! but a lot of things can get wrong with an engine!"

"I'll pay for it—it was my fault."

"Oh, nonsense! Besides," she glanced sideways at him, "a wife's money is her husband's. So you can consider it as coming out of the family budget."

"But we're not going to be—"

She interrupted hurriedly: "Here, give me your coat. You must wear a hat, darlin', or you'll catch cold." She tossed the garment on the back of a chair, and did the same with her own. "Aren't you going to help me with my galoshes?"

"Oh, I'm sorry." He pivoted to kneel in front of her.

When he arose her arms were about his neck. But he unclasped them, and went to sit on the divan.

"Jimmy-Lew—" Ellen eased down beside him and reached timidly to stroke the rumpled, unruly curls of his bowed head. She had to be content that he did not withdraw from her light touch.

"Jimmy-Lew," she said again, presently, "I know how you feel. . . . All your bright visions of what you considered your life work here have been shattered by—by this terrible thing that has happened. But, darlin', don't let it change you—No, please don't interrupt me," she pleaded as he brought his stormy eyes to bear on her at last. "Please let me finish."

He withdrew into his shell once more, his elbows on his knees, bronzed hands twisting restlessly about each other. But eventually, as the girl talked on, the hands came to rest and his head dropped against her breast. Some power of wisdom outside herself seemed to dictate her words, and all the while her cool fingers pressed the boy's hot, brooding face closer.

"We have so hard a time to see through this depressing present, dear. I know it is hard . . . *hard*. But remember you said you saw unborn generations when you stood before your classes? That is true—only, we can't veer with every ill wind that blows upon us. Great things are not accomplished like that, darlin'. It takes time—as it took time to uproot us and plant us here three centuries ago; as it took time to bring us through all kinds of anguish to this present."

"But we are living *now* . . . ," the boy said, dully, and started as he recognized the words to be those Gladys had used in arguing with him.

The girl smiled her calm smile.

"What is Now," she asked, "but Tomorrow's Yesterday and Yesterday's Tomorrow? It is such a small thing. Don't think I'm trying to be bookish, darlin', or that I'm trying to rationalize away this thing that we must meet . . . meet anywhere we go. I'm not. But I'm willing to face it, not run away from it. I don't think that just education alone will wipe it out; but I do believe that education is one of Time's powerful instruments toward a cure. Darlin', if we let this racial thing blind us to the rest of living, we'll be lost."

Jimmy-Lew shook his head. "What right have I," he asked, "or any other man here in this town—or in America, for that matter—to marry a woman whose children I can give no protection from a lynch mob?"

She lifted his face and lingeringly kissed him. "There's more to Now than worrying about the big problems, darlin'," she said. "We've love to give each other, and the right to live here in these Low Grounds, as your grandfather calls them. We belong here as much as the other groups of Americans, Jimmy-Lew. We're no more or less than the other Americans. We're just people . . . all of us . . . north, south, east, west . . . white, black, brown, yellow . . . we're just people . . . Americans. . . . And in our working, our loving, our sorrowing, and our dying we are making the America of Now and Tomorrow, just as we helped to make it Yesterday."

The boy buried his face against her and whispered, holding very tightly to her:

"Maybe . . . maybe . . ."

About the Author

"A real story of real people." That is what *Kirkus Review* wrote about *These Low Grounds*, Waters Edward Turpin's first novel from 1937. He wrote two other novels, *O Canaan!* (1939) and *The Rootless* (1957), in addition to plays, short stories, and poetry.

It was Dr. Turpin's mission to portray African Americans as courageous human beings who helped shape the United States. His love of story was fostered by his maternal grandfather, who talked about the struggles of Black people on the eastern shore of Maryland. The novelist Edna Ferber, who hired Dr. Turpin's mother as a cook and household manager, mentored him as well.

He ended up earning a BA in English from Morgan College (now Morgan State University) and an MA in English and an EdD from Columbia University, and he taught at colleges in West Virginia, Pennsylvania, and Maryland.